THE
LAWLESS
FRONTIER

BOOK YOUR PLACE ON OUR WEBSITE AND MAKE THE READING CONNECTION!

We've created a customized website just for our very special readers, where you can get the inside scoop on everything that's going on with Zebra, Pinnacle and Kensington books.

When you come online, you'll have the exciting opportunity to:

- View covers of upcoming books
- Read sample chapters
- Learn about our future publishing schedule (listed by publication month *and author*)
- Find out when your favorite authors will be visiting a city near you
- Search for and order backlist books from our online catalog
- Check out author bios and background information
- Send e-mail to your favorite authors
- Meet the Kensington staff online
- Join us in weekly chats with authors, readers and other guests
- Get writing guidelines
- AND MUCH MORE!

**Visit our website at
http://www.kensingtonbooks.com**

THE
LAWLESS
FRONTIER

Randy Denmon

PINNACLE BOOKS
Kensington Publishing Corp.
www.kensingtonbooks.com

PINNACLE BOOKS are published by

Kensington Publishing Corp.
850 Third Avenue
New York, NY 10022

All Kensington titles, imprints, and distributed lines are available at special quantity discounts for bulk purchases for sales promotions, premiums, fund-raising, educational, or institutional use.

Special book excerpts or customized printings can also be created to fit specific needs. For details, write or phone the office of the Kensington special sales manager: Kensington Publishing Corp., 850 Third Avenue, New York, NY 10022, attn: Special Sales Department, phone: 1-800-221-2647.

Pinnacle and the P logo Reg. are U.S. Pat. & TM Off.

ISBN 0-7860-1834-8

First Pinnacle Printing: September 2006

10 9 8 7 6 5 4 3 2 1

Printed in the United States of America

To my family, for putting up with me
all these misspent years.

ACKNOWLEDGMENTS

Thanks for Jim Fitzgerald, my agent, and
Gary Goldstein, my editor, for helping me get published.

"Give me chastity and continence, but not yet."
                              —Saint Augustine (354–430)

Prologue

I never met my grandfather. He died under the Mexican sun. Alone. Nothing to keep him company but the lingering image of his fiancée, a woman who, unbeknownst to him, was carrying his unborn son. He lay there bleeding in the dust, until memories became dreams and dreams a swirling road into the hereafter.

What he saw on his way to his Maker, I can only imagine. But he died on his own terms. He died without fear, without regret. He died like a man.

Myles Jefferson Adams was gunned down in 1914, a peripheral victim of the bloody, sprawling Mexican Revolution. Everything I know of him I know from family stories, from vintage newspaper clippings on the war, and from his partner at the time, a man as inscrutable as my grandfather was predictable.

Stewart Cook, his mysterious partner, died shortly after I met him for the first and only time, a retired lawyer living out the twilight years of his life in rural Texas. But before he passed away, I spent a week with him and his wife at their ranch, chewing the fat and learning the lore that grew up around my grandfather.

Mr. Cook left to posterity one small diary, barely the size of a paperback. His wife gave it to me after he died. Leatherbound, its pages yellowed with the years, it still smells like adventure.

He and my grandfather lived in a different era, one that had more in common with the century preceding it than with its own. When I read the pages of Mr. Cook's journal, I feel like I'm reading the dreams of a lost generation. What would my grandfather say to me today? Would we speak the same language?

What follows is his story. Forgive me any chronological deformities or lapses in detail. I have pieced together what I could, relying equally on firsthand testimony and secondhand inspiration, the latter of which has persisted like fragrant sage in the desert heat. In the end, my grandfather's story is as much legend as it is fact, a quest that unhinges the deepest longings of our collective unconscious.

As for the war, I won't even pretend to understand its murky depths. It began as a revolution, pitting agrarian reformers and their peasant armies against a decades-long dictatorship that had brought modernity and material comfort to a privileged few. It soon spiraled into a full-blown civil war, and by the time President Woodrow Wilson ordered U.S. Navy "bluejackets" to pacify Veracruz in April of 1914, three factions, including Pancho Villa's Constitutionalists in the north, were vying for control of the heart of the Mexican Revolution.

A year later, the country, already bludgeoned and battered by years of unrest, collapsed into sheer anarchy. It could no longer be called a war between the landowning haves *(hacendados)* and the landless have-nots *(guerrilleros)*. Internecine bloodletting and further splintering of the parties had blurred the previously black-and-white divisions into something decidedly more gray. And Mexico's very soul was at stake.

Against such a backdrop, my grandfather's story seems pretty straightforward. He was just trying to do the right thing.

Chapter 1

Upriver from the mouth of the Tamisi, a decrepit riverboat stalled in the still waters. As the engine fell silent, a wayward gull lit on the bow, and its gray speckled wings, fluttering softly in the sudden hush, woke the man sprawled across the deck.

Stewart Cook lifted his straw hat from his eyes slowly, grudgingly at first, and squinted at the mid-morning glare. He turned and saw the gull, still perched on the bow. It was standing on one leg and had buried its beak in its wing.

Stewart sat up groggily, and the bird hesitated perhaps a second before taking flight. The American watched it arc away from him until it had crested the canopy of trees on the river's edge and disappeared from sight. As it did, Stewart remembered where he was—and where he was headed. He stood on wobbly legs a moment and then shuffled toward the cabin. The boat swayed gently in the water as the top of its hull dipped nearly even with the river's surface.

Myles was waiting for him in the doorway.

"Why are we stopping?" Stewart asked. He could feel a wave of heat escape the doorway as he glanced past Myles into the cabin.

Myles smiled nonchalantly at his partner. "Sorry to interrupt your beauty sleep. Lord knows you need plenty of it."

"Why—"

"Why are we stopping?" Myles interrupted. "I heard you the first time. Boat's broken down. And we're thirty miles from the nearest creature that walks on two legs."

Still trying to shake off his nap-induced fog, Stewart let the words sink in. They were stranded. Going nowhere. He clenched his jaw and swallowed hard as he stifled the urge to protest. He had never been one to waste words, preferring instead to spend them sparingly. Half Mexican, half Texan, the former-artilleryman-turned-attorney-at-law was hell-bent for Santiago, and he didn't have time for this delay.

He had begged and cajoled Myles Adams into leading this expedition into Mexico's forbidding and remote northern interior. He had played his final argument like a trump card, knowing deep down that Myles would never let him make the trip behind enemy lines alone. And Myles had bit. The former lieutenant colonel from New Orleans, now a liaison officer for the U.S. War Department and a part-time arms and people smuggler, was a study in contrast. He was battle-hardened and world-wise, with the unmovable cool of someone who had seen death up close without flinching. But he also had a soft heart and the gift of gab, and he fancied himself quite the ladies' man. Sometimes Stewart found him downright annoying.

Stewart brushed past him and entered the cramped, muggy cabin, where he found the two men Myles had enlisted for the journey: Sergeant Bill "Bones" Bates and Antonio Diaz. They were standing side by side, staring at the boat's spartan instrument panel.

Antonio turned to see Stewart and smiled reassuringly. "Do not worry, Mr. Cook," he said in his singsong Mexican accent. "We will help you save your girl."

Antonio was a well-connected member of the local landed gentry: pompous but affable, as overly formal as he was crass, someone who stood to lose everything—including his life—if the war continued to unravel in favor of the revolutionaries. He had the tools at his disposal—a riverboat and a Model-T pickup truck—to get the Americans where they needed to go.

"She's not my girl," Stewart replied, barely opening his mouth to form the syllables.

"No?" Antonio began. "Then why are we going to the trouble of . . ."

Myles, who had followed Stewart back inside and was now leaning against the doorjamb with his arms folded and a cigarette in his mouth, shook his head, signaling Antonio to stop while he was ahead.

Stewart felt his forehead burn with anger and embarrassment. He had no idea why he was risking life and limb for a girl he had never kissed, a girl he had been fond of for most of his life but somehow had never managed to court. All he knew was that she was in danger. Alexia Garcia lived with her family in the remote village of Santiago, just outside of Monterrey. Both towns were only days—perhaps hours—away from being overrun by the bloody Mexican Revolution. Even if his feelings for her were confused, Stewart knew he couldn't leave her to such a fate.

But their rescue effort appeared stillborn, the casualty of a twenty-four-foot riverboat whose unpainted, waterlogged wooden hull looked as porous as any sponge. They had only managed to travel a dozen or so miles upriver from the Gulf of Mexico. Stewart could feel his quest slipping away from him already.

As the other three men exchanged knowing glances, Stewart straightened himself and walked over to the small wooden hatch that concealed the motor at the riverboat's stern. He opened the hatch, and white-hot smoke rushed out to fill the cabin.

"Doesn't smell like oil," he said between coughs as he backed away from the smoke. "Encouraging."

"I feel better already," Myles quipped. "Better let me have a look at that. I'm the engineer here."

Stewart stepped back to make room for Myles.

"Go out there and see if you can find something to push us out into the middle of the river," Myles said. "If we sit over here on this bank, the mosquitoes will be awful menacing."

Stewart relayed the message in Spanish to the captain, who was lazily tying the boat up to a willow tree on the riverbank. The Mexican captain, Stewart knew, would be paid the same no matter how long the trip took; he was just transporting so much cargo. Five feet tall in his rubber-soled shoes, he was a rugged-looking character who knew not one word of English.

"Bones," Myles said, turning to Sergeant Bates, "see if you can find something up there to make an anchor out of."

"Sure thing, Boss," Sergeant Bates said.

"I got it," Stewart said irritably, waving off the sergeant.

Sweat glistened on his forehead as Stewart left the cabin to search for a makeshift anchor. The sun was only a few hours above the eastern horizon, but he could feel the day already growing sultry. As the riverboat settled at the bank's edge, the breeze that had accompanied it was suffocated. They were dead in the water.

Stewart returned to the cabin empty-handed and, feeling powerless to do anything, watched as Sergeant Bates grabbed an old rag and handed it to Myles, who was clearing a spot on the floor so he could take a closer look at the engine. It was still billowing steam.

"Go see if the captain has any tools," Myles told the sergeant.

"The engine must have overheated," Antonio said.

Myles flashed a crooked smile. "Now that's a divine statement."

A moment later, Sergeant Bates reappeared with a toolbox. The sergeant was Myles's ever-loyal assistant—a six-foot-two-inch skeleton with skin, ready to ride and die at the colonel's orders, a veteran, like Myles and Stewart, of the Spanish-American War. He was as steady as rain in November.

"What you think, Boss?" he asked as he handed the tools to Myles. He took off his dirty white straw hat and began to fan himself with it.

"I don't know," Myles said. "I'm going to have to get down there for a better look." He removed his pocketknife from his trousers. "Hand me that lantern over there."

Myles set his pocketknife on the engine, lit the lantern, and got down on his back. He grimaced and put his hands above his face to shield himself from the heat.

"I'll be back in a minute," he said as he slid into the small space beneath the motor.

Stewart stepped up to have a look for himself. He did so without all the dramatics, and stuck his hand into the engine compartment to check the status of a few rubber hoses. "What do you see down there?"

Before Myles could answer, Stewart accidentally knocked his pocketknife off the motor. It clanked loudly against the engine as it plunged downward, finally tumbling to a stop on what Stewart hoped was the wood planking and not Myles's face.

"Cut that out before you screw something else up!" Myles bellowed from beneath the engine. "You're getting shit in my eyes and blocking my light!"

"Right," Stewart said, and backed away from the engine.

"If you want to do something useful," Myles said, "go get my pack of cigarettes."

Antonio, sweating profusely and wincing at the confusion, savored a long drag from his cigarette and then handed it to Stewart to pass to Myles.

"I said *my* cigarettes, not Señor Jefe's," Myles grumbled without returning the cigarette.

Myles spent a few more minutes under the engine before emerging. Once erect, he wiped the sweat from his face and the dirt from his short-cropped blond hair as he spoke. "We got a hole in the radiator."

Stewart rummaged through the toolbox the sergeant had retrieved. "Don't see much in here that's gonna fix it."

Myles walked over to look for himself, but came to the same conclusion.

"Can we fix it?" Antonio asked.

"Relax," Myles said. "It's not Armageddon. I got something in my bag of tricks that will probably fix it. Toss me your pack, Bones."

The sergeant complied, and Myles retrieved a small bottle from the pack and opened it. "This stuff here will plug that hole," he said as he studied the contents of the bottle.

"What is that, Colonel?" Antonio asked, curiosity replacing anxiety on his face.

"Liquid cement." Myles picked up a small stick from the bed of the boat and began to stir the bottle's contents.

"*Colonel,* huh?" Stewart said sourly.

"That's right, lawyer."

"You were a *lieutenant* colonel," Stewart said, "and only for a passing moment, if I recall."

"I'm still a colonel," Myles said defiantly. "I'm just on official leave. The current administration's policy is to keep a low profile down here. My work is unofficial. When I get back to the States, I'll be reinstated."

Stewart knew well Myles's role, on and off the record, in the current war. His connections made him indispensable. For Myles had somehow managed to stay in the good graces of the revolutionaries *and* the *hacendados,* using his charm and likable nature to steer clear of the bloodletting. Just the same, throwing a quick barb the "colonel's" way—a habit picked up while the two were serving in the Philippines—had become second nature for Stewart. He felt compelled to dig into his former comrade-in-arms even when all he wanted to do was get moving.

Antonio leaned over Myles's shoulder and peered into the bottle of liquid cement. "Are you sure it will work? It looks like it has been in there for years."

"It's a little old," Myles acknowledged, stirring the bottle, "but it will still work. You stir it up and them little chemicals in there will harden up like a rock. One time when I was building the Panama Canal, I was up scouting a lake, and the fuel tank of this little skiff I was in sprung a leak. What was worse, there was a big storm coming in. I pulled out some of this stuff, and the next thing I knew, I was back at the dispensary frolicking with the nurses."

Stewart frowned and then plopped down beside the sergeant on a wooden bench. The tension on the boat began and ended with him. He knew as much, but he couldn't bring himself to be hopeful. "Jack-of-all-trades," he mumbled as he wiped the sweat from his brow.

"Yeah," Myles said. "It don't matter if I'm jimmying a lock on a house or cajoling one of Antonio's daughters back home from some pompous social event."

Antonio laughed heartily beneath his graying beard, his plump belly jiggling. In his full military field dress—a bogus uniform absent any insignia—the old man looked lost on the dilapidated riverboat. He was an overdressed bull's-eye descending into the devil's playpen. But he clearly had no fear. The Revolution could not cure him of his flamboyancy, much less kill it.

As Stewart studied Antonio, he wondered why the Mexican had agreed to help him. For Myles and Sergeant Bates, loyalty was enough. It was, in fact, everything. But for Antonio, something else was fueling his generosity. Enlightened self-interest, perhaps. That, Stewart thought, or self-*preservation*. Antonio had promised, with the help of the captain, to deliver the three Americans deep into the Mexican interior, a world away from their coastal base in Tampico and plenty close to the front lines. Even if he was only along for the first leg, the journey promised to be more risky for him, an aristocrat traveling in the countryside, than the others. But he owed Myles as much; he might need the colonel's people-smuggling services himself if the war continued to turn sour for the aristocracy.

Stewart turned to Myles and rejoined the conversation. "After building the Panama Canal, this should be nothing."

"I didn't build it by myself," Myles retorted. "I had some able-bodied help, which is a step up from the straits I'm in now." He reached into the boat's toolbox and pulled loose a white overcoat, which he donned in solemn fashion, neatly buttoning its belt around his waist. "Bones, hand me that big new cigarette lighter of yours."

"Boss, you look kind of like a scientist in that white coat," Sergeant Bates observed.

"That's because I *am* a scientist," Myles replied, and tested the cigarette lighter. "With an intricate knowledge of the chemical and physical laws that govern the universe."

Stewart stood up. "Don't encourage him, Bones. He's no scientist. And no gimmick will deliver this bucket of bolts. I'll be lucky if I get to Santiago this month."

"You're about the most pessimistic son of a bitch I've ever met," Myles said. "You know that?" He didn't wait for a response. "This job is going to take two hands. Get down here beside me and hold this cigarette lighter while I plug this hole."

Stewart leaned against the door frame and gazed up at the sky. As the riverboat plowed through the still black water, its low rumbling stirred huge flocks of blackbirds and egrets.

The long white plumes of the egrets sparkled against the mass of blackbirds as swarms of each trailed away into the hinterland, a black-and-white exodus silhouetted against the clear blue sky.

Myles's liquid cement had held. The riverboat's engine and radiator were chugging together again, spoiling the tranquil river but lifting the spirits of Stewart and the crew, who, to a man, were drinking in the cool breeze.

They had long since passed an area just outside of Tampico where the mouth of the river was cluttered with large petroleum tanks and refining facilities on its banks. Upriver and beyond the coast, scattered haciendas had punctuated the riverbanks. Since then, nothing.

The river ran northwest through the coastal morass known as the Huasteca, and then into the upper highlands. The area was poorly named; the ancient people who bore its name had found it so useless they rarely entered it.

As they rounded a slight curve in the river, Stewart spotted an adobe ranch house sitting atop the high bank. Its bright red-clay-tiled roof contrasted sharply with the golden hills behind it.

The captain slowed the motor, and the boat glided easily to the bank. He looked up at Stewart and spoke in Spanish. "I am going to stop here and see if they have anything that needs to go upriver."

Stewart jumped off the boat to stretch his legs, with Myles and Sergeant Bates following him ashore. Sergeant Bates grabbed the bowline and tied it to a hitching post sunk in the bank. A weathered wooden sign nailed to the post read HACIENDA CORRAL.

"I will not be gone long," the captain said, and started up the steep bank toward the ranch house.

"Anything to drink or eat up there?" Stewart asked in Spanish as he and Myles followed the captain up the bank.

The building was nothing more than an old ranch house converted into a storage facility. One end of it was a small living quarters, with the remainder used to store goods. No one was in sight, but two mangy dogs roamed the dirt lawn.

The captain stopped in the yard to look around, and then hollered to see if anyone was home. The front door of the living quarters was open, and he turned to look at Stewart and Myles.

"Anybody here?" Myles asked.

"I do not think so," the captain said as he approached the open door. "I will go see." The captain had barely stepped over the threshold before hurrying back outside, his eyes full of fear. "There are two dead men in there!"

Stewart rushed past him to the door. He stood silently for a few seconds in the doorway as he stared at the victims, both lying dead on their cots, a bullet through each man's forehead. As he looked closer, he noticed that both men had mestizo characteristics and wore familiar cattle-working clothes. The blood had not yet dried on their foreheads. He touched the arm of one of the men. It was still warm.

"They've only been dead a couple hours," he said, looking up at Myles. "Probably in here taking a siesta. Never even saw it coming." He stepped outside and yelled down to the boat: "Bones, fetch Jefe."

"I told you before we left," Myles said, "this Mexican bush is a wild and woolly place. We're going to deal with this all the way to Santiago."

Stewart walked back inside and knelt beside one of the beds. He shook his head and looked at one of the dead men before staring back up at Myles. He had not put much credence in Myles's earlier warnings. Myles was not a fibber, but his reputation as a first-rate storyteller—and his perennially low-key disposition—made it difficult for even his closest friends to read him.

Things had changed since Stewart had last been home. A

native of Victoria, on whose outskirts his father still ran a ranch, Stewart was the son of an American and his Mexican wife. He had grown up primarily in Mexico before leaving home for Texas and volunteering for the U.S. Army. More than a decade later, with his stout five-foot-seven-inch frame, olive skin, and jet-black hair, he could pass for a full-blooded Mexican. But he no longer recognized Mexico. The fervor that gripped his country of birth was as alien to him as it was to Myles and Sergeant Bates. He felt lost. And the high stakes of his gamble to rescue Alexia and her family were finally hitting home.

"Let's go outside," he said.

On the front lawn, Stewart watched as Myles studied a pair of horse tracks in the dirt lawn. He looked up to see Antonio and Sergeant Bates cresting the bank's steep rise, with the sun blazing overhead.

"Colonel?" Antonio asked breathlessly.

"There's two dead men in there," Myles said from one knee. "Been shot in the last few hours. Go see if you recognize them. Bones," he said, turning to Sergeant Bates, "go see if you can find a shovel. We'll bury these boys before we go."

Stewart followed Antonio inside. "You know these gentlemen?"

"They look like some of Luis's men," Antonio said after brushing the bangs from the face of one of the victims. He looked around the small room. "It was probably robbery. There is a river station and fuel stop about an hour upriver. We can stop there and ask if anyone knows anything about this."

Outside, Sergeant Bates and the captain had begun digging a pair of shallow graves behind the house. Neither spoke in the stifling heat.

"Need some help?" Stewart asked as he was joined by Myles and Antonio.

"You bet," Sergeant Bates said, tossing the shovel to Stewart.

Stewart glanced over at Myles, who offered an encouraging nod. He paused and squinted up at the sky. There was no one he trusted more than Myles.

The five men labored silently in the dust, each taking his turn with one of the two shovels. The ground was hard. The graves would be shallow indeed.

Chapter 2

"Is she worth it?" Myles asked.

Stewart could sense in Myles's voice that the question wasn't really directed at him, but instead signaled an inner battle going on in his partner's gut. How far would Myles go to help his longtime friend?

Both men had taken off their sweat-soaked shirts to dry them in the sun. They stood on the bow as the riverboat chugged upstream, its engine droning on reassuringly. Myles stood a good five inches taller than Stewart, whose olive skin accentuated Myles's pale complexion, and whose stout upper body contrasted sharply with Myles's slender but soft-in-the-middle frame. Stewart was dressed in denim trousers and cowboy boots. Myles wore knee-high pull-on leather boots and a pair of khaki cotton pants with canvas knees sewn into them.

Most women found Myles, despite the recent softening of his midsection, strikingly handsome. He had light blond hair, sapphire eyes, and an agreeable complexion. He oozed a rugged, optimistic sort of charm: a bit rough around the edges, but positively endearing to the ladies.

Stewart, on the other hand, was more of a mystery— to himself and to everyone around him.

"She must be," he finally answered. "Otherwise, you wouldn't be here."

"Hey, I'm not here for her. There's no way I'm letting you wander off into the bush alone. If the revolutionaries don't put you against the wall, the thugs and profiteers riding behind them will slit your throat. You don't know what you're getting into."

"What choice do I have?"

"None, I reckon. This damn war is making life miserable for everyone, especially the folks trying to maintain order. Alexia's father—hell, her whole family—will be in danger. Sheriffs and their families usually don't get too much sympathy from rebels. Anyway, you must feel *something* for her. It's obviously mutual. Otherwise, you wouldn't be dragging me into this—and she would have hitched up with someone else by now. Ever since you left home, whether you were off on the other side of the globe fighting in some godforsaken war or up in Texas hitting the books for law school, she's stayed put with her folks—waiting. Your regular visits back home sustain her."

"You don't know that," Stewart said, turning to Myles in time to see the incredulous look on his face.

"Stewart Cook, for someone as learned in the law as you are, you'd think you had enough brains to read a woman." Myles shook his head. "Give her a ring, and get it over with. If you wait too long, she might just start courting someone else."

Stewart nodded slowly. "A ring might be the only way I can coax her to leave with me. I've been trying to get her and her family to move to Texas for as long as I can remember."

"Well," Myles said before taking a swig of water from his canteen, "she's obviously stubborn. Doesn't have any idea what a pain in the ass she's turned into. She might just be as thickheaded as you."

Stewart shifted his glance upriver. "Looks like Antonio's river station."

A small wooden dock with a fuel tank resting atop it came into view, followed by two old stone buildings. One was a general store and the other a cantina.

"Grab your shirt," Myles said as he pulled his white cotton button-up shirt, its buttons still fastened, over his head. "And bring your pistol."

As the captain pulled the boat up to the small dock, a young man in his early twenties ran out of the store to catch a rope from Sergeant Bates. He tied the boat off as Stewart stepped onto the dock.

"Fill the boat up with gas," Stewart said in Spanish, surveying the two stone buildings and their surroundings.

The sun was just now setting, but thirty minutes of lingering daylight remained. Two horses were tied up outside the cantina.

"Bones," Myles said, "go over there and take a look at those horses. Let me know if one of them has a small chip on the front of his back left hoof. We'll be in the saloon."

"Will do, Boss," Sergeant Bates said.

"Do you want me to wake up Antonio?" the captain asked as Myles and Sergeant Bates stepped onto the dock.

Myles turned back to the captain. "Get him up," he said, and straightened his pistol belt around his waist.

Stewart led the way into the musty cantina and squinted. A dozen or so wall-mounted candleholders, each housing the stub of a flickering candle in its wrought-iron cradle, cast long, fluid shadows. The warm candlelight provided as much light as the saloon's four windows, now blue-black in the half-light of dusk.

As Stewart walked toward the bar, the wood plank floor, which was covered with a quarter inch of dust, creaked conspicuously beneath his feet. Two men sitting at one of the establishment's three wooden tables looked up, and the middle-aged Mexican woman tending bar gave him a nod as Myles entered behind him.

"We'll take two tequilas," Stewart said, dropping a few pesos on the bar. He leaned sideways against the bar and indiscreetly stared at the two men sitting at the table. They were both in their forties and had Creole facial features, stringy hair, and unshaven faces and mustaches. They wore American cowboy hats, as opposed to the more common sombrero, and each had a dusty bandanna around his neck.

Stewart watched as Myles gladly accepted his shot of tequila and downed it with a welcoming grimace.

"What you boys doing way out here in the middle of nowhere?" Myles asked obligingly.

"Just passing through," one of the men said before turning up the shot glass in front of him. He refilled it from a half-empty bottle, which sat next to one already bone dry. "What's it to you?"

Stewart gazed at the two men and then at Sergeant Bates, who had arrived at the front door. The sergeant looked past him and nodded to Myles before walking to the other end of the bar.

"We came across a hacienda down the river a piece," Myles said. "Two dead bodies there. You fellas wouldn't know anything about that, would you?" He turned his back to the bar and fronted the two.

"Nope. We came in from the north," the man said. He backed his chair away from the table a few inches. "You the law around here?"

"I'm the law wherever I go," Myles said without blinking. "You shouldn't go lying to me. One of those horses outside makes the same tracks we saw at that hacienda."

Stewart noticed Antonio saunter into the bar and halt in the doorway, the smile on his face fading.

The man doing the talking slowly stood to get a better look at Myles and Stewart. He then glanced over at Sergeant Bates, who was a few paces down the bar.

"I don't see any badges," he finally said. As he spoke, a metallic click came from under the table, where his partner had remained seated.

Without pointing their weapons at either of the two men, the three Americans slowly drew their pistols.

"We're not looking for a fight with a couple of drunk gauchos," Myles said. "But if you boys want one, we'll end it in a hurry."

The man standing laughed loudly. "You threatening us?"

Myles didn't answer.

Stewart's eyes narrowed. He hadn't spoken since ordering the tequila. His temples wore beads of sweat. He knew what was coming.

As the man searched the Americans' eyes, his bravado evaporated in the dim saloon. He jerked his eyes from Stewart to Myles and back to Stewart.

"Here we go," Myles mumbled just loud enough for Stewart to hear.

The man grinned and started to draw. But his pistol never cleared its holster. Stewart's gun coughed smoke, and a blood-black circle grew in the center of the man's forehead, just beneath the rim of his cowboy hat. He fell with his arms at his sides, twisting downward in a lifeless heap, his hat still on his head.

The single shot's concussion brought the man's partner to his feet, and Myles and Sergeant Bates each put a bullet in his chest. He fell onto the table, knocking it over on his way to the dusty planks. With gunfire still ringing in his ears, Stewart watched as two tequila bottles clanked between the two dead men, eventually spinning to a stop.

Then, silence.

The Americans glanced at each other through the smoky haze with their pistols still extended. Antonio, his mouth open, remained frozen in the doorway.

A giddy, sickening sensation pulsed from Stewart's chest to his throat.

"You all right back there, ma'am?" Sergeant Bates finally asked, lowering his pistol and walking behind the bar. He gently lifted the barmaid from the floor while Myles filled four shot glasses, the last of which he handed to the barmaid.

Stewart grabbed the bottle and one of the shots. He sat down on a stool beside the bar, turned the glass up, and stared at the two dead men on the floor. "We need to get to Santiago," he said in a raspy voice. He poured himself another shot and drained it.

Myles sat down next to him and steadied his gaze at Stewart. "I didn't mean to get in a fight. I was just going to report them to the local sheriff. Looks like we saved the Mexican justice system some paperwork."

Stewart exhaled slowly through his mouth. His blood had gone cold. He knew his partner could see it in his eyes.

Myles downed his shot and kept talking, no doubt hoping to somehow bring Stewart back. "That was about the quickest, easiest, and most casual justice I ever administered. I haven't shot many men that I didn't feel a little bit guilty about, but I must confess, I don't have any remorse for these two. Hell, they were so drunk, I don't think they could've drawn their pistols. Jefe," he said, turning to Antonio, "here's your robbers."

"You gringos work fast," Antonio said, shaking his head. "Gabriella, do you have anybody to help you haul these men outside?"

The barmaid barely nodded.

"Good," Stewart said, suddenly finding his voice. He set his shot glass down on the bar and stood up. "We're running behind schedule. Let's get moving." Blue twilight flooded the cantina as he brushed past Antonio and out the door.

Chapter 3

Stewart stood alone on the bow. The eerie glow of dusk had given way to a moonlit night, and the riverboat seemed to be gliding on utter blackness. The river, wherever it was taking them, spoke only in rippled tones, its plate-glass surface plowed under by the riverboat and buried by a throaty hum.

They had traveled beyond the lowland swamps and into the rich savanna grasslands of the eastern slope of the Sierra Madre Oriental Mountains. With midnight approaching, the river had narrowed to a third its size and the current had picked up considerably.

"What's on your mind, partner?"

Stewart turned to see Myles, canteen in hand.

"Thirsty?" Myles asked, not seeming to need, for the moment anyway, an answer to the first question.

"Yeah."

Myles unscrewed the cap and handed him the canteen.

"Thanks," Stewart said before taking a long drink. He wiped his mouth and looked up at Myles.

Myles said nothing, and Stewart smiled wryly as he realized how well his partner knew him: Sometimes, the only way to get Stewart to speak his mind was to let him come to it in silence.

"I'll never get used to killing," he finally said.

"Me neither."

"I thought we left all that behind in the Philippines. Almost didn't bring a gun. I only brought it for insurance. Never thought I'd use it, especially this soon."

"At least you know what you're up against now," Myles said. "You're doing the right thing, going after Alexia. But it's not gonna be easy. You haven't fired your last bullet. If it ain't the carpetbaggers that are preying on the chaos, it'll be the revolutionaries. We'll have to watch ourselves, that's for sure. But once this is over and you're back in Texas, you can store your gun somewhere it can collect dust."

"What if I'm not good enough? It's been a long time."

Myles laughed. "Stewart, my friend, that ruffian in the saloon didn't even have time to burp up his tequila before you put a bullet between his eyes."

"He was drunk."

"Well, consider him a practice run. From here on out, we'll watch for sober gunslingers, too. Hell, I'm not worried. Ever since you shot up half the Spanish Army and saved my sorry ass a half dozen times, I've never doubted your marksmanship."

"I only saved you once. And I was lucky."

"You call it luck, I call it skill. It don't matter one way or another 'cause I'm still here, and you're the reason for it."

As they spoke, the captain eased off on the engine, and the riverboat drifted toward the bank. Slowly, the small river station of Hacienda Calles appeared out of the darkness. A ghostly adobe building emerged above a dirt ramp and ten-man wooden ferry. Just ahead, a bridge spanned the river, linking east to west, and four large haciendas acted as spokes to the station's hub.

They could see a lantern glowing in the window of the adobe building as the captain pulled the riverboat next to the embankment beside the ferry. The captain silenced the engine, and with it the riverboat's headlight.

"Start her back up!" Stewart heard Myles holler in the sudden darkness. "We need that headlight!"

Antonio jumped out of the boat first and marched up to the small building, swearing angrily at its occupants the whole way. He opened the door and barged in without knocking.

Stewart looked at Myles, and both men laughed.

"Looks like it doesn't bode well to piss off that Mexican," Myles said as they started walking toward the small building to see what had inspired all the Spanish expletives.

Inside, Antonio was still distraught. Two of his subordinates were sitting on their cots, rubbing their eyes and cowering under his verbiage.

"I told you to keep someone on guard at all times!" Antonio screamed, pacing the floor and wringing his hands. "Can you two do nothing right? That truck would make a fine booty for any of the bandits that frequent these river stations! And merchandise is not all that is being stolen. We found two men with bullet holes in their foreheads this morning because neither one saw fit to post a guard!" Antonio tried to collect himself. In a somewhat gentler—but still firm—voice, he asked, "Did you fill the truck up with gas?"

"Sí, jefe," one of the men stammered. "But we have a problem."

"What?" Antonio asked, his tone implying there was no answer that could possibly please him.

"We promised it to the Campbell family."

Antonio's face burned red. But his expression softened just as quickly. "What is wrong? Is it the baby? Why do they need the truck?"

"They don't need it, *jefe. You* need it. Some squatters moved in on their house two days ago. They're getting out. They asked for your help."

"But I do not know how to get there by myself," Antonio protested.

"They sent a map over the mountain," the man said, retrieving a homemade map from beneath his cot and holding it out for Antonio's inspection.

"Antonio," Stewart interrupted, "we don't have time for this. We need that truck."

Antonio ignored Stewart. He took the map and slowly unfolded it, seemingly mesmerized by the turn of events. He sat down on a chair and looked up at Myles, his voice tentative at first. "Mr. Campbell is a gringo. He and his Mexican wife have two daughters and an infant. I have known them for years. They are good people. Colonel, this . . . this is what you do. You smuggle people out of the country. This is why your government sent you here to 'observe' the war. These people need your help. Please! Help me get them back here to the river, and I will take it from there."

For the first time, Stewart thought, Antonio actually looked noble. Passion flamed in his eyes, and his previously cartoonish uniform gleamed with resolve. There was more to the old man than just pomp and circumstance, after all.

"I don't go," Myles said, nodding in Stewart's direction, "unless he goes."

All eyes fell on Stewart.

"We can't," he said softly, realizing that he couldn't say no to Antonio or the Campbell family. "We . . . " He closed his eyes and shook his head slowly. "We . . . ah, hell!" He turned for the door and tried to slam it behind him, but it kicked open after he banged it shut with too much force.

"Don't worry," he heard Myles say inside. "He's coming. We're all coming."

Chapter 4

"Load up and let's get moving," Myles said, tossing his cigarette off the dock. "Captain, tie your boat off and stay here until we get back. I don't give a damn if it's a week. Jefe, your men will make sure he gets fed and watered and fill his boat up with fuel while we're gone." Before Antonio could answer, Myles was issuing another order. "And Captain, make sure to drain that river water out of the radiator and find some well water to replace it with."

"There is a well out back," Antonio offered.

Myles, at last, was in charge. He still wasn't sure about their ultimate destination. But the fact that Stewart was willing, albeit grudgingly, to take a noble detour encouraged his own sense of chivalry. They were doing the right thing, he thought, even if the road ahead was impossible to make out. And he was ready to throw the full weight of his expertise—not to mention his personality—behind the expedition.

Ahead of him, Stewart and Sergeant Bates climbed into the back of Antonio's Model-T pickup truck, a fancy testament to modernity and wildly out of place in the Mexican outback.

"Impressive, Antonio," Myles said as he eyed the laminated wood panels and wagon-wheel tires. "This buggy looks brand-new."

"Almost," Antonio said proudly of his Ford. "It is two years old. Barely broken in."

"I'll say," Myles said. "The chrome on the radiator and headlight housings is as shiny as my backside in the dead of winter."

As he was about to climb into the doorless passenger's side, Myles caught Stewart's stony gaze from the truck bed.

"Relax, we're gonna get there," Myles assured him. "Like you said, we need this truck."

From the river station, they traveled inland on a long, straight dirt road that was, for the first twenty miles, reasonably maintained. Myles stared through the windshield into the darkness. Ankle-high green grass and a few scattered oak trees on the road's shoulders flickered in the truck's headlights. But beyond the glowing road, sheer blackness awaited them.

The road to the Campbell ranch led into cloud country, a lush oasis of green in the middle of northern Mexico's otherwise barren interior. Moisture coming off the gulf collided with the high mountains to the west and dissipated downward, providing some of the richest and most worked pastureland and cropland in all of Mexico. The farms all had efficient roads, and they were making good time.

That is, until Antonio hit the brakes.

"Why is he slowing down?" Stewart hollered from the wood-paneled bed.

"Cattle!" Myles hollered back.

The truck came to a complete stop, and Antonio started cranking on a manual horn, the business end of which was blaring away from atop the aluminum hood.

"That's a very unpleasant tone," Myles said, wishing the cab had doors.

Antonio grinned and kept cranking. "It's just as bad in back."

"Tell Jefe in there that the next time we see cattle, me and Bones will get out and run 'em off," Stewart hollered once more from the truck bed as the small herd of cows rumbled off the road and into the brush.

Myles turned and smiled; Stewart and Sergeant Bates were staring back at him with their hands over their ears.

They continued on for another hour, eventually turning onto a dirt road at the base of some foothills.

Myles banged on the back glass. "Jefe says it's about to get bumpy."

The narrow, lightly used dirt road led up into the mountains to the west of the Tamisi Valley, winding its way piecemeal up the hills along a small creek and then up switchbacks on a steeper mountainside. The latter portion of the road was no more than a rock ledge cut into the side of the mountain, and was so tight and treacherous Antonio couldn't clear first gear. But he pushed each corner as fast as he could, paying little mind to the harrowing cliffs plunging downward from first one side, then the other, of the road, which was only a few feet wider than the truck. With Myles quietly clutching the leather seat beneath him, the aristocrat waxed political on his country's future.

"Most Mexicans are adamantly opposed to any U.S. intervention in the internal affairs of our country," he said as he negotiated a hairpin turn. "But my constituency—landowners, businessmen, and the bourgeoisie—are starting to rethink their position. The war is going badly for us. We fear for our safety if the Americans do not get involved. The Marines sitting offshore back in Tampico may be our only hope."

"Uh-huh," Myles said, his eyes widening at the sight of another drop-off, visible only as sheer blackness just feet from where he sat.

Antonio grinned at Myles's obvious discomfort and continued his monologue.

"But," he said, pausing for effect, "I'm afraid the Marines are only in Tampico to protect the oil wells and refineries. While you've been helping the U.S. consulate evacuate American families and businessmen and other foreigners, we Mexicans fear we will be left to the mercy of the rebels."

Myles managed a nod as he fixed his gaze straight ahead.

"It could be worse," Antonio said with a chuckle.

"What?" Myles asked.

"Take a look at your friends."

As Antonio leaned into another hairpin turn, Myles braved a hurried glance behind him, and caught sight of Stewart and Sergeant Bates scrambling to the uphill side of the bed.

Finally, they crested the escarpment and found flat, open terrain atop the mountain. Antonio picked up the speed some, and Myles loosened his grip on the leather seat cushion. They drove on for another ten minutes, and then turned off on an even smaller side road leading back down a small draw on the backside of the mountain, where Antonio stopped.

"We're here," he said and got out.

"We're here?" Myles repeated. "I can't see that we are anywhere."

"Colonel, I thought you were a seasoned warrior," Antonio said as he helped Sergeant Bates out. "Do not tell me a little ride up into the mountains gets you spooked."

"I've survived too many artillery barrages to die because some old Mexican drove his truck off the side of a mountain," Myles replied as he lit up a cigarette. "That said, if we can't fit everybody in that truck on the way out, I won't have any problem walking off this mountain."

"I might join you," Stewart said, and jumped out.

Antonio laughed, startled, it seemed to Myles, by the Americans' frankness to someone of his political stature.

He pulled a large box out of the bed and set it on the ground. Opening it, he found a small lantern and beckoned the three men to join him. "Please, come over here and take a look at this."

He lit the lantern and unfolded the small hand-drawn topographic map on the ground.

Myles looked over at Stewart, who had grabbed his pack and was gazing up at the clear sky in an attempt to get his bearings. In this solitary backcountry hundreds of miles from the contamination of city lights, the stars were in glorious abundance. Myles marveled at them.

Since the group had left the river station, the temperature had dropped twenty degrees, and all now donned field jackets. In stark contrast to the oppressive mugginess of the lowlands, a cool, dry breeze blew—so dry it could be smelled.

"No need to worry about all those stars and directions," Myles said as he sniffed at the mountain air. "You're with me. Come on."

Stewart followed Myles and Sergeant Bates over to Antonio as he continued to pick out reference marks. There, they knelt on the ground beside Antonio, and the three gave the Mexican boss their complete attention.

"We are right here. The gringo and his family live here." Antonio pointed to a small X on the map. As he spoke, steam escaped his mouth. "They are supposed to be in a little cabin here up in the hills. From the looks of this map, it is about ten miles from here."

"That map looks kind of shady," Myles said as he stared intently at it.

"Trust me," Antonio said, looking up at the three men. "Bob Campbell knows his property."

"I don't have any doubt that that map is an accurate portrayal of where that cabin is in relation to everything else on the map," Myles said. "But I'm a little concerned about where *we* are on the map. Hell, we might not even *be* on that map!"

"We are right here," Antonio reiterated, stabbing his finger at two arbitrary points on the map. He then stood up and pointed to two mountaintops on the horizon, barely discernible in the moonlight.

"I feel better already," Stewart said.

"Let me have a look at that map," Myles said, picking the map up off the ground.

The map had no north arrow and delineated only a few streams, mountaintops, and ridges. It did have a few measurements locating the cabin with reference to one of the streams and a few mountaintops, including the one they were currently on.

"Bones, get your compass out and give me a bearing on those two mountaintops," Myles said. "Jefe, is there somewhere around here we can see down the other side of this mountain? A good lookout?"

"There is a pretty good point just up the hill," Antonio said.

Before he could get the words out of his mouth, Stewart had started up the hill. Myles grabbed Sergeant Bates's pack, and he and Antonio followed Stewart. Myles walked slowly, attentively studying the map as he held the lantern high enough to read. He arrived to find Stewart perched atop a large boulder, looking out off the mountaintop.

"What do you see?"

"A lot," Stewart replied as he continued to search the valley below.

Myles looked out into the vast expanse of open highland extending as far as the eye could see. In the darkness, no particulars could be seen, but the enormity of the area below could be discerned.

Stewart opened Sergeant Bates's pack to retrieve a pair of binoculars. He looked through them out into the valley. "I can't see anything out of these."

"Yeah," Myles mumbled inattentively. "I think Uncle Sam got taken to the cleaners on those glasses. Some Yankee up in

Boston really pulled a fast one on us." He had sat down on the ground and was painstakingly looking back and forth between the map and the valley. "I hope old Bob down there is a better farmer than he is a map drawer."

"He's probably been down here so long, he's starting to turn Mexican," Stewart said, putting his hand on Antonio's shoulder to indicate the comment was not personal.

"Is that what happened to you?" Myles asked and stood up. Sergeant Bates had arrived, and Myles wanted to have a look at the bearings he had taken. He studied the map and the bearings for a few seconds in an attempt to correlate the two. "This map isn't worth a damn."

"Why the hell didn't he just ride out?" Stewart asked Antonio. "Let you pick him up at the river."

"Ride out to where?" Antonio asked, still looking at the map. "All the farms on the other side of the mountains are deserted, and nothing is going down the river."

"This is what we're gonna do," Myles said as he made eye contact with the other three. "We know that the cabin is on a creek somewhere down there. I only see three possible creeks." He pointed to the cabin's proximity to a creek on the map. He then looked out at the terrain below and pointed to three overgrown shrub lines heading out into the valley from their current location. One shrub line was directly below them, and the two others a few miles to the north and south, respectively. "Those are probably creeks. As soon as the moon comes up a little more, two of us will go down the one to the south, and two will go down the one to the north. We'll meet up at the middle creek about ten miles west of here and work our way back here. As soon as it gets light enough, we'll pick a spot out there somewhere to meet. Stewart, let's draw a couple of accurate maps from here. Bones has the two bearings for this location, so in case we get lost, we can get back here. I'll take Bones with me."

"Okay," Stewart said, nodding.

"We'll take the southern route," Myles said as he handed the small piece of paper with the bearings on it to Stewart. "Write down these bearings. Let's try not to deviate from the plan, if possible."

"Why didn't we bring some horses?" Stewart asked.

"Quit bellyaching," Myles said. "This is gonna be a cakewalk compared to the mess I've let you talk me into. A week from now, you'll wish you were back here stumbling around this peaceful mountain."

Chapter 5

"I wonder where they're at," Myles said.

He was lying on his back in two feet of rye grass, lounging in the shade beneath a group of small hackberry trees at the rendezvous point. Dappled sunlight flickered through the treetops above him as the leaves rustled in a cool morning breeze. He looked at his watch pessimistically.

"Maybe they got lost," said Sergeant Bates, who lay nearby, hidden in the rye grass.

"Or that old Mexican pulled up lame."

"Maybe they found them."

"I hope you're right, but I'm a little more inclined to believe scenario A or B," Myles said. "I reckon I could crawl up on that hilltop and see if I can see them. What do you think?"

"You're the boss."

"It sure is comfy down here. That hilltop is a long way up there. I wouldn't have any problem staying right here all day, but I better get up there. It might preclude some grief on our part." Myles stood up, put on Sergeant Bates's pack, and started for the base of the small rock-covered hill. He stopped and looked back at Sergeant Bates. "Go fill up the extra canteens in that creek over there. Meet me up on the hill."

The trudge up the hill was more taxing than Myles figured it would be. At the top, he flopped down on his back in an effort to revive himself. As he panted for air, he struggled to remove his small canteen from its pouch on his hip. It was wedged between his thigh and the ground, and could easily have been removed by sitting up. Instead, he wriggled in the rocks and jerked on the canteen in a time-consuming but less stressful routine until it came free. He then drained the half-full bottle into his mouth and rolled three revolutions to a rock rim on the edge of the summit, where he took up a prone position.

From there, with the aid of his binoculars, he scanned the sparse valley below until he spotted a horse train. A handful of horses, tied together in single file, were moving deliberately in a southwesterly direction. Some were loaded down with luggage and supplies; others were carrying women in white dresses. They had no chance, Myles lamented, of even passing within a couple miles of his current location. He took a second look at the train to confirm its members, but only had to look but a moment. The bright red jacket of Antonio's bogus military uniform could not be mistaken. Stewart was there somewhere—probably the man out in front guiding the train.

"You see anything?" Sergeant Bates asked, arriving at the hilltop without breaking a sweat and breathing no heavier than usual.

"Yeah," Myles said. He looked at the sergeant sideways. "Give me that."

Before Sergeant Bates could figure out precisely what *that* was, Myles snatched his canteen, satisfied in the knowledge that his was already empty and the sergeant clearly didn't need his.

"The good news," Myles said between gulps, "is it looks like they've found Mr. Campbell and his family. The bad news is they're heading out into the unbeknownst." Myles picked the glasses back up to take another look. He had stopped puffing from the climb and could focus now on the problem at hand.

"Where at?" Bates crawled up beside him.

"Over there," Myles said as he handed the glasses to the sergeant and pointed. "You see 'em?"

The chaparral below, brown and dry in contrast to the plains just to the east, was barely fit for cattle grazing. The sage, mesquite, and yuccas dotting the landscape did little to hide the easily unsettled dust the horses were kicking up.

"That's them all right." Sergeant Bates put the binoculars down. "You want me to go and fetch them?"

"I suspect they'd be halfway to Mexico City before you caught them."

Myles rolled over and stood up. Once on his feet, he spit a piece of grass from his mouth and brushed at the dust on his face and clothes. He turned to see the sergeant stand as well, taking his cue, as usual, from him.

Sergeant Bates sized up his boss and smirked. "What the hell happened to you?"

Myles didn't respond.

"They're getting farther away every minute," Sergeant Bates pointed out.

"Let me think just a second," Myles replied. He pulled out his pistol and discharged the nine-round magazine into the air. As he fired with his left hand, he lifted his binoculars to his eyes with his right to see if anyone in the caravan had noticed.

"They hear you?"

"Doesn't look like it. Looks like all I did was squander those rounds. The wind's blowing pretty hard in our direction." Myles scanned the valley below. "You got your rope in that pack?"

"Yeah," Sergeant Bates replied, checking to make sure. "Why?"

"There's some horses in this pasture down here. Maybe we

can catch one and ride it over there to get them. Let's get going, lest they wander out of sight."

Myles slapped Sergeant Bates on his bony shoulder and briskly walked down the hilltop in the direction of a small fenced pasture at its base. A few horses rummaged in a semi-shaded grove.

"Whose are these?" the sergeant asked.

"Beats me."

"Which one should we take?"

"That one," Myles said, pointing to a tall sorrel gelding. "If someone bothered to take his manhood, he must be broken in."

"I hope so," Sergeant Bates said. "He's awfully big."

As they slowly approached the horse, they separated, with Sergeant Bates keeping his lasso by his side and trying to look harmless.

The gelding looked up from the grass and snorted.

"Well, we've got his attention," Myles said, feeling his heart skip a beat. "You better make good with that lasso."

The sergeant's first attempt fell short, as did his second and third. But the horse stayed put. He seemed disinterested in the comedy unfolding before him.

"Throw it farther!" Myles chastised Sergeant Bates. "You throw that thing like a woman."

The sergeant tried again, this time overshooting the mark by a good ten paces.

"Not *that* far!" Myles said.

With Myles offering plenty of criticism but no help, Sergeant Bates tossed the lasso another half-dozen times before finally snagging the gelding, which didn't respond.

"Damn!" Myles said. "That horse is so tame we could've walked up to him and put the rope around his neck without him so much as noticing we were here."

He made a primitive bridle out of the rope and, with the sergeant's aid, struggled to climb atop the horse. He heard

Sergeant Bates groan under his weight, and looked down to see the sergeant holding the horse's bridle and pushing him up at the same time.

Once settled in on top, Myles spent a few minutes caressing the horse's neck and talking softly to him. Sergeant Bates was still holding the bridle and waiting for Myles to give him a signal to let go. But Myles couldn't bring himself to do so; he was enjoying making the sergeant wait.

"All right," he finally said. "Lead him a couple of rods. If he acts right, let him go."

Much to Myles's relief, the horse was well behaved and even responsive to the bridle. Myles made a turn with the gelding and smiled. "Let me do that again," he said, "just to corroborate my findings."

After instructing the sergeant to return to the hilltop, he took off at a gallop in the direction of the horse train. He couldn't wait to rib Stewart for his faulty sense of direction.

Stewart was leading the train when he spotted Myles on the horizon riding toward them. He motioned for Antonio and Bob Campbell to stop the horses.

"Who do you think that might be?" Antonio called ahead.

"That surly Irishman," Stewart hollered, stepping forward a few paces. "Self-proclaimed womanizer and jack-of-all-trades."

Myles arrived at a full gallop, bringing the gelding to an abrupt stop alongside Stewart and stirring up a dust cloud. He frowned through the dust. "I should have known better than to send a lawyer and a politician off on their own. Where the hell are you headed?"

"The meeting place," Stewart said without flinching. He could tell Myles, by stopping the gelding a few inches from his face, was hoping to provoke a reaction. But he did his best to look unmoved as he stared up nonchalantly at Myles.

"You're headed due west," Myles said. "To where, I know not." Myles guided his horse over to the family of five. Mrs. Campbell was a short Creole woman in her thirties, and her young daughters, in their teens, each wearing a white dress and straw brim hat like her mother, bore a resemblance to both parents. "No need to worry now, ladies. I've arrived to save you from your fate."

Bob, a stoutly built American with big hands and a rancher's firm grip, introduced himself and reached up to shake Myles's hand.

Myles returned the gesture. "I'm Colonel Myles Adams." He looked at the horses, which were weighed down with an assortment of boxes and bags. "Did you leave anything at home? Well, Stewart," he called ahead to his partner, "at least you got 'em."

Stewart frowned and wiped the dust from his eyes; if Myles only knew the half of it. "That compass I bought in Tampico before we left only points in one direction: north."

"You must have got it at the store around the corner from your hotel," Myles said. "I should have warned you about that." He circled the group of horses and then tickled the stomach of Bob's baby girl. "Good morning, missy."

The baby, who was sitting in the lap of Bob's oldest daughter, started crying.

"Never met a woman yet who liked you touching her," Stewart grumbled.

Myles gave up trying to pacify the baby girl and rode back to Stewart, who, still standing several paces apart from the others, was losing his patience by the minute.

"What do you think?" Myles asked after dismounting.

"This ain't the way to Santiago."

Myles smiled and squinted in the mid-morning sun. "Bones is at that hill," he said, pointing at the bluff he had just ridden down from. "It's about three miles. If we push on, making it back by dark is tenable. You think those horses will make it?"

"Bob says they're rested and fed," Stewart answered. He removed his white straw hat and ran a hand through his jet-black hair. "We'll take them as far as we can."

"So you're okay with getting these folks back to the station?" Myles asked, catching Stewart's gaze.

"Can't leave 'em here," he said with a huff. "And we need that truck."

Myles turned to the group. "Bob, I know you know your horses and the country. But I was an officer in the United States Cavalry, and there ain't no way these horses are going to make it where we're going packed like this. Everybody is going to have to walk. We're going to distribute this stuff evenly between your horses and this one. If we do that, we should be at the river by dark."

"Okay," Bob said gruffly. "My girls are tough. They'll do what they have to if it means we'll make it out of here." He turned to help his family.

"I wouldn't be celebrating just yet," Myles said. "We may get those horses up the mountain, but it's the ride down the other side in Jefe's truck that's going to be the biggest hurdle. After that, you might just decide you would've been better off staying here and taking your chances with some of Pancho Villa's bandits. I'll probably walk out myself."

Chapter 6

"You know what I think?" Myles asked.

Stewart shook his head. He felt relieved that they had found Sergeant Bates and had made good time, with the sergeant leading the group back to the truck and the two of them bringing up the rear. The sun had yet to set over the valley below, and he could see clearly the small side road they had followed the night before—and the Model-T pickup still parked where they had left it—just up ahead. But he wasn't in the mood to listen to Myles ramble.

"I think we don't need that truck," Myles said. "Where we're going, we need a few good horses and plenty of ammo. If we run into mechanical difficulties with that truck, or if we hit a bad stretch of road that ain't fit for an automobile, we'll be wishing we were horseback."

"You're just now saying this?"

"I just now thought of it."

"Typical," Stewart groused.

"Hey, I don't have to be here, you know. I'm doing this out of the goodness of my heart. It's not like you're paying me." Myles stopped, and the gelding he was leading almost bumped into him. "Are you?"

Stewart turned and glared at him. "Where are we gonna get the horses?"

"From Bob. He doesn't need 'em where he's going. He and his family will probably take a steamer out of Tampico. Antonio can leave us right here. With us three out of the picture, they'll have plenty of room for the girls and the baby. Bob and his two eldest daughters can ride in back with the luggage, and Mrs. Campbell and the baby can ride up front with Jefe."

"You're finally starting to make sense."

"It's what I do," Myles said as they joined the group waiting for them at the truck. "I make sense of the senseless. I—" He stopped abruptly.

"What is it?" Stewart asked. Something in the valley had caught his partner's attention.

"Where are my binoculars?" Myles asked absentmindedly.

"I've got both of ours," said Sergeant Bates, who had been waiting for them beside the pickup. He handed Myles the pair they had used earlier in the day, and then trained his own binoculars at the valley below.

"What do you see?" Antonio asked. He was resting against the pickup, which was facing back down the hill and perched on the side of the small draw where they had parked the night before. From where he and the others stood, they had a commanding view of the valley below.

"It's probably nothing," Myles said, still fixated on something in the valley. "Then again . . ."

Stewart felt a twinge of fear—and a healthy dose of annoyance. "What is it?" he asked impatiently.

"I see a dust trail," Myles said. "And six men on horseback."

He looked up from his binoculars at the same time as the sergeant, and the two men exchanged glances.

"This area," Myles drawled, "is full of marauding bands administering vigilante justice and appropriating what they deem theirs. It is best to be circumspect. Whoever it is, I think they may have some interest in us. They've stopped. They're too far to make out, but they must have seen us."

"They saw the truck," Stewart said.

"Maybe," Myles said. "Either way, we'll know who they are soon enough. Looks like they're headed this way." He turned around to face everyone. "It's probably nothing, but let's be on the safe side. Bones, take these ladies and hide them in that little creek bed over there. No offense, but attractive young ladies consorting with gringos can sometimes make some of these devious lads indignant. Hide your tracks so as not to arouse any suspicion, and take Antonio with you. That precious uniform he has on may do the same."

"Don't worry, ladies," Bones said as he took the petite Mrs. Campbell by the arm. "There's nothing to be concerned about. It's better to be safe than sorry." The sergeant, with Antonio following, ushered the ladies in white dresses up the road to some thick brush covering a small creek. As he returned, he brushed his tracks with a tree branch along the way.

Stewart retrieved his rifle from the cab and gave it to Bob, thinking the husky rancher looked antsy but ready to spar if need be. "Can you shoot this thing?"

Bob nodded, and Stewart went over a few brief necessities for employing the rifle.

"Just keep it nearby and ready, Bob," Myles said as he climbed into the truck bed. "Don't hold it."

Sergeant Bates climbed up in the truck beside Myles and looked through his binoculars at the group of horsemen. "If my vision's not failing me," the sergeant said, "I believe that's Jorge Trevino."

"Really?" Myles said as he returned his binoculars to his eyes. "I believe you're right."

"That scoundrel is easy to spot with all that silver jewelry on," Sergeant Bates said.

"You know him?" Stewart inquired as he turned to look at

the group. He could see a bright red bandanna on the head of one of the lead men—and sparkling reflections from his attire.

"Yeah," Myles said. "He's one immoral, pestilent bastard. Heads a small group of banditos. They're a product of the war, not part of it. Their only conviction is themselves, usually wrung from somebody else's blood. They're likely up here plundering some of these abandoned farms. If it's any consolation, Jorge should know better than to mess with me." Myles put down his binoculars. He removed his pistol from its holster and laid it on top of the cab's flat black roof in front of him. "Nonetheless, be ready. He's dogged and given to anything, especially if he's been drinking."

The banditos, riding up the backside of the mountain, arrived from the opposite direction from which the Americans and their Mexican friend had come the night before. They rode uphill at a gallop until they were twenty paces short of the truck, where they stopped abruptly. They sat quietly on their horses, deliberately inspecting the four Americans. They were a middle-aged crew, all armed. Several held rifles in their laps. Their makeup was diverse, with one of the gentlemen redheaded and another slightly grayed. They were in common dress suited for travel, and most wore a smaller version of the sombrero fit for riding.

Jorge sat in the middle of the group, half a horse in front of his men. A red bandanna covered his bald head, and he had a six-inch goatee. Tawdry silver jewelry adorned his neck, waist, and both wrists, shimmering in the setting sun.

"I thought we already ran all you gringos out of the country," he finally said, breaking the silence. "Looks like we still have some work to do, boys." He squinted as he studied the Americans, their silhouettes framed by the setting sun.

"You won't have to concern yourselves with us much

longer," Myles said. "We're on our way out. You'll be able to rape and pillage all you want before long."

The group's horses stopped fidgeting, and Myles's voice seemed to cave in on itself as it pierced the stifling tension. He and Sergeant Bates stood in the bed of the truck, exposing only their top halves. Stewart, with his shirt off and his brawny exterior exposed, stood beside the truck on the driver's side. He glanced briefly at Bob, who was on the passenger's side.

"Colonel Adams, somebody's going to cut off that slanderous tongue of yours someday," Jorge said. "I hope it's me." His eyes were wild and intimidating, and he spoke with unconcealed fury. "Maybe today I will get my wish."

"If you've got a problem with me, you know where to find me," Myles said. He took his eyes off Jorge and addressed the other men. "These people are leaving. They're looking for no trouble. They *want* no trouble."

Jorge clicked his heels against his mount and rode forward slowly, his spurs jingling rhythmically. His men followed, but stopped a few paces short of the truck as he circled to its rear, effectively sealing off the Americans.

Stewart watched as the banditos encircled him and the others, and he could feel the walls closing in on him. He slowly stepped back a few paces so he could keep an eye on Jorge. He hoped no one could see the sweat building on his brow.

"What you got hidden in those bushes back there?" Jorge asked, looking down at the road behind the truck and then at the creek bed.

"It ain't any of your business," Myles said as he turned around to face Jorge.

"Have you seen Carmen lately?" Jorge asked with a devilish grin.

Myles's eyes narrowed.

"I thought she was your woman."

"She *is*," Myles asserted.

"Well, seems like a man should be with his woman, especially when the countryside is burning around her. I hear Victoria will be lucky to last another day. The rebels are ready to burn it down." Jorge leaned to his left slightly and spit tobacco juice on the gravel road beneath him and his horse. "I'd hate to see her take up with a group of marauders like us."

As his men laughed, Jorge spurred his mount violently. He turned around and galloped past the truck and back in the direction he had come. As he did, he pointed his revolver skyward and emptied its chamber.

Stewart watched as the banditos rumbled down the road and out of sight. He grabbed his shirt, which was hanging from the truck-bed railing, and knelt down to wipe the sweat from his face.

"You look worrisome," Myles said. "What you thinking about?"

"Santiago," Stewart said. "Who's Carmen?"

"My mistress. Weren't you listening?"

"Do you think Jorge was telling the truth about Victoria?"

"Maybe. He's a sorry lot. It's tough to tell whether he's coming or going."

"What happened between you two?"

"A better question would be *who* happened between us."

"Carmen?"

"You catch on fast. Bones and me were in Victoria a year or so ago when I met Carmen. It was love at first sight for her."

Sergeant Bates laughed.

"Hey," Myles said, glaring at the sergeant, "*I'm* the one telling the story here." He turned his attention back to Stewart. "Anyway, we met at a saloon. I was fixing to ask her to dance when Jorge and his boys came stumbling in. Apparently, he had already had his eyes on her earlier that night. But she made it obvious she'd rather be with yours truly. She's a

cultured woman with refined taste in men. Jorge didn't have
a chance. He's been trying to scare up a fight between us ever
since."

"How?"

"By harassing Carmen. He's been trying to court her since
our first run-in, always asking her to dance and making a fuss
about it in front of everybody. But she's too good for him, and
he knows it. I don't think he even wants her no more. That
crazy malcontent's just trying to get under my skin. That, or
he just can't get enough rejection. Either way, he knows I can
take him, which explains why his posse keeps getting bigger.
I reckon he feels safer in numbers."

"Why'd you have to fester him up like that?"

"He wasn't going to mess with us. He thought we were a
bunch of Creoles. After they shot that Scotsman a few weeks
ago, Villa gave strict orders not to harm foreigners." Myles exhaled a long breath of air. He lit a cigarette and gave one to
Sergeant Bates. As he did, he wiped his face against his shirtsleeve to remove some of the sweat from his cheeks. "I must
confess, I was starting to have my doubts. If we didn't have
those ladies with us, I would've shot him dead on the spot and
took my chances with his amigos. It probably would save
twenty or thirty lives down the line. You better get used to his
type. The closer we get to Santiago, they'll be the norm, not the
exception."

Stewart put on his shirt and looked up at the darkening sky.
His father had probably made arrangements to get the family
out of Victoria. But he had to be sure. "Myles," he said, "my
folks are in Victoria."

"I know that. We gotta go through there to get to Santiago
anyway. Might as well stop in on 'em. While you do that, I'll
check on Carmen. Bob, mind if we borrow a couple of your
horses?"

Bob still seemed shaky from the near-confrontation with

Jorge. "Sure," he stammered. "Can't afford to ship 'em to the States with us anyway."

"Much obliged, Bob. Now how about you go on back there and get your family so we can say our good-byes and get on with our respective journeys."

As Bob walked down the road, Stewart turned to Myles. "You're some kind of diplomat, Myles. I don't think I want to be around the next time you run into Jorge."

"He is a scary bastard," Myles admitted. "I'll give you that."

"Don't fret over it," Sergeant Bates said. "Somebody else will shoot him before long."

Bob returned with his family and Antonio. From the ditch, the women had been unable to witness the episode but had listened to every word. Both of Bob's oldest daughters and his wife were visibly shaken. Antonio was helping revive one of the daughters, and Bob the other.

"You arrogant Yankee," Bob's wife said to Myles from beneath her scarf. "You can get yourself killed, but leave my family out of it." She removed her hat and swatted Myles across the head with it.

Stewart smiled broadly and let go a rare laugh. His partner had a way of relieving the tension, sometimes unintentionally. Myles nodded at the angular-faced Sergeant Bates, who was grinning from ear to ear.

"That's why I don't have a wife," Myles said. "Here I've trekked halfway across Mexico to save a woman and just backed down a group of rogues, and all I get is grief." He reached down to place Mrs. Campbell's hat back on her head.

"Antonio," Stewart said, still laughing, "this is where we get off. It was a pleasure meeting you."

Antonio nodded as he and Sergeant Bates helped the Campbell women into the truck. His brilliant red uniform was coated in a layer of dust now, but he still looked as regal as ever.

"Don't worry, Jefe," Myles said. "Jorge won't bother you so long as he thinks we're still around. Just make a beeline for the river station and get these folks to safety."

"Are you sure you three know what you are getting into?" Antonio asked, sounding fatherly in his concern, Stewart thought.

Stewart let Myles, who was smiling wryly at him, answer. "I think we have an inkling," Myles said.

Chapter 7

Stewart teetered in his saddle as he stared at Myles through half-shut eyes. He wondered if he looked as dog-tired as the man staring back at him: eyes only narrow slits in a sea of red dust, lips chapped like furrowed fields. He craned his neck gingerly to look at Sergeant Bates, a gritty skeleton on horseback.

They had ridden all night, stopping only to water their horses. Exhausted and unkempt, they stopped under Victoria's welcoming arches in the luminous dawn.

"I never wanna see another cattle ranch or damned henequen plantation as long as I live," Myles said, gingerly pulling his gloves from his hands.

"They all look the same in the dark," Stewart muttered.

"At least we made good time," Sergeant Bates offered. "We're not that far off course, either. We were heading north anyway, which was pretty easy to do once we found the rail corridor."

"It would have been easier had a troop or cargo train passed by," Myles groused. "We could have hitched a ride the rest of the way. But nothing. Not one train. What were the odds of that happening?"

"Pretty good," Stewart said, "considering there's a war on."

Victoria stood on a hot, dusty seaward plain a thousand feet above sea level and a hundred miles from the coast. But the morning, at least, was cool, unlike their coastal base in Tampico, where the thermometer had never dipped more than a few degrees, even overnight.

"Well, boys, we've been two nights now without much more than a wink," Myles said. "It'll take the better part of a day to find us some fresh horses and organize supplies for the rest of the trip." He shifted in his saddle and turned to Stewart. "I know you're antsy as hell to get to Santiago. You probably wanna just ride through your folks' ranch on the way to rescuing your girl. But we're putting down roots tonight."

"The hell we are," Stewart said weakly. His body ached for sleep, but he knew he would never be able to rest until they had reached Santiago.

"Listen, partner. You know I'm in it for the long haul. But you need to rest up and recoup. So does Bones. He's practically asleep in his saddle. Anyway, we're not even halfway to Santiago. And this was the easy part of the trip. Looks like Jorge was exaggerating some. The war hasn't found Victoria yet. But you can rest assured it's raging just a few miles north of here—and all the way to the Rio Grande. For every mile we head north, that's one more mile into hostile territory. We're staying put tonight. Bones knows a hotel on the north end of town where you two can stay. We'll ride out of here tomorrow at first light."

"Where are you gonna stay?" Sergeant Bates asked.

"Carmen's apartment," Myles said as he patted the gelding. "We've got some catching up to do."

"Oh, no, you don't," Stewart said. "The last thing we need is a hungover, lovelorn lecher leading us into bad country. You're saddle sore as it is. If I'm resting up, so are you."

"Fine," Myles said. "Have it your way, lawyer. I'll bunk with you two tonight. But that doesn't preclude me from conducting what was to be a nocturnal visit in the light of day."

Stewart closed his eyes as he drained what was left from his canteen. "Just save something for the trip north."

"That, my friends, I will do," Myles said. "I'll see you at the hotel tonight. But don't count on me before the clock strikes midnight. My lover awaits me."

Stewart and Sergeant Bates held their horses, and Myles rode off to meet his destiny in Carmen's arms.

"What are you gonna do?" Sergeant Bates asked Stewart as Myles faded from view.

"Check on my father," Stewart answered. "You?"

"I need a good meal, a shave, and a bath. Not necessarily in that order. Then I'll see about supplies for tomorrow. This might be the last chance we get to take stock."

Myles stopped at a gurgling fountain at the city's over-grown gardens and tied his horse to the wrought-iron rail around it.

"Drink up, friend," he said, and jogged down a narrow alley that led into a tangled maze of four- and five-story buildings that blocked out the rising sun.

He slowed to a walk, studying the apartments until he found the one he was looking for. He removed his boots and tucked them under his right arm.

"Here we are, love," he said.

He climbed an empty trellis to the second-floor balcony and slipped inside, where he found Carmen still sleeping inside.

She was a pure feminine image, he thought, sleeping peace-fully in the half-light of her drab studio apartment. Twenty-three years old and easily one of the most beautiful women in Victoria, she lay facing the balcony, her long eyelashes gently closed in dream sleep and her curly shoulder-length brown hair tumbling free atop her pillow. She stirred as he approached.

Myles stopped and removed his holster, draping it over a

chair by the bed. He started to unbutton his shirt, but was cut short when Carmen opened her stunning brown eyes and propped her head up on her delicate wrist.

"If you think you can just ride into town and have me whenever you want," she said as she leveled her gaze at Myles, "you're mistaken."

"Still as sassy as ever, I see," Myles said.

"I'm not going to fall for any of your chicanery, if that's what you mean." She paused, and then whispered, "I missed you."

Carmen Cologan had the virtue—or the fault, depending on one's perspective—of never being able to hide her inner thoughts and feelings. Myles marveled at her a bit before taking a seat in the chair next to the bed.

"I figured as much," he said. "I've always left an indelible impression on the ladies."

Carmen laughed lustily, exposing the brilliant whites of her eyes as she rolled them. She sat up in bed and pulled the covers up to her neck. "You need a bath. Why don't you go down the hall and clean up while I make some coffee?"

"Now you're talking, sweetheart," Myles said, and stood up. But she wasn't about to let him off that easily.

"When are you leaving?" she asked.

"What do you mean? I just got here."

"Yes. Which means you'll be leaving soon. I'd like to know when you're leaving now, if you don't mind."

"I really am smitten with you, lady," Myles said, hoping to duck the question.

"When?" Carmen asked.

Myles sighed in resignation. "Technically, tomorrow morning. I'm staying tonight on the north side of town with Bones and another old friend from the cavalry. We're headed to Santiago at first light."

"Santiago?" she asked in disbelief. "What on earth for?"

"A girl," Myles said. "Stewart Cook's girl. Even if he

doesn't know it yet. We're helping him track her down before she gets into any trouble with the revolutionaries. Her father's a sheriff. She and her whole family will be fair game."

"Isn't Stewart Cook the one who saved your life in the Philippines?"

"That's him."

"So he's the other old friend from the cavalry?"

"Right."

"You're going to get yourself killed, Myles Adams."

"Now look, lady," Myles said. "You haven't showed me an ounce of affection yet, and now you've already written my obituary. I think I deserve a little better than that."

Carmen didn't blink.

"You see," Myles said, searching for the right words. "I'll be fine. This is just a little hunting trip. After which, I'll be back here—ready to whisk you out of here before the rebels turn Victoria into a tinderbox."

She paused before responding. "Go take a bath, Myles," she said with a smirk. "You stink."

Stewart pushed open the door of a small one-room building just outside the city's center. He found his father sitting at his desk at the family hacienda's administrative headquarters. The dusty office was furnished only with a file cabinet, a handmade wooden desk, and the chair upon which Mr. Cook sat. The room's four windows, inset in unfinished stucco walls, were open in an effort to coax the cool morning breeze inside.

Mr. Cook looked up from his work and removed his gold wire-rimmed spectacles. Unlike Stewart, he claimed a strictly English heritage, albeit by way of Texas, and lacked any native qualities. Despite his years of working the land, he possessed a refined appearance, his stately gray hair and tall, thin figure lending him a scholarly air. He wore a business suit, not rancher's clothing.

"Get my telegram?" Stewart asked.

"I did," his father answered, and stood up to shake his hand. "Looks as though you've made it this far in one piece. Where's Myles?"

"With a lady friend."

"Ah, I see. I trust he'll be marrying that young woman. Miss Cologan needn't have her reputation soiled by the likes of that second-rate charmer."

"I'll believe it when I see it. So you know about their tryst?"

"I do. As do most of the townspeople. What about you? Is marriage in your and Alexia's future?"

The question caught Stewart off guard. Everyone, it seemed, knew better than he did how he felt about Alexia. "Right now I'm just trying to get her out of harm's way."

"That sounds chivalrous," Mr. Cook said. "But are you sure you're prepared for what lies ahead? There are risks involved, I'm sure you're aware."

"I am."

"Well, I would have thought that her father Julio would have left by now, what with him being sort of a fickle fellow and all. Not much of a fighter, I suspect. But apparently, they've already locked him up."

Stewart lifted an eyebrow in surprise. "What?"

"There's more. Your Alexia is too stubborn to leave. Why did they have to move to that squalid little village, anyhow? They should have stayed here in Victoria. Had they done that, you two probably would be married and raising your own brood by now."

Stewart's eyes widened, the whites accentuated by his soot-covered face.

"Here," his father said, standing up and offering Stewart his chair. "You look like you need to sit down."

Stewart accepted the offer. "When did you hear about Julio?"

"The day after I got your telegram. Last week."

Stewart stood back up. "I've got to get to Santiago."

"You look like the walking dead," his father counseled him. "I would suggest a day's rest first."

"You sound like Myles."

"Hmm. For once, I find myself in agreement with your friend."

"I guess I'm lucky to have his services," Stewart said. "He's a first-rate soldier, even if he is an incurable slouch."

"Robert E. Lee, he is not," Mr. Cook agreed. "But you'll need him where you're going." He gazed at his son over his wire-rimmed spectacles. "You didn't need to check on us, by the way. But I'm glad you did."

"Any news on the war?" Stewart asked. He was glad the dirt covered his blushing cheeks.

"The U.S. Marines landed at Veracruz last night—have secured the town—but they killed a couple hundred Mexicans in the process. All over the country, both sides are irate. They want to run every gringo out of the country, but they're too worried we might come in on one side or the other. Worse yet, Villa is about to subvert Monterrey. The Federals have all but thrown in the hat. It will only be a week or two before he's here." Mr. Cook looked out the window into the street. "This whole country is falling apart at the seams. The commoners are squatting on all the farms north of here. I can't say that I wouldn't be doing the same if I were one of them, but I cannot excuse their other deeds. Rage is the order of the day. For generations now, the peasants have been defiled and betrayed and shown a level of indignity we can't even imagine. You sow that, and this is what you reap. But the carnage I cannot understand."

Mr. Cook continued to gaze aimlessly out the window at the sparsely populated *zócalo*. He seemed preoccupied, Stewart thought, with something far, far away.

"I have secured the services of a boat to take about forty people to Brownsville," Mr. Cook said.

"You leaving?" Stewart asked, hoping his father would say yes, but knowing the answer ahead of time.

"No, I will stay here and look after the farm." Mr. Cook returned his eyes from the window. "They will not harm me. But your mother, brother, and the girls will go. I will try to get a few friends out of here, if I can."

"When is the boat leaving?" Stewart asked.

"In three or four days. It's still in Brownsville now. You should visit your mother and siblings at the ranch. Then I would suggest getting some rest before you leave. Be careful, son. These are dark days, indeed. I have a feeling this whole affair is going to end much worse than any of us could ever imagine."

Chapter 8

With Carmen behind him on the gelding, Myles rode toward the Cook family farm just outside of town under the baking late afternoon sun.

Mr. Cook had profited mightily from the large henequen farm, which he had owned for thirty-five years. Unlike most of the other struggling farmers in the region, he ran it like a business, fairly and efficiently. He paid and treated his workers well and had earned their respect as a result. He had even built a small school on the hacienda to educate the children of his employees, who were envied by most of their peers.

The neighboring landowners, meanwhile, respected Mr. Cook as well. But they'd had little interest in creating the same conditions he had provided for his workforce. And now, they stood to lose their land—and possibly their lives—to these same workers when Victoria fell to the revolutionaries, who would no doubt encourage the hapless laborers to emancipate themselves with the blood of the *hacendados*.

Myles and Carmen rode up a narrow dirt road framed by two rows of immense sabino trees that led to the main house. The ornate residence, a spacious one-story edifice several hundred years old and made of thick brown limestone, had a bell tower at one end and was fronted in the center with a patio and stone arches. Laid out around it were the smaller and less sturdy buildings that housed servants and equipment. The grounds were as well groomed as any military installation.

The couple dismounted at the house, and Myles tied off the gelding. He led Carmen to the front door and knocked.

"No one's here," Carmen whispered.

"Nonsense," Myles said. "They're just otherwise occupied. Follow me."

He pushed open the front door, and Carmen followed him into the house's vast living room. As she looked around in awe, he paused in front of a photograph on the wall near the entryway, momentarily transported to another time and place.

"That's you," Carmen said, finally taking notice of the yellowing black-and-white photograph. "You look so young. And innocent."

"Young, sure," Myles said, laughing. "Don't know about the latter. It's a picture of me and Stewart in the Philippines. I looked pretty sharp in my Class A uniform, if I do say so myself."

They followed the sound of several voices to a veranda off the kitchen, where they found Stewart's mother and his three sisters preparing some bread on a stone table.

"I reckon it's just my lucky day," Myles said as he peeked around the corner, "to stumble upon four comely women like this."

The Cook women turned to see who had cunningly sneaked up on them.

"Well, now!" Stewart's mother gasped as she put down the bowl she had in her hands. "To what do we owe the honor of a visit from the *frontera*'s most famous gringo?"

Myles chuckled self-deprecatingly and walked over to greet her. He had always had a soft spot for Stewart's mother since meeting her shortly after the war.

Mrs. Cook had flour on her hands, and tried to avoid leaving it on his shirt as she embraced him with a hug and a kiss. She turned to see Carmen. "And who's this charming creature? You must be Carmen. What a sight to behold!"

Carmen was standing in the kitchen entryway, radiating grace, as always. "Pleased to meet you, Mrs. Cook."

Myles bent over to give Mrs. Cook's thirteen-year-old twin daughters Isabelle and Maria a big bear hug before introducing them to Carmen.

Mrs. Cook then called to her other daughter, who was washing her hands at the sink. "Elena, you're not going to come over and greet Myles and his friend?"

Elena dried her hands and turned to welcome Myles and Carmen.

Myles, who had been visiting the family from time to time since his assignment to Mexico, had not seen the seventeen-year-old in three years; she had been off to school on the East Coast. He was taken aback by her burgeoning womanhood. He glanced sheepishly at Carmen, hoping she hadn't caught the awkward expression on his face.

Though American citizens, Mrs. Cook's daughters were Mexican in every sense of the word. And they looked just like their mother, with long black hair, dark brown eyes, and a tinted but creamy complexion that had been passed on from generation to generation under the southern sun. They each wore a white apron, accentuating their resemblance.

Mrs. Cook's forty-nine years could hardly be perceived, Myles thought; she had the resilient beauty of a thirty-year-old. She was Mexican by birth, but had grown up in Corpus Christi, Texas, where she and Mr. Cook still maintained a residence, no doubt a boon to them now that Victoria was doomed to crumble beneath the weight of the revolution.

"You sure don't look like you've aged much, Alice," Myles said, turning to Mrs. Cook. While others might not have been able to get away with such informality, Myles was the master of knowing just when he could stretch the social norms. And he delighted in it. "I believe all your daughters are going to turn out as pretty as you."

"I've aged, even if it doesn't show," Mrs. Cook said in a tired voice. "In the last couple of years, I have put on twenty years."

"Well," Myles said, "if you don't have gray hair now, you will when you get through fighting the men off of these girls."

"I doubt that. But it's probably going to kill their father."

The daughters laughed in unison.

"You're probably right," Myles said. "That's going to be tough on him."

"What brings you two by?" Mrs. Cook asked.

"Just here to pick up Stewart," Myles said. "Thought we'd take him to the carnival in town, maybe get his mind off his troubles. That is, unless he's resting, in which case I don't want to disturb his beauty sleep."

"Not to worry," Mrs. Cook said, dusting the flour from her hands. "He's as restless as ever. He napped for about an hour, and now he's down at the pink house working up a sweat. I'm sure he wouldn't mind a visit."

"Thanks, Alice." Myles reached for the back door.

"Nice to meet you all," Carmen said.

Mrs. Cook grabbed Carmen's hands in hers and kissed her warmly on the cheek. "It was our pleasure."

Myles and Carmen exited the veranda into the well-manicured courtyard that stood between them and the pink house, a small one-room boardinghouse that had been used to house servants at one time. They walked under the cool shade of towering sabino trees and paused in front of a one-hundred-year-old fountain surrounded by yellow orchids.

"It's beautiful here," Carmen said, slipping her arm under Myles's.

"Not a bad place to call home," Myles agreed.

As they approached the pink house, Myles stopped and leaned on a wooden fence surrounding the house's small lawn.

Stewart was on all fours in the front yard, trying to uproot some deep-taprooted weeds with an old wooden hoe. He didn't look up, too preoccupied with the weeds, Myles knew, to come and greet them. Instead, he went after each weed with something just short of a personal vendetta, his bare, broad shoulders glistening with sweat.

"If this doesn't beat anything I've ever seen," Myles finally said, shaking his head. "A well-reputed lawyer spending the afternoon on his hands and knees, chopping weeds."

Stewart discarded the broken hoe on the ground and stood up. "Who's your friend?"

"An angel of mercy," Myles said. "We've come to deliver you from your troubles. Clean yourself up and let's go."

"Go where?" Stewart asked, squinting up at the late afternoon sun.

"Carnival."

"No, thanks. Gonna finish up here and then get some rest at the hotel." He blinked at the ravishing Carmen and then returned his gaze to Myles. "You said you were gonna spend your whole day . . . indoors."

Carmen blushed and then spoke up. "We thought you might enjoy one last night out before . . ."

"We get shot up?" Stewart asked. He frowned and turned to Myles. "Marines landed at Veracruz last night."

"I heard. Did the Mexicans leave?"

Stewart shook his head. "Nope. They're fighting us. We've taken the city. About a hundred casualties. Gonzales has attacked Monterrey. The locals have thrown the American consul in jail."

"What about Tampico? That's where the three thousand Americans are."

"Fletcher has half the fleet at the mouth of the river. He has a battalion of Marines with him. They're evacuating all the foreigners. I suspect we'll occupy the city to protect the oil wells and refineries."

"You sure look troubled. You should have known this was coming."

"More worried about the road to Santiago."

"What's it look like up there and in Monterrey?" Myles grabbed Carmen's hand, interlocking their fingers, and led her into the small house.

"Will hold out for a few days. Maybe a week. Who knows?" Stewart started to pace, pausing to light a cigarette before following Myles and Carmen inside. "The clock's ticking."

Myles paused and turned to look at a wood-framed edition of the *El Paso Times* hanging on the wall. Headlining the front page was a large article on the Mexican Revolution written by Stewart.

Myles spent a few minutes scanning the article's contents. He knew that for years, Stewart had been doing everything in his power to alter America's indifference to the appalling atrocities occurring just south of the border. He had long advocated American intervention in Mexico. Not to intervene in the ongoing war, but to transplant American democracy and capitalism. In his opinion, the current course was American exploitation backed by the Mexican government. The article on the wall propagated those sentiments.

"Whose side are you on in this war?" Myles mumbled as he scanned the article.

"I really don't know," said Stewart. "After four years, my opinion is more ambiguous than ever. I was hoping it might settle out somewhere in the middle, but I'm afraid one of the extremes is going to prevail." Stewart had a pronounced integrity in his voice.

"I wouldn't get too worked up. There's nothing you can

do about it. I came down here with a bunch of virtuous ideals myself. I've since been hardened to the cold reality. My only conviction now is preservation." Myles continued to read the article. "When did you get so down on the gringo?"

"I've never been down on the gringo, and you're taking that article out of context. The gringo promotes civility, prosperity, and freedom wherever he goes. But it can't be all taking and no giving."

Myles looked up from the article with a grin, satisfied he had sufficiently stirred Stewart. He looked over at a full crate of books lying on the floor. There was another stack of books beside the crate. "You packing?" He walked over to the crate. "You got any good books in English?" He reached into the crate and looked through a few books.

"I don't have anything with pictures in there, if that's what you're looking for."

"No, I'm looking for something that might invigorate my intellect." Myles continued to thumb through a few books looking for some pictures. He found only text.

"You mean something for the uncultured and bankrupt masses?"

"Yeah. I don't want to read any of this crap."

"Try the *Arabian Nights* there. It might suit you." Stewart pointed to a book in the crate, and Myles grabbed it. He curiously flipped through a few pages and then put the book under his arm. "If you need some help with any of the deeper themes, let me know."

"I'll let you know if I need any assistance." Myles sat down at the table beside Carmen and glanced at Stewart. "Bones is gathering up our supply pack right now. We'll leave first thing tomorrow morning, but we can't just ride off into the bush, roughshod. We're going to have to work our way up there cautiously. This invasion is a bad deal. It will make life much more difficult for us. It's certainly going to encourage bad blood between Americans and Mexicans."

"The Marines shouldn't even be here," Stewart grumbled.

Carmen stepped in. "What are the chances of you finding this woman you are so determined to save? Have you even heard from her?"

"Sent her a telegram a few days ago," Stewart said defensively before looking away. "No response."

Carmen waited for an answer to her first question.

"Maybe one in three."

Myles shook his head. "I'm going to tell you this right now. I'm not going to get myself or Bones shot for this girl. You need to sit down and decide if you're willing to take that chance before we leave. I mean it."

Stewart glanced at the two and relented. "All right," he said. "Let's go to your damn carnival."

Myles stared in disbelief at the throngs of people celebrating at the foot of the seventeenth-century stone church abutting Victoria's plaza. If war was raging on the city's doorstep, no one had bothered to tell the city's residents, most of whom were defiantly, perhaps somewhat desperately, staging the annual parade and festival at the city's center. Revelers spilled out into the side streets from the town's *zócalo*, and the grand ebony trees shading the park were filled with colorful streamers fluttering in the mild evening breeze.

"Bones," Myles called out to Sergeant Bates, who had rented a carriage and, with Stewart at his side, was chauffeuring Myles and Carmen into town. "Let's ditch this buggy while we can. There's no room ahead."

"Already thought of that, Boss," Sergeant Bates said while carefully threading the horses through the crowd to a hitching post beside the church.

As they waded into the sea of people, Myles glanced over at Stewart, whose skin had turned a muted gray and was bathed in sweat.

"Maybe we shouldn't have invited him," Carmen said, grabbing hold of Myles's arm.

"Nonsense," Myles assured her. "He just needs to loosen up for once. Isn't that right, partner?" he called to Stewart ahead of him.

Stewart turned back to look at Myles and Carmen. "What?"

"I was just telling the lovely lady next to me that you need a drink."

"No, thanks," Stewart said testily, and plowed through the waves of colorfully attired fairgoers.

They walked through a buzzing labyrinth of carnival booths, food stands, and mariachi bands, the latter of which were camped at every street corner and intersection, tunefully invoking the giddy festivities. A giant steel Ferris wheel, or "pleasure wheel," as the locals called it, towered over the heart of the *zócalo,* an interminable line snaking away from its entrance.

"Let's go get some fairy floss," Carmen said gleefully.

"Fairy floss?" Stewart said. "What the hell is that?"

"Sugar," Myles said. "You'll see."

They stopped at a small stand and watched as the vendor, an animated man who seemed part salesman, part circus ringleader, poured several cups of white sugar and a few drops of red food coloring into a glass-topped machine that melted the ingredients into liquid before spinning them in a large doughnut-shaped mechanism. The melted sugar, now pink, poured through tiny holes in the doughnut hole, emerging on the other side as wispy strands.

Myles ordered four sticks, and the vendor dipped the first into the contraption with exaggerated flare, whisking it inside the doughnut for a full minute and then removing a fluffy-headed treat. He handed it to Stewart, who looked dumbfounded as he took it.

"You eat it," Myles said. "It's food."

"I know that," Stewart said, pulling off a piece of the fluffy pink candy and stuffing it into his mouth. He grimaced slightly as he swallowed.

"Too sweet for you, eh?" Myles kidded Stewart before handing a stick to Carmen.

As they walked on, Sergeant Bates led the way, clearly relishing his own share of the sticky, decadent treat. "Pardon me," he mumbled with his mouth half full after accidentally bumping into someone in his path, all the while still focusing on the rapidly disappearing cotton candy in front of him.

"Stewart," Carmen suggested, "let's go play some games."

"What do you want to play?" he asked.

Myles, expecting a gruff reply, was surprised by the response. Maybe Stewart was loosening up.

"Let's try this one right here," Sergeant Bates said.

They were standing in front of what amounted to a ball-throwing contest. The booth's attendant had stacked heavy steel jugs in a pyramid, and each contestant was required to knock them down with a ball.

"How do I win?" Sergeant Bates asked in Spanish.

"If you knock down one stack of jugs, then you win one of those," the boy in charge of the booth said as he pointed to a small handmade doll on the wall behind him. "Two, one of those," he said, pointing to a medium-sized doll. "And three, one of those." The grand prize was bigger than the others.

"I'll try for all three," Sergeant Bates said as he reached into his right pocket for a handful of change. "I don't like to mess around."

He laid five pesos on the table, and the young man set three balls in front of him.

"I forgot how much of a rebel you are," Myles said with a laugh.

The three stopped to watch Sergeant Bates take a stab at the rigged contest. After two misses, he reared back for his final throw and hurled the ball at the jugs as hard as he could, his skinny right arm flailing wildly on the follow through. But his final attempt barely tipped over one of the steel jugs.

Before the lone jug even hit the ground, the young man working the booth had snatched up the five pesos from the counter in front of him and asked Sergeant Bates if he wanted to play again.

"That was symbolic of your entire life," Myles said from behind the sergeant. "Quick, ugly, and uneventful."

"You're right," Sergeant Bates said, bristling at the criticism. "It was symbolic of my life. I cut right through all the crap and laid it all on the line."

"You, Bones, are a gambler," Stewart said as the foursome moved on to another booth.

"When you run with him," Myles said, "you better have your wits about you."

The sergeant shook his head and grinned resignedly, and the three men laughed in unison.

"Let's go win one of those big dolls," Carmen said.

Myles took her hand. "All right, we'll win one right here."

The booth in front of them varied only slightly from the last, this one requiring the contestant to knock a stack of thimbles over with a small wooden projectile from a slingshot.

"Step up here," Myles said to Carmen as he pulled some money out of his pocket and gave it to the booth's custodian, a man in his fifties.

Carmen missed on two of her three attempts, not winning anything. But she did so with gusto, laughing unabashedly with each shot.

"Let me try that," Myles said, proudly stepping up and

wrestling the slingshot from Carmen. He squinted at the thimbles stacked in front of him and slowly exhaled through his mouth.

"I hope you're better with that thing than you are with a rifle," Stewart said.

Myles, oblivious to Stewart's attempt at breaking his concentration, took aim and toppled the pyramid of thimbles on his first attempt. The small group erupted in cheers, with even Stewart hollering jubilantly at his partner's success, and the attendant regretfully removed one of the large dolls from the wall behind him.

Myles nodded in Carmen's direction, and the man gave her the doll.

"Gracias," she said, bowing politely while trying to contain her enthusiasm.

Myles paid for another turn and took aim once again. He hit the center thimble in the bottom row a second time, and the pyramid came tumbling down.

As the attendant handed Carmen her second doll, Myles, swelling with pride, plunked a few more pesos on the counter. But the man waved him off.

"No more for you," he said in broken English.

"You're fouling up their rigged game," Sergeant Bates said.

"Fine," Myles said. "We'll just have to find another booth to exploit."

Carmen, whose arms were loaded down with the two oversized dolls, protested. "Oh, no, Myles, you've done enough damage for one day. Let's ride the pleasure wheel."

"Sounds good to me," Stewart said, leading the way to the back of the line.

"Is there a law against yelling 'fire' in a crowded plaza?" Myles quipped. "Maybe we could cut this line some."

They waited their turn impatiently, trading barbs and passing the time in unruly fashion, until finally reaching the front of the line.

Myles and Carmen sat down on the small wooden bench attached to the colossal wheel. Stewart and Sergeant Bates sat on the bench behind them.

"Please squeeze together tightly," the man working the wheel said to Myles and Carmen as he pushed down on a wooden board securing them and Carmen's two dolls on the bench.

"Kind of like buttoning your pants, isn't it, Colonel?" Stewart called out from the bench behind Myles.

As the steam-powered wheel slowly lifted them skyward, they caught peekaboo views of the city's glowing rooftops in the sudden twilight. The swarming energy beneath them faded until it was nothing more than a muddled humming, incoherent background noise to the four floating a hundred feet above it.

The wheel stopped when Carmen and Myles's bench reached the top. They could hear Stewart and Bones jostling beneath them. Carmen's face grew ashen.

"What's wrong?" Myles asked.

"Do you have to go?" Carmen asked, her voice barely above a whisper.

Myles stared into Carmen's bewitching eyes. She seemed to have lost all enthusiasm in the rarified air above the carnival.

"Yes, I have to go," he answered. "It makes me feel warm for you to be leery, but Stewart is going with or without me. He'll never make it without me. Maybe we will help a few deserving people find a way out of this calamity." Myles looked at Carmen and tried to detect the assurance he was hoping to induce. He found only anxiety. "I'll be fine," he heard himself saying.

"You promise?"

"I promise," Myles said, pulling Carmen toward him even

tighter. "In the meantime, I'm going to see to it that you and your family get on a boat for Texas this week. I may not be back before you leave. You may not see me again for a while."

A breeze rocked the Ferris wheel gently, and as they began their descent, he could feel her trembling in his arms. He, too, felt his soul shudder as the ride came to an end.

As they stepped off the Ferris wheel, Myles turned to see Stewart and Bones, who were watching stone-faced as the man removed the restraining bar from their bench.

"Hey," Myles said, directing his comments to Stewart as they approached, "loosen up a little. We're leaving in the morning. Everything's going to be all right."

Whether or not he believed his own advice, Myles, as always, was determined to lead. It was the only role he knew. "Now," he said, "let's go watch the fireworks."

Sergeant Bates secured a tiny plot of lawn in the center of the *zócalo* from which to watch the show. "When do they start?" he asked as the four got comfortable on the cool grass.

"Nine-thirty," Stewart answered. "But that's Mexican time."

The words had barely escaped Stewart's mouth when a loud boom erupted from behind the church and the first volley of fireworks could be seen streaming skyward. The jammed *zócalo* grew quiet as the fireworks burst over the church's lofty steeple, illuminating the spires against the dusk and seducing the crowd below. With each progressive explosion, the masses looked up in amazement at the cascading fireballs, and the *zócalo* flickered between total darkness and pyrotechnic brilliance. The colorful crowd seemed to move and react as a single living entity, gasping at the ongoing display.

Stewart, never one to relish a moment too long, turned away from the spectacle and gazed at Myles and Bones. He wondered if they or anybody else at the festival had any idea how their lives would be changed forever over the next few weeks. He felt fortunate that he and his entourage would be allowed to leave. But he also felt shame, for theirs was a luxury owed entirely to birth. He could have easily been a Mexican citizen, trapped in the revolution that was maiming this beautiful country, unable to grab hold of a different fate.

The sky grew dark as the last of the fireworks fell to the earth, glowing embers snuffed out before they hit the ground.

Chapter 9

As Stewart and Sergeant Bates took the carriage back to the hotel, Myles and Carmen strolled through the crowded streets to Pancho's, a local restaurant, cantina, and seedy brothel just down the street from the central plaza. Usually, the three enterprises of the establishment were segregated, but for the carnival the owner had masked the more lewd aspects of the tavern and opened the entire place to revelers.

The festival week afforded unescorted women of aristocratic lineage the luxury of touring the city unhindered, and few passed up the chance to see why Pancho's was so alluring to Victoria's men.

Myles led Carmen into the smoke-filled restaurant, and found that the tables had been pushed into a corner to make room for dancing, the patrons moving gaily to the melody of a mariachi band. The women wore white cowboy hats and long white dresses, the latter adorned with colorful beads and stripes and tailored especially for the occasion. The men, meanwhile, all dressed like Mexican cowboys.

As he and Carmen paused in the foyer, Myles felt the stares of many in the room. Americans were a rarity in Victoria. There were only a dozen or so American families mixed in with the city's twenty thousand residents. Myles's blond hair gave him away as an American everywhere he went.

"Let's try the bar," he hollered over the mariachi band.

Carmen nodded, and they made their way to the bar behind the restaurant. The bar, noisy and cramped, was even more crowded with locals celebrating the festivities. Myles began to perspire heavily as he pushed through the crowd and found Carmen a seat at the bar.

Like the rest of the ladies in attendance, Carmen was dressed in full costume, the gritty bar accentuating her dainty figure and intoxicating grin. She was a beacon of beauty and vulnerability in Victoria's seamy underside. But her smile had faded suddenly.

"Let's go someplace else," she whispered to Myles.

"We just got here," Myles protested. Then he caught sight of Jorge sitting with his men across the bar in a dimly lit corner. Jorge had his back to the wall and was eyeing the couple at the bar.

"Well," Myles said, "look what the cat dragged in. Jorge and his posse must have followed us to Victoria. I think that miscreant is gunning for me."

"It's me he wants," Carmen said, tugging on her lover's hand.

Myles put his arms around Carmen and, after looking squarely at Jorge, turned back to his lover and kissed her on the lips.

"Quit teasing him. He's going to end up killing you, thinking he can have me then. If he does, what will become of me?"

"I'll never let that happen," Myles said. "You can't show fear to a man like Jorge. It emboldens him." Myles turned to the bar. "Bartender," he said in Spanish, "we'll have a bottle of tequila and two glasses."

The bartender complied, and Myles drained back-to-back shots of liquid courage.

"Are you sure you know what you're doing?" Carmen asked.

"I didn't survive the Philippines so some scoundrel could put one in my back," Myles said. "Men of Jorge's stunted demeanor are easy enough to deal with so long as you keep 'em on a short leash. He's a coward beneath that permanent scowl and all that fancy jewelry." Myles downed another tequila and grabbed Carmen's hand. "Come on. Let's dance."

"All right," Carmen said hesitantly.

Short on sleep and long on alcohol, Myles was already talking with a discernible slur as he clumsily led Carmen back to the adjoining restaurant-turned-dance hall, winking at Jorge and his men as he walked by. He looked back to see Jorge grinning a Machiavellian smile.

In the restaurant, the exuberant crowd sang along to the chorus as the mariachi band sloppily plowed through another folk song promoting the Picota, a local dance in which the women lifted and flared their long skirts as they twisted around their partners.

Myles and Carmen entered just in time to join in the final chorus.

"That was fun," Carmen said as the song came to an end. She put her arms around Myles's neck and leaned her head back to look up at him.

Myles gently reached down to brush her hair away from her deep brown eyes. "You're a fetching sight, I'll give you that."

"You're not too bad yourself, Colonel," Carmen said.

The band started up again, this time improvising a slow waltz.

"You should see me with nothing on but my boots," Myles said, and spun her away from him with one hand.

"Are you forgetting this morning?" Carmen said with a laugh as she returned her arms to his neck. "I saw you with nothing on but your boots. And I wasn't that impressed."

"You ready for me to take you home and ravish you again before I go?"

"Not really. You haven't paid me enough attention yet."

"If this relationship is ever going to work, you're really going to have to start putting some honesty into it." Myles pulled Carmen close to him and covered her smirk with a light kiss.

Carmen locked her eyes on his. She was irresistible when her eyes glistened with such resolve. "You ever going to make a respectable woman out of me, Colonel Adams?"

"I don't know if I want to marry you after all," Myles fibbed. "I'm young and handsome, and you can go a month without sleeping with me. What's going to happen when I'm old and fat? You could probably hold out for years."

Carmen laughed as Myles grabbed her hands and pushed her an arm's length away.

"You wouldn't like it in New Orleans, anyway," he added. "We don't put up with insolent women up there."

"If that's the case, how come you fell for me so easily?"

"You know," Myles said, "all the women in New Orleans are beautiful and smart. You're not going to have every man you see doting over you." He pulled Carmen to his chest and caressed her neck with his right hand.

"I don't believe you," Carmen said as she twirled Myles around. "There are no women as beautiful as me." She was starting to wear the enjoyment of once again seducing Myles.

"Well," Myles confessed, "I reckon I'm going to have to take you with me in a couple of weeks anyway. I can hardly bear the thought of one of those generals having his way with you. We'll get married then. I promise."

"Good. Now that that's settled, you need to go get some rest. I'll come see you in the morning before you go—when you're a little more sober." Carmen looked at Myles's watch and then kissed him on the lips briefly.

"You sure you don't want to come over to the hotel and visit with me for a little while?" Carmen was backing away from Myles and letting his hands go. Myles grabbed Carmen around the waist and playfully lifted her up on his shoulder. "I've had about all this seductive behavior I can stand for one night."

"You know I would love to, but you need to get some rest," Carmen replied as Myles released her to the floor.

"These Mexican women down here sure are hard on their men," Myles said in Spanish to the four band members. They had finished playing and were casually observing the couple. "Are they all like that?"

"*Sí, señor,*" one of the men said, and the others laughed.

Myles drew Carmen close to him once again. But she removed her head from beside his and leveled an austere gaze at him.

"Promise me one thing before we get married," she said as her voice cracked.

"You name it," Myles said cavalierly, slow to recognize the sudden shift in mood.

"Don't get yourself killed."

Chapter 10

Stewart had been asleep for some time when he felt his face warm from the heat of the just-lit kerosene lamp on the nightstand next to him.

"You're late," he mumbled from his bed without opening his eyes. "Turn off that lamp."

"I had to take Carmen to her folks' house on the other side of town," Myles slurred. "Jorge's in town and spoiling for a fight."

Stewart chewed on the news for a moment. "What a surprise," he finally said. "Now turn off that fucking lamp."

"I will as soon as one of you boys moves over and lets me in," Myles said belligerently. "I only see one bed."

"All they had," Stewart grumbled. "Take the floor."

Myles shuffled to the bed. "Don't make me jerk one of you off that bed."

Stewart was lying on his back with no shirt on and his eyes still closed. Sergeant Bates lay motionless and asleep beside him. "This is the last time I'm going to tell you," Stewart said, his voice rising in intensity. "Cut the light and shut up."

He heard Myles strike another match to light a cigarette. "Scoot on over and make a hole for me."

"If I have to turn that lamp off," Stewart said slowly, annoyed that he was having to waste this much breath, "it's not gonna be pretty."

"I'm shaking in my—"

Before his partner could finish his sentence, Stewart had jumped out of bed, bear-hugged him with both arms, and slammed him onto the hardwood floor with such a jolt it knocked the mirror off the wall behind the door and woke the slumbering sergeant.

Myles grunted as he collided with the floor. His tall, thin anatomy was no match for Stewart's short and stocky 210-pound frame.

As Stewart manhandled Myles, he stole a quick glance at the bed to see the sergeant grinning and rubbing his eyes. Then Stewart stared back down at Myles and slowly let go of his arms. "You're going to stay right here, and you're going to shut the hell up. Or I'm going to wear you out."

He stood up cautiously and looked down at Myles.

"Is that all you got?" Myles asked and kicked Stewart in the chest with the bottom of his boot, knocking him back onto the bed.

Stewart slid to the floor and shook his head as he tried to regain his bearings. "Bones, give me a hand," he said matter-of-factly. "The quicker we do this, the quicker we can go back to bed."

Sergeant Bates got off the bed and stood beside him. "What do you need?" the sergeant asked, looking down at Myles without enthusiasm.

"Get his legs," Stewart said. "I'll take care of everything else."

Myles was lying on his back with his feet in the air. As Sergeant Bates approached, Myles started jerking his legs in rapid motion, like he was frantically pedaling a bicycle.

He kicked the sergeant two times in the face and then stared at Stewart. "Now this is my last warning. I'm going to end up hurting one of you," he said, and gave Sergeant Bates another swift kick, this time in the arm.

Stewart lunged into the mass of moving muscle, wrapped his arms around Myles's waist, and flipped him over onto his stomach. He then threw his ass onto Myles's legs, grabbed his right arm, and pinned it into the small of his back until he stopped squirming.

"Now, you're going to lay here and shut up," Stewart said between gritted teeth, "or I'm going to break this arm. Understand?"

When Myles made no response, Stewart forced his arm farther up his back. "Understand?"

"All right!" Myles said. "Let go of my arm! That's my shooting arm. I might need it this week to shoot a bandit off you."

Stewart relaxed as he listened to Myles pant beneath him.

"Don't think I'm not still going to get into that bed," Myles said.

Stewart, himself breathing heavy now, looked up at Sergeant Bates, who was wiping the blood from his punctured lip. "Bones," he said, "go over there and pick the bed up. We're going to shove him under there. He can run his sewer all he wants in there."

Myles vainly resumed the scuffle. But he was impotent beneath Stewart's weight, and Stewart could feel the struggle in him fading.

The bed was nothing but a mattress lying on top of a heavy wooden box. The inside was dead space under a heavy board supporting the mattress. Sergeant Bates lifted the bed up a few feet, and Stewart shoved Myles under it with little trouble. The sergeant quickly dropped the wooden frame, and he and Stewart jumped onto the bed to give it added weight.

"Guess I'll be the one to turn the lamp off," Stewart said, and extinguished the kerosene flame. "Don't worry. He can't get out."

"We're never going to get any sleep now," he heard the sergeant say in the dark next to him.

"He'll quiet down eventually," Stewart assured him.

He listened to Myles wriggle beneath them, hollering and struggling to get out. And he laughed along with the sergeant as the mattress rose and fell with each kick.

"You guys have got to let me out of here!" came Myles's muffled cry. "There's no way I'm going to make it until morning without having to take a piss!"

"Good night, Colonel," Stewart said.

Morning came all too early in the cramped hotel room.

At first light, Stewart sat up slowly and sniffed at the stale air. "Stinks in here."

With Sergeant Bates stirring beside him, he got up and walked to the room's only window.

"What time is it?" the sergeant asked groggily as Stewart opened the shades and let in a flood of early morning sunshine.

"Time to get moving," Stewart answered. He opened the window wide and waved his hand in front of his nose. "Why don't you let the colonel out? I'm gonna grab a bath down the hall."

The sergeant hesitated. "You don't wanna be here when I let him out?"

"Nope. Gotta get moving."

Stewart's playful, if manic, edge from the night before had evaporated in the morning light. As he thought about the distance still between him and Santiago, he felt his muscles stiffen, the anxiety that had been following him returning in full force. He had no more time for sophomoric pranks.

"Whatever you say," Sergeant Bates replied as Stewart left for his bath.

* * *

The sergeant stared at the bed apprehensively. He slowly lifted it and peered into the claustrophobic space.

Myles lay on his back with his hands aside his waist and his eyes closed.

Sergeant Bates recoiled at the awful stench that had been trapped beneath the bed all night. "Morning, Colonel," he managed to say, backing as far away as he could without letting go of the mattress, which he had propped up on its side.

Myles opened one eye and then the other.

The sergeant was almost afraid to ask the question. "Did you—?"

"Yes, Bones," Myles said in a hoarse voice. "I pissed on myself. What else was I supposed to do?"

Myles was holding perfectly still, but Sergeant Bates was ready to bolt.

"Don't worry, Bones," Myles said. "I'll forgive you. On one condition."

The sergeant felt a familiar, sinking sensation in the pit of his stomach. Myles was about to exact his revenge.

"If you help me collect a little revenge from that Mexican," he said, "I'll forget your own role in this unfortunate incident."

"Okay, Boss," Sergeant Bates said tentatively, the hesitation in his voice as palpable as the stink of urine wafting up from Myles.

"Where is he?" Myles asked.

"Who?"

"The surly Mexican."

"Oh, Stewart. He's, uh, down the hall taking a hot bath."

Myles lay motionless a moment before his eyes twinkled and a smile spread across his face. "Bones," he said, "fetch me his things, would you? Grab his towel, too."

Sergeant Bates left the room and snuck into the bathroom, where he heard Stewart hard at work with the scrub brush behind the curtain. He silently grabbed his clothes and his towel and returned with them to the room.

"Did he see you?" Myles asked.

"No, sir. Too busy getting clean."

"Okay, Bones, this is what I want you to do. First, fetch me a pail of water, a washcloth, and some soap. I gotta clean up and get dressed before old Stewart finishes his bath. While I'm doing that, I want you to round up the horses and supplies you paid for yesterday. You did take care of all that, right?"

"Sure did," the sergeant said. "I'll get you that pail and soap."

"Don't forget the washcloth!" Myles called out to him as he left for the front desk.

"Ah, hell," Stewart said.

The murky water had turned lukewarm. He stood up and reached for his towel but found nothing. Peering from behind the curtain, he saw the empty chair where his clothes had been.

"Bastard!" he huffed. He looked around frantically before pausing to collect himself. "This'll have to do," he said as he pulled down the curtain, which he proceeded to fold over once and then wrap around his waist.

He tiptoed to the room, thankful that sunrise was still only about twenty minutes old. The hotel was dead quiet, its patrons still asleep.

"Very funny, Myles," he said as he swung the door open to their room. "Now give me my clothes back."

His jaw dropped as he viewed the empty room. Everything was gone, including his pack. The bed had been hastily made. In the middle of the room a galvanized steel bucket half full of soapy water sat with a washcloth hanging from its side. He leaned over the bucket and found a bar of soap floating inside.

He walked to the window and searched the alley below.

Nothing.

"Well, I'll be," he said. "This beats anything he ever pulled in the service."

He sat down briefly on the bed, but then his anxiety got the better of him.

"We don't have time for this!" he bellowed as he rushed out of the room.

He stomped downstairs to the lobby, and the clerk looked up from his coffee in disbelief.

"What are you staring at?" Stewart groused, not bothering to speak Spanish. "Never mind. Did they pay you?"

"*Sí, senor,*" the clerk said. "But . . . I am afraid I will need that before you go." He pointed to the curtain.

Stewart looked down confusedly. He then looked back up at the clerk, who seemed to be scowling and smiling at the same time. "Fine," he said, "but I'll be needing your paper."

He grabbed a newspaper from the counter and, after dropping the curtain, quickly covered his loins with the day's headlines. He then pushed open the hotel's front doors and ambled outside, giving the astonished clerk a first-rate view of his gleaming backside on the way out.

On the street, Myles and Sergeant Bates sat atop their horses facing the hotel, with Stewart's horse and the packhorse waiting beside them. His father, too, was waiting at the curb to see the group off, as was Carmen.

"You ready to go, partner?" Myles asked with a straight face. "We've got a long day's ride in front of us."

"I could use some clothes," Stewart said testily.

"I'll say. You look like you just got out of the bath." Myles turned to Carmen. "Avert your eyes, darling. This is a spectacle unbefitting a woman betrothed."

"What?" Stewart couldn't believe his ears. "You're not cut out for marriage. Hell, they've probably got laws in Louisiana to keep your type from procreating, anyway."

"You're the attorney," Myles responded. "You'd know better than me. Mr. Cook," he said, turning to Stewart's father, "we'll be back in a few days. We're not going to get into anything over our heads. But if for some reason we don't get back here before that boat leaves, put Carmen on it."

"You can count on me to look after your fiancée, Myles," Mr. Cook said.

Stewart adjusted the newspaper slightly as his father turned to look at him standing naked in the hotel entrance.

"As for you," Mr. Cook said, "I would suggest taking this little adventure of yours a little more seriously henceforth. The revolutionaries have little regard for foolish antics. We are in the midst of a war, in case you haven't noticed."

Stewart felt a wave of indignation wash over him. "Trust me, Father," he seethed, "no one wants to get on with this more than I do."

He let the newspaper drop, marched over to his horse, and reached into his pack for a change of clothes. Modesty be damned.

Myles knew Stewart well enough to know he had pushed him too far. He stifled a laugh without breaking a smile and then gazed down at Carmen.

She chuckled quietly. "You're terrible, Myles Adams. You know that?"

"Yeah, I know," he said, dismounting to bid her farewell. "But I've got a heart of gold."

"Yes, you do," Carmen said, her voice trailing off as a tear streaked down her face.

"I'll only be gone a couple of days," he said as he gently cupped her soft cheeks in his hands. "Then you can have me forever." He looked away awkwardly and cleared his throat. He knew better than anyone what awaited them.

As she buried her head in his chest, he felt a strange sort of distance forming between them, as though both of them knew something neither had the courage to speak. He kissed her softly, and then took hold of her hands, tenderly pulling them from his neck as he stepped away.

"You about ready, boys?" he called out to Stewart and Sergeant Bates.

"Sure are, Boss," the sergeant answered.

Myles turned to see Stewart dressed now and sitting atop his horse. "Well, all right," he said to his freshly bathed friend. "Looks like we're ready to ride."

Chapter 11

Before Myles mounted his horse, he walked over to check Sergeant Bates's packing. Myles and Sergeant Bates were well supplied and equipped for extended travel in Mexico. During their earlier work, they had frequently gone into the bush for weeks without supply. Sergeant Bates had saddled his and Myles's horses and supplied them amply with things of necessity. He had also packed a third horse with some supplies. The third horse would serve as a backup and lug a few essentials. On it were a small two-man tent, some pots, and two large leather bags for carrying water. Most of the food would be foraged or purchased along the way.

The saddled horses carried his and Myles's personal belongings. They consisted of a pair of Springfield 1903 rifles, two boxes of ammo for them and their sidearms, a spare change of clothes, a blanket, mosquito net, hammock, binoculars, and maybe of the most value, Myles's map collection for the area. His maps, originally made by the U.S. Army and later updated by some of the American mining companies in the area, were of better quality than either of the warring factions' maps.

Myles then retrieved a small leather bag from his horse. The bag contained American twenty-dollar gold coins. Myles had learned that under the current circumstances nothing was of more value than this. If he got in a bind, this might get him out of it. In the war-torn regions of the country, the Mexican peso had little value, and to the peasant bandit, American dollars meant almost nothing.

Finding all in order, Myles placed the money bag in a saddlebag. "Bones, did you pack some of that seasoning we got from that old Mexican in Saltillo?"

"Yeah, I did," Sergeant Bates said from his horse.

"How much beef jerky did you pack?" Myles asked, climbing onto his horse. It had starting walking off. Stewart had just untied it and had started riding away. "You know it normally takes a small wagon train to feed this Mexican we got with us."

Sergeant Bates grinned and spurred his horse.

"Feel better now that we're back chasing your damsel in distress?" Myles called out to Stewart as they slowed to a trot beside him.

Stewart nodded but said nothing.

"I'll bet it feels good to be wearing something besides a newspaper, too," Myles said. "Talk about saddle sore. We're going to stop by Engracia and pick up Felipe on our way out of town. He may come in handy."

"I sent him a message yesterday that we'd be coming through this morning," Sergeant Bates said.

"Who's Felipe?" Stewart asked bluntly.

"Felipe Canova—my local guide, and a damned good one, too," Myles said. "Really knows the country."

On their way out of Victoria, the three Americans passed between two Federal posts guarding the north side of town. The forts were teeming with soldiers, all solemn faced and hard at work moving sandbags, stacking ammo, and sighting the artillery. The frenetic pace of their work seemed to weigh them down as if it was with a sense of foreboding, as though the soldiers knew they would ultimately be overrun. The somber mood stood in stark contrast to the carnival atmosphere in the city's center the night before. The burdened look on their faces seemed a portent of things to come.

It took the Americans about two hours to reach the thirty-person farming community of Engracia. It was a pleasant little village lying amid mango groves fifteen miles north of Victoria, but apart from any major roads. As they casually rode into the five-house village, Myles noticed twenty or thirty people crowding the small plaza. He studied the humble houses.

"Something's up," Sergeant Bates said.

"I think you're right," Myles answered as the group slowly rode into the plaza. Myles studied the mob. Most appeared to be poor squatters having recently arrived from the north, but five or six were on horses and forcing their way into some of the houses. "Look's like there's somebody trying to get fed and housed at Felipe's." Myles quickly dismounted. The front door of Felipe's small two-room wooden house was kicked in, and Myles could hear some loud voices inside. "Y'all come on."

Myles led Stewart and Sergeant Bates toward the doorway at a quick time. The sound of their boots on the wood porch amplified their entrance. Inside, they found two men scouring the small kitchen, and another pointing his pistol at Felipe, who was sitting down in a chair.

Myles stopped just inside the front door and cautiously pulled his pistol from his holster, drawing aim on the man pointing his weapon at Felipe. Stewart and Sergeant Bates stood behind him, but neither drew weapons.

"Drop the gun, right now," Myles said calmly.

Myles's statement got all three men's attention, and the six men spent a few seconds quietly inspecting each other—the only sound the door rocking and squeaking from a light gust. The pilferers were middle-aged, of European blood, and all wore dirty clothes and unshaven faces.

"What do you want?" one of the men in the kitchen asked in an amused tone, continuing to eat from a large bun. He spit casually on the floor, and none of the three made urgent moves to comply with Myles's orders.

"You didn't hear me?" Myles said loudly, making no effort to hide the irritation in his voice. "I said drop the gun." He pulled the hammer back on his pistol with his thumb, producing a metallic tick.

The man pointing his pistol at Felipe swung his gun around toward Myles. "Who the hell are you?"

In response, Myles shot the man's right hand. The shot removed the pistol from his grasp and produced a loud shriek. The earsplitting noise of the shot rang through the house, jolting Stewart and Sergeant Bates, who pulled their pistols. As the echo of the shot subsided, the room fell quiet, except for the shuffling of feet on the wood plank floor as the three Americans repositioned at the ready.

Myles looked at the man he had shot. The bullet had impacted the pistol. There was no blood. He stepped to the man, kicked his pistol, now on the ground, to a safe distance, and then violently grabbed him. He shoved him against the wall. "I'm Colonel Myles Adams, United States Army, and this man is Felipe Canova, Sergeant of Scouts, United States Army, and if you three don't get the fuck out of here in the next few seconds, you're going to meet your Maker this afternoon" Myles grabbed the man by his shirt and threw him out the door.

Myles turned to the other two men in the kitchen and nodded his head to the door. They quietly walked out of the room and into the crowd that had gathered around the house.

"What are you so stirred up about?" Stewart asked, lowering his pistol. He looked at Sergeant Bates with a smirk on his face.

"I've just about had enough of this place for one lifetime," Myles said as he helped Felipe to his feet. "You all right?"

"I well," Felipe replied.

"It's *I'm* well, not *I* well," Myles said, and picked Felipe's hat up off the floor. He put it on Felipe's head and inspected the man he had not seen in over a month. Felipe was of common mestizo stock and humble origins. He had black hair, brown eyes and skin, a quiet man who rarely spoke unless prompted, and bore a look as if he had spent his thirty years painstakingly employed in menial tasks.

"Felipe, you're making me look bad. I was just bragging on you this morning, and here I have to rescue you from a group of hoodlums."

"They are just hungry men," Felipe replied in Spanish. "We all can do things like that when we are hungry."

"You ready to go?' Myles asked. "This is Stewart Cook."

"I ready," Felipe replied, and followed the other three outside.

"Get your pistol. From the looks of it, you'll need it before you get back home." Myles walked back outside to inspect the simple crowd. They were now encircling the horses.

Less than an hour out of Engracia, the four men were riding toward a small pass in some hills. It was a fifteen-foot-wide draw that afforded effortless passage through the foothills ahead.

Since leaving Engracia, Stewart had been listening with one ear to his partner's jabs. He might be inclined to respond in kind, he thought, if they weren't being followed. He had sensed the presence of someone else on the trail ever since leaving the village limits.

"How long do you think they've been shadowing us?" he asked Myles, knowing he didn't need to preface the question.

"Oh, I don't know," Myles said casually. "Probably since Felipe's. Maybe before."

"Should we double back on 'em?" Sergeant Bates asked.

"Don't need to," Myles said. "I have a hunch they've already taken a shortcut and are waiting for us a ways up ahead."

Stewart put a gloved index finger to his lips and pointed fifty yards ahead, where two men were poorly concealed behind a stone outcrop above the pass. He pulled back on his reins and waited for the other three to draw even with him before speaking.

"Good hunch," he whispered.

"Speak of the devil," Myles said quietly, and dismounted. "Let's creep up this mountain a little to have a look."

Following Myles's lead, the other three dismounted and started up the adjacent hillside at a jog. Before they could climb to the top, three men on horseback suddenly appeared below, sending all four scampering for higher ground.

"Take cover!" Myles grunted as the men on horseback unleashed withering fire on the hillside.

They dove behind a small ridgeline twenty yards above their attackers and sat with their backs against a four-foot-high fold of loose stones and earth.

"Two guesses!" Myles groused, pulling his hat down tightly around his ears as bullets kicked up dirt from the escarpment and threw it onto the ambushed men.

"Jorge!" Sergeant Bates hollered. "Let's take him out once and for all."

Stewart stole a peek at the men below, earning another rapid volley in the process. "How do you know it's them?" he shouted above the gunfire.

"Simple," Myles said, checking his pistol to make sure it had a full magazine. "The little peckerwood is gunning for me. This has his signature all over it. Heaven forbid he actually met me face-to-face in a fair fight. He'd rather try his hand at an old-fashioned ambush."

Sergeant Bates raised his pistol over the ledge and took a few blind shots. Stewart and Felipe, who had more cover and a better angle on their attackers below, joined the sergeant and felled one of the men from his horse.

The other two men returned fire as they raced into a thick cluster of sage at the entrance to the pass.

Stewart and Felipe poured gunfire into the entrance in their wake.

"Cease fire! Cease fire!" Myles hollered, scurrying to the sergeant's side to steal a better look. "You aren't doing anything but wasting bullets!"

As Stewart and Felipe halted their fire, the group heard the sound of a horse baying.

"Got one of their horses," Stewart said. He and Felipe were lying beside each other reloading their pistols.

"Quiet," Myles said. "I hear 'em."

Stewart watched as Myles turned toward the sage thicket and cupped his hand around his ear.

"What are they saying?" Sergeant Bates whispered.

"Hard to hear over that suffering horse," Myles quietly replied as he paused to listen again. "But it sounds like they're yelling for their buddies to come over and help them. Must be those two Stewart saw in the pass."

"Where's Jorge?" Stewart asked.

"I don't know," Myles answered hastily. He paused a moment, and Stewart could see him sizing up the situation. "Okay, boys, let's get these two while they're isolated."

"Why don't we just stay here?" Stewart asked as he stared at the sage thicket. "Let them charge us or run off." He wiped his sweat-covered face with his sleeve. "Those are real bullets."

"Believe me," Myles said, "I'd like to do just that. But

they're not going anywhere, and I'm worried they'll shoot our horses." He turned to look at Stewart. "You're the one who's in the big hurry."

"I'm not in that much of a hurry," Stewart said, returning his partner's gaze. He could see Myles's wheels turning as his partner looked past him and then down at their horses pacing nervously below.

"I'd like to just make a run for our horses and get out of here," Myles said, "but that's too chancy. Wouldn't take much to shoot us."

Myles, too, was sweating. But Stewart could tell he was relishing the opportunity to command once again. The former lieutenant colonel spoke quickly and to the point as he brushed the dirt from his forehead.

"This is what we're going to do. Me and Felipe are going to move up this hillside where we can see the pass and those first two bandits. Stewart, you and Bones move down there and take cover. Then fill that thicket with bullets. That'll flush 'em out. When they come by us, we'll either shoot them or let 'em go. Probably shoot 'em, just so we won't have to deal with them anymore. Let's go before those others show up."

"Where's Jorge?" Stewart asked again, still hoping for some reassurance.

"I already said I don't know," Myles said. "If he's still here, we'll know soon enough." He slapped Stewart on the back and then hurried up the hill and out of sight.

As Myles and Felipe disappeared from view, Stewart fought off a brief moment of panic. He turned to see Sergeant Bates scampering down the hill toward the thicket. "Ah, hell!" he said, and followed the sergeant to the edge of the sage.

As the two men squatted behind a boulder, Stewart slowly lifted his head up to peer into the brush. He couldn't see anything beyond the first few feet of the sage, the depth of which was tangled in shadows. The draw had fallen deathly silent.

He glanced at Sergeant Bates, who was sweating from his long forehead but looked as steady as ever, and then pointed at the thicket and counted down to one with his fingers.

At one, he and the sergeant rose quickly and filled the sage with a magazine each. As they reloaded, they heard some shots coming from the direction where Myles had gone.

Stewart was tempted to run to wherever the gunfire was coming from, but he knew Myles would skewer him for ditching the plan. He calmed himself long enough to study the sandy ground and locate the tracks of the two horses the men had been riding.

"Nobody here," he said. "Would have at least hit a horse. Come on."

He followed the tracks into the sage, with Sergeant Bates close behind. Shortly, the horse that had been baying appeared, now dead, and they reached the end of the thicket.

Stewart peeked into the pass. He instantly saw the two men in question; they were riding back out of the pass and toward the thicket—and straight at him and Sergeant Bates.

As the sound of the horses' hooves grew louder, Stewart turned to the sergeant, put his finger over his lips, and then gestured that there were two. He raised his pistol and dove onto the open ground.

Before Sergeant Bates could fire a shot, Stewart had downed both men from their horses, needing just two bullets as he drew a bead on each in succession.

"Damn!" the sergeant said, panting in excitement. "I forgot how good you are."

Stewart knelt on one knee and threw up. "Make sure they're dead," he muttered, wiping his mouth.

He watched Sergeant Bates inspect the first man, who had likely died before he had hit the ground. His head was turned awkwardly in Stewart's direction, and Stewart could see a bullet hole in his left temple. His eyes, though still open, wore the frozen expression of death.

As the sergeant walked to the second man, Stewart noticed the man's chest still rising and falling as he labored to breathe, a bullet hole in his chest. He recognized the man's profile, although his nose had been cut in the fall and was bleeding.

"Where's Jorge?" the sergeant asked softly in Spanish.

"He can't hear you," Myles said. He and Felipe were approaching from the thicket with their horses in tow. "He's all but dead."

Stewart stood up on wobbly legs and tried to look composed.

"I swear, you must have an allergic reaction to shooting that pistol of yours. It's getting worse every time you use it. Next time," Myles said as he put a hand on Stewart's shoulder, "aim at something other than their vitals. Would have been nice to pump this fellow for some information before we put him out of his misery."

Both men flinched as the sergeant fired a round into the man's head.

"Speaking of which," Myles said. He and Stewart turned to face Sergeant Bates, whose pistol was still smoking. "Can't stand to see a man suffer, can you, Bones?"

"Nope," the sergeant said. "I hope you'll do me the same favor if it ever comes to it."

"It never will, Sergeant," Myles said forcefully. "Not if I can help it."

"We heard gunfire back there," Stewart said. "What happened to the other two *pistoleros*?"

"They didn't like getting shot at from on high," Myles said, and knelt beside the dead man. "We ran 'em off without much of a fight. Probably thought it was all of us, what with me being such a deadly aim and all. The shots sent these two back in your direction."

"Jorge?" Stewart asked.

"I never did see my old friend Jorge. But this here's one of his men. I recognize his scowl."

"Stewart took 'em both with two shots," the sergeant said.

"And you were worried about being rusty," Myles said as he stood up and frowned at his partner.

"You wanna bury these men, Boss?" Sergeant Bates asked.

"Well," Myles ruminated, "it would be the decent thing to do, even if they weren't exactly law-abiding citizens. Anybody pack a shovel?"

Chapter 12

While Sergeant Bates finished burying the bandits, Myles walked his horse to a small creek to water before departing. The stream was just on the front side of the draw, bottoming a wide, barren valley.

As the horse buried its mouth into the clear water, Myles pulled his watch from his pocket and looked at it pessimistically. Overhead, the sun seared down from a blue, cloudless sky. "We need to get going. Daylight's—"

Suddenly, two startled birds flushed from the creek bed, and Myles heard several gunshots and wild screaming in the distance. He looked out across the valley, a wide plain only covered with brown rocks and dotted with a few grass patches. On the far slope of the valley were a half-dozen men on horseback, just now topping the ridgeline. They were massed together, racing roughshod down the hill and firing their pistols skyward as they howled.

"Looks like we're not done here yet," Myles said in an excited tone, quickly mounting his horse. His companions did likewise. Myles pulled his knife from his belt and cut the rope tethering the packhorse to his mount. He spurred his horse violently and lunged forward in the saddle to help the mare forward and into the creek. "Maybe we can outrun them—our horses are probably better than theirs. Last time I wait around to bury these thugs."

Sergeant Bates had been the first to cross the brook, and led the four back in the direction they had come, at a full gallop. Myles, with Felipe riding beside him, leaned forward on his horse and whipped her on the shoulder with his reins. His hat blew off and hung over his back, its chin string snug around his neck.

As Myles pulled up beside Stewart, he turned to sneak a glimpse behind him. The six horses had crossed the creek and were in hot pursuit. Over the sound of his running horse, he barely heard a few more gunshots.

"Jorge's leading the bunch," he yelled. "Split up."

Without waiting for a response, Myles jerked on his reins, veering off to the right. His horse stumbled briefly, but quickly recovered. The move forced Felipe, on his right, to do the same. Myles pulled his pistol from his holster and hunkered low over his horse's neck. He then looked back again and took several wild shots. "There's three. Think we're separating, but our horses will wind shortly."

Felipe glanced at Myles and then fired a shot to his rear without aiming, his pistol upside down over his shoulder.

Myles joined him and fired a few more rounds before turning his attention ahead to look for some cover. There was little in sight, and the jarring ride scrambled his vision.

"There. That round-top," Myles yelled. The loud, repetitive sound of hooves thumping and buckles rattling drowned out his words. He pointed with his pistol to the end of a ridge with a few trees and some sage, a half mile ahead.

Felipe nodded, slapping his horse's rump a few times with his reins. The action sent him out a neck in front of Myles.

It took about three minutes of hard riding to reach the round-top. Approaching it, the two made running dismounts that stirred the dust. Myles swiftly removed his rifle from its holster on his horse and retrieved his saddlebags. He then slapped the horse on the rear and whistled loudly to send both animals into the brush.

Felipe disappeared into the sage. Myles followed.

"Here," Felipe said, ducking behind a horse-sized boulder. He peeked over the cover and fired two quick shots.

"You can't hit 'em from here," Myles said, breathing hard. He stood exposed in the thicket looking back down the hill. The three horses were charging in his direction, but still a quarter mile away. "It will be two or three minutes before they're in range."

Myles squatted in the loose rock. He pulled a box of ammo from one of the saddlebags and checked to make sure his rifle was loaded. He studied the small covered area for a few seconds. The pebble-strewn promontory was a quarter acre in size, covered with a few trees and scattered sage. It did not look ideal for defense, but visibility was unimpaired in all directions.

"I'm going to move to the other end of the brush. Keep them from flanking us. You stay on this end."

Felipe nodded, peering over the boulder, pistol at the ready. His eyes danced, the whites easily noticeable against his dark skin, shaded by his hat.

Myles hustled to the far end of the hilltop, where he took up a prone position behind a rock outcropping. He placed his pistol and binoculars on the rock ledge and then rested his rifle beside them, quickly butting it to his shoulder and checking the rifle's action a few times. He removed some dust from it with a handkerchief before pivoting the rifle side to side a few times to confirm his field of fire and freedom of movement. He put the riders in his sights. They were still too far to hit—five or six hundred yards down the hill.

"Don't shoot until I do," he yelled to Felipe as he removed his gloves.

"Okay," Felipe replied.

"When I start shooting, shoot the horses. We'll have them then. Then shoot the bandits." Myles wiped some excess perspiration from his eyes. Then he put his left hand under the stock, pulled the rifle firmly to his shoulder, and placed his finger on the trigger. His targets were only two hundred yards down the hill, still racing toward him. *Not a very bright bunch,* he thought to himself as he put the chest of the center horse in his sights. He paused his breathing and squeezed the trigger. The lead horse stumbled to the ground, producing a loud squeal as it fell. Its rider plunged over the horse's neck to the ground, face-first. Myles quickly bolted another round into the rifle.

The other two riders yanked back their reins, their horses coming to skidding stops. They wheeled around and fired a few pistol shots into the thicket, forcing Myles to flinch. He regained his position and felled a second horse as he heard Felipe firing rapidly with his pistol. The shots dropped the third horse.

Myles bolted another round into the rifle's chamber. The first man to hit the ground was scrambling to take cover behind his dead horse. A shot by Myles threw him to the ground, on top of his dead horse.

Felipe, having reloaded, began firing another nine-round volley. The shots were winging off the ground around the remaining two bandits, one of whom was pinned under his horse and struggling to free himself. A carefully aimed shot from Myles ceased his movement.

"Where's the other one?" Myles yelled from behind the boulder.

"Lying behind the horse on the left," Felipe yelled back. "I'll go get him."

"No," Myles yelled emphatically, quickly reloading the rifle. "Don't stand up."

Myles peeked over the boulder. The third horse had not

fallen broadside to him, but at an angle insufficient to hide a man. Myles grabbed his glasses and spied the horse. The lower legs of a man protruded from behind the dead horse. Myles returned the rifle to his shoulder. He took careful aim and squeezed the trigger. The shot produced a loud groan. A quick second did the same, and he saw two legs fluttering.

Felipe fired another reckless volley into the dead horse. "We get him?"

"Probably," Myles yelled back. "Just sit tight. I don't know if any of them are dead. But you don't have to worry about them charging us."

Myles removed the rifle from his shoulder and took a deep sigh. His heart was throbbing. As his mind settled from the excitement of the chase, he scanned the vast expanse below for further trouble. Out to his right, he saw some movement— horses, over a mile away and riding hard toward the round-top. He quickly picked up his binoculars. It was Stewart and Sergeant Bates. The lanky sergeant, riding awkwardly upright in the saddle, was easy to recognize.

"Here comes the cavalry. Late, as usual," Myles mumbled to himself, taking up a more leisurely position behind the boulder. He took a drink from his canteen and wiped some burning gunpowder from his right eye. A cumbersome pebble had settled in his boot, and he raised his foot trying to shake it free.

Abruptly, Myles's respite was broken by the hawing of two horses in the brush behind him, followed by several shots from Felipe's direction. Myles instinctively turned. His stomach lurched, and thoughts raced. He grabbed his pistol, bowed low, and quietly shuffled through the sage toward Felipe.

From the bushes, he saw a man kneeling over Felipe. It was Jorge, his shiny jewelry instantly recognizable. Myles slowly walked out of the sage, revealing himself. He extended his pistol and cocked its hammer. The hammer click broke the silence. "You're going to hell, now."

Jorge, still squatting over Felipe, turned to Myles, his eyes as wide as the big sky behind him.

Myles paused a few seconds, then pulled the trigger. Instead of the satisfying sound of a blast, all the action induced was another click. Stunned, Myles blinked his eyes in disbelief.

Jorge stood and smiled, his hands dangling at his waist, just inches from his holstered pistol. He glanced into the valley below to see Stewart and Sergeant Bates riding hard at him but still five minutes away. "Too bad about your friend. Wish you could have seen it."

Myles's veins pulsed with rage as the two stood a dozen paces apart. His mind went dizzy as it searched for a solution. He looked down at Felipe, lying on his stomach with a single bullet hole in the back of his head. Fresh blood covered his black, oily hair. Myles fought off an urge to charge Jorge.

Jorge let out a loud roar of laughter and pulled his pistol from its holster on his hip.

Myles dove for cover behind some rocks in the thick sage, bullets spraying around him as he hit the ground. He quickly shoved another magazine into his pistol and blindly returned fire.

Jorge dashed into the brush thicket, and Myles fired three shots in his direction. Return fire sent Myles back to the ground.

Myles lay still, staring into the sage for motion over his panting breath. Believing he saw some movement, he fired two more shots. He heard Jorge whistle and fire two more rounds. Then he heard a horse running away. He scrambled into the thicket on his hands and knees. His and Felipe's horses were on the ground, panting heavily with blood oozing from gunshot wounds in their sides. "Shit!"

Myles dashed out of the thicket. Jorge was riding away, full speed. Myles raised his pistol and fired, but Jorge was already out of range. He threw the pistol to the ground and sprinted back to get his rifle, twenty yards away.

He grabbed it and fell to the ground where he could see Jorge. The valley behind the hilltop was a quarter mile wide, and Jorge was already halfway to the safety of the next ridgeline. Myles calmly raised the long-range sights on the rifle, turning a small screw on the sight a few times. He then licked his thumb and checked the wind before securing the rifle to his shoulder. Jorge was just a tiny image in his sights, partially distorted by heat waves drifting above the ground.

Myles sighed deeply and fired two rounds. To his surprise, the second shot felled Jorge's mount. Myles squinted his eyes, trying to figure the distance. Seven or eight hundred yards, he guessed.

Jorge scrambled to his feet and started running for the ridgeline.

Myles cynically fired three more shots without careful aim. With each, Jorge ducked and weaved as he continued running. Finding amusement in this, Myles quickly reloaded. Far to his left, he saw two horses riding to Jorge's aid. He turned around. Stewart and Sergeant Bates were now less than a minute from arriving.

Myles aimed more carefully and fired twice more at Jorge. One shot caused him to dive to his left before quickly returning to his feet. Myles looked at the two horses racing toward Jorge. They still had a quarter mile to cover, but Jorge was only fifty paces from the safety of the next rim.

Myles returned the rifle to his shoulder. He lay as still as possible and focused his eyes. The valley was deathly quite. Jorge had reached the ridge and stopped running. He turned toward Myles, who heard the echoes of an angry scream cascade across the valley. He could see Jorge waving his arms. Myles fired. Jorge turned and slowly walked over the ridge and out of sight.

Myles put all of his energy and fury into a long scream, so loud it resonated off the valley wall two times. He let his upper body, which had been resting on his elbows, fall to the ground. The disappointment had sapped all his energy.

As Myles languished in despair—his head buried in the ground—pistol fire disrupted his thoughts. He turned to see Stewart and Sergeant Bates pumping finishing rounds into the three bandits Myles and Felipe had felled earlier.

Stewart guardedly led Sergeant Bates onto the round-top. Both carried their pistols in their shooting hands. Stewart gazed down at the spent ordnance scattered on the ground, a nervous feeling falling over him. The smell of gunpowder was heavy. He looked and listened. There was only the sound of sage ruffling in a slight breeze.

He gently spurred his horse and moved through a couple of chest-high bushes until he saw Myles sitting on a boulder and staring down at the ground, his forearms resting on his knees. Stewart walked his horse to Myles and casually leaned forward onto his saddle horn.

"You all right?" Stewart asked, disturbing the hush.

Myles looked up at Stewart and Sergeant Bates. "Slow but sure."

"Where's Felipe?"

Myles nodded his head toward the other end of the hilltop.

Stewart turned in the saddle. From atop his horse, he could see Felipe lying flat on the dirt. Sergeant Bates got off his horse and walked over to Felipe. Stewart followed. "What happened?"

"It matters not," Myles said softly. He stood and followed Stewart. Sergeant Bates turned Felipe faceup, and Myles knelt beside him. He put the back of his hand against Felipe's cheek and caressed it briefly. All stood silent for a few moments before Myles spoke again. "A finer or more modest man has never walked this land."

"He have any family?" Stewart asked.

"Just a mother," Myles replied, reaching down and removing a gold chain and cross from around Felipe's neck. He sighed deeply, put the cross in his shirt pocket, and then took a seat on a knee-high boulder. He had his back to Stewart and Sergeant Bates as he stared out at the horizon. "We should have just left him at home. This was no business of his, anyway. It was Jorge. He killed him because of me."

"Jorge!" Stewart said. "Did you get him?"

Myles did not respond.

Stewart watched Myles's distress for a couple of minutes, forestalling an urge to grab Felipe, quickly dig a grave, and move on. He knew this was inappropriate, but his desire to get to Santiago as quickly as possible seemed to override all immediate need or piety. He walked his horse over to inspect the two slain horses. "You want to go after him?" he asked, not at all wanting to hear a positive response.

Myles took a deep breath. "You can't imagine how bad I want to do just that. But we'll just have to let him go for now . . . if we want to get to Santiago in time to do any good. His days are numbered. Sergeant Bates, go see if you can find that packhorse. We'll redistribute everything on the three horses we have until we can buy another horse. We're finished burying these bastards. The coyotes can have them."

Chapter 13

As Myles led the way north, the road became increasingly congested with each passing mile. He tried not to stare as peasants in search of food and shelter trudged southward, their faces etched with the horror of the war at their heels. Spanish-Mexicans fleeing retribution and Federal regulars retreating before the advancing revolutionary army swelled the peasants' ranks. The road was soon teeming with desperate refugees, all of them heading south, *away* from Santiago.

"Get the feeling we're headed in the wrong direction?" Myles quipped as a steady stream of refugees poured by the three men. "Bones, might be a good idea to ride on ahead and scout who's coming our way. We have nothing to fear from Federal soldiers, but an armed, hungry soldier who's been under fire for God knows how long might be inclined to any unpredictability."

"Sure thing, Boss," the sergeant said, spurring his horse ahead of the other two men.

As Sergeant Bates rounded a bend in the road and disappeared from sight, Myles and Stewart slowed to make room for a family in rags, the mother and her six children clearly carrying everything they owned on their backs.

The peasants swarmed the blond-haired American and begged him for food and money.

Myles, as softhearted as he was coolheaded, reached down to the woman and handed her a handful of gold coins from his saddlebags.

"Keep that up, and you'll be broke," Stewart warned as the family resumed its march southward.

"I know that," Myles said. "Guess I couldn't help myself. Look at these poor people."

The peasants, many of them wounded or lame, looked hollowed out, their ghostly eyes a searing indictment of the carnage they had just escaped. The soldiers and bourgeoisie in their midst looked only marginally better.

Hungry, exhausted, and often barefooted, the Federal soldiers bore wounds of their own. Most wore light-colored pants and shirts, usually beige or gray, some donning light jackets, and many wore leather ammo belts that crisscrossed their chests. The lucky few were still accompanied by their *soldaderas,* female companions who followed the soldiers on foot, carrying food, cooking utensils, and bedding. The soldiers, wearing black leather boots, slip-on sandals, or nothing on their feet, could usually be distinguished by their hats, which looked like military cadet hats, each with a black bill, a flared beige top, and a two-inch white band between the two. The hats were a cheap way to create a uniform. They cost very little, but were easily identified by their commanders on the battlefield. Officers of any responsibility typically wore a full uniform, complete with a sword. None had passed their way thus far.

The Spanish-Mexicans, meanwhile, though physically in better condition, wore fear on their faces. They no doubt knew that their lives, if the revolutionaries won the war, were forfeit.

As Myles and Stewart continued on, they found Bones

waiting for them at the sacred village of El Chorrito, whose church had been built in front of a cave containing a rock formation that bore a striking resemblance to the Virgin Mary. The village, which sat near a large waterfall, boasted one of the only freshwater springs for fifty miles and was usually manned by a small garrison of Federal troops. Most of the southbound refugees had no knowledge of its location, even though it was nestled only a few miles off the road. It would be a good place to eat lunch and replenish their canteens.

"Find anything of interest?" Myles asked Sergeant Bates as they entered the village's outskirts. "Or have you just been passing the time until we got here?"

The sergeant nodded toward an elderly priest of Spanish ancestry who was standing across the road and consoling a middle-aged woman outside her gated manor. She was on her knees and nearly hysterical, weeping openly.

Myles dismounted and approached the two.

"Good afternoon, Father," he said. "Can you tell us anything about what's going on around here?"

The priest did not respond, instead continuing to console the well-dressed and fair-skinned woman.

Myles cleared his throat and asked in a softer voice, "What happened to her, Father?"

"A group of men came through here a couple of hours ago and abducted her daughter," the priest finally replied. He pulled the woman's head closer to him and brushed her hair with his hand.

"She lives in this big house?" Stewart asked from his horse.

"Yes, she is the wife of the local *político*. He has been off at the front for weeks."

"Please help me!" the woman pleaded in perfect English. Still on her knees, she crawled over to Myles and threw her arms around his legs. "They took my daughter this morning!"

she cried as she looked up at Myles plaintively. "They cannot be far."

Myles shifted his weight to his other leg and looked uncomfortably at the priest. He liked playing the role of hero, but this was too much. "You got any idea what happened?"

"She says it was three rugged-looking men on horseback. They took off in that direction." The priest pointed down a main road that led east out of town.

The woman stood up and faced Myles, tears still streaming from her eyes. "Please help me. I will give you anything, even myself." She turned from Myles to his companions on horseback.

"What do you think?" Myles asked, looking across at Stewart. "It's your choice." The woman's beauty and urbanity aided her cause, Myles thought, and he wondered how lovely her daughter must be.

"I see three sets of horse tracks," Stewart said hesitantly as he looked down at the road from atop his horse. "Maybe we should check it out."

"Okay," Myles said casually, trying to mask the anxiety in his voice, "we'll go see if we can find her. Señor, you know anything about what's going on around here?"

"Monterrey has fallen, and the *insurrectos* are infiltrating hacienda country. The Mexican Army left here two days ago."

"Thank you, Father," Myles said.

The priest nodded to the men and gently took the woman's arm to lead her back to the gated manor.

Myles climbed back atop his horse and joined the eastbound road, which led toward farmland on its way to the coast. If the rebels already had Monterrey, he surmised, surely Santiago was about to fall, if it hadn't already. If the rebels stayed true to form, they would put any surviving Federals up against the wall and round up any of their supporters: officials, lawmen, bureaucrats. Stewart had to be thinking the same thing: Alexia and her family might disappear before they could reach Santiago.

After a few yards, Myles stopped his horse and got off to study the tracks. "Looks like one horse has two riders."

"She sure looked shook-up," Stewart said, arriving beside Myles.

"So would you if a bunch of thugs made off with one of your sisters," Myles said as he remounted his horse. He turned to see the uneasiness his statement produced on Stewart's face.

The three followed the tracks for a half hour until they stopped at a small creek beside the road. There, they crossed the shallow stream and briefly scouted the opposite bank in both directions in an attempt to determine where the horses had exited the river.

"It looks like they used this stream to cover their tracks," Sergeant Bates said as he followed the bank, scanning the ground. "If they've got any sense, they didn't get out for a couple miles."

"I suspect you're right," Myles said, and got off his horse to water it in the stream. The midday heat had all three men perspiring heavily. Myles splashed some water on his face and looked up the riverbank, silently pondering their options.

Stewart dismounted beside Myles to refill his canteen. "What're you thinking?"

It was time to make a decision, Myles knew. They had two choices, both of them far short of ideal.

"We could doubtless follow this creek until we find these gangsters," he said as he continued to water his horse. "Might take a day or two. If we do, we can probably shoot up all the bad guys and save this girl. They didn't take her to kill her—at least not until they use her up. But it's not going to get us where we're going any faster. I know it doesn't seem very Christianly, but we're going to have to decide if we want to save this girl or the one we came up here for. It doesn't matter to me. We'll do whatever you want."

Stewart groaned and removed his hat. "You sure have a sadistic way of putting things."

"I don't like it any more than either of you," Myles said. "This will probably haunt me for years, but it's just the way it is. We have to make a choice."

"Damn it!" Stewart kicked the water and spooked his horse. He held his hat up against the sun, shading his eyes as he looked up the river. "Don't feel like playing God," he said bitterly, "deciding who lives and who dies."

"We didn't do anything wrong," Myles assured him. "We didn't start this war, and we sure as hell can't stop it."

Stewart put his hat back on and closed his eyes.

"Look," Myles said, searching for the right words, "me and Bones—we've been making these decisions for a couple years now. It's never easy. Trust me." He looked up at Stewart, who had stuck his left foot in his stirrup and climbed back in his saddle.

"You're right," Stewart said. "We best move on."

Chapter 14

"Well, boys," Myles said, "it looks like we've reached the end of the road as far as leisurely travel is concerned."

The three rode side by side, with Sergeant Bates and Stewart flanking Myles in the middle, as they slowed their horses to a walk on the outskirts of Linares.

This was orange country, and the golden flood of twilight was pouring through the surrounding orchards, which ran east to west as far as the eye could see. Even out of season, the oranges could still be plucked and eaten. Collectively, they had so far withstood war's plunder, their fleshy undersides glowing provocatively in the setting sun.

"That was leisurely?" Stewart quipped, shifting positions in his saddle.

After watering their horses in El Chorrito, they had traveled all day, making good time as they crossed several ridges on a small mountain road that was virtually inaccessible to foot traffic. With the inhospitable limestone pass behind them, they entered Linares, now bursting at the seams from an influx of refugees and Federal soldiers.

An old man, his back bowed under the weight of his belongings, stared numbly up at the Americans. He was slowly making his way through the throngs of beleaguered refugees crowding the main avenue.

Nuns tended to the homeless refugees and scurried about the old church abutting the town's *zócalo*. A dozen bodies were lined up in the church courtyard, each covered with a clean white sheet. Two Federal soldiers searched the horizon from the cupola above.

"Downright cheery atmosphere," Myles said as he took in the town's weighty gloom. He pulled up on his reins, pausing to study a makeshift infirmary and a platoon of Federal soldiers billeting in the plaza. "Rekindle any memories?"

Stewart nodded as he stared at a moaning soldier receiving treatment in the infirmary. A doctor, armed only with a bone saw and a half-empty bottle of chloroform, disappeared inside a nearby tent.

Sergeant Bates, also no stranger to war's carnage, did his best to seem unmoved. "What are the chances of us finding a hotel room here?"

"We'll get a room in the hotel," Myles said as he got off his horse. "I'm a paying customer there." He pointed to a run-down hotel at the far end of the *zócalo* and then turned to face the sergeant. "Bones, go find the commander of that platoon and bring him into the saloon. I want to talk to him. Pay him if you have to."

"At this rate, we'll need a week to get to Santiago," Stewart grumbled as he followed Myles toward the hotel.

"I tell you," Myles said earnestly without looking up, "this has been about the worst day I've had in a while. I sure hope it's not an omen of things to come."

Myles and Stewart entered the crowded hotel lobby and managed to secure a room—at three times the normal rate. Then, after turning their horses over to the hotel's valet for boarding and feeding, they walked to the saloon, where they found only a few occupants, most of them Federal officers.

"As far as I can tell," Myles said discreetly from the entrance, "the biggest problem with the Federal Army is its officer corps. They spend more time drinking and wallowing in excess than they do commanding."

Stewart frowned. "Like those three?"

Three officers, each in a drunken stupor, were entertaining a pair of the saloon's courtesans. Myles swiped an almost empty bottle of tequila from the bar and walked over to the officers' table.

"You girls take a break," he said, grabbing one of the girls by the arm and lifting her out of her chair to make room for himself.

"That is not necessary," a young lieutenant at the table slurred.

"Major, I'm Colonel Myles Adams, United States Army," Myles said to the elder of the three officers.

Stewart removed the second girl from her chair and sat down beside Myles.

"Don't tell me," the major huffed. "You're the advance party of the U.S. Army, here to save us!" He laughed loudly, and was joined by the two lieutenants beside him.

"Afraid not," Myles said somberly as he poured himself a shot of tequila. "What's the situation here?"

The major, a short, chubby, and somewhat unsavory man in his forties, regained his composure and replied in a more official tone. "We're reforming a defensive line from here to the coast."

"Don't you think you should be doing something other than getting drunk right now?" Myles asked as he turned the shot of tequila up and finished it.

"Why?" the major asked unrepentantly. "They won't be here for a week. They're having too much fun pillaging right now. And by this time next week, I'll probably be dead anyway. What's there to get in a hurry about?"

The war had been convulsing for the last three years. As each side recaptured the momentum, the other absorbed its enmity. Each act of cruelty birthed another, the second more salacious and vindictive than the first.

One thing was certain: Any Federal officers captured would be put in front of a firing squad, immediately and without trial. The common soldiers, for their part, were given the option of changing sides or being shot. The Federals, of course, were equally as guilty when it came to committing war crimes, but not as apt to take their revenge out on the public at large.

"Señorita, you can return now," the major hollered across the bar to one of the courtesans the Americans had excused.

"Good luck, Major," Stewart said as he and Myles got up. "You're gonna need it."

Sergeant Bates had entered the saloon, and was quietly observing the table from the bar.

"I couldn't find the commanding officer," the sergeant said as Stewart and Myles approached the bar. He looked at the drunken officers at the table. "What are they up to?"

"They're commanding their troops," Myles said, "in quite an unbecoming manner. They'll probably get what they deserve in a week or so. Sergeant Bates, before we hit the hay, buy us another horse. I'll ride that bay. He's pretty well behaved."

Stewart removed his pistol from its holster and beat it on the bar a few times.

A barmaid appeared from behind a door at the rear of the bar. "Colonel Adams," she said in Spanish. "I'm surprised to see you."

"We would like a couple of beers," Myles said, "if you can find the time."

The young lady walked to the other end of the bar.

"How do you know her?" Stewart asked as he stared at the girl. "Something about her looks strange."

"Her name is Iliana," Myles said, and lit a cigarette. He leaned back on the bar to look at the girl over Stewart's shoulder. "She's one of my ex-mistresses. She looks strange because of her height."

Iliana was a girl of mestizo parentage, slim, with darkly tanned skin, full facial features, long black hair, and brown eyes. The only physical feature that distinguished her from the two thousand unfortunate females outside was her height. Totally uncommon for a mestizo, she was almost five feet, eight inches tall—an Amazon in these parts.

"You see how she smokes that cigarette?" Myles mused. "Takes those long drags? That's because of me. When I met her, she didn't even smoke. After our first night together, she started smoking. Now, whenever she sees me or thinks about me, she has to have that nicotine."

Stewart shook his head and laughed quietly.

"What?" Myles asked. "You don't believe me?"

"Bones," Stewart said, and nodded in Myles's direction, "tell him what I told you the other day. I don't feel like explaining it twice."

"Uh," Sergeant Bates stammered, "what Stewart here told me, Colonel, was that you often stretch the truth a bit."

"Just a tad," Stewart said, measuring an imaginary inch with his thumb and forefinger.

"He says just exactly when the story goes from fact to pure fiction is anybody's guess," the sergeant added.

Myles feigned insult and repeated his last question. "You don't believe me? Get her over here and ask her. She'll corroborate my story."

Iliana was currently walking in their direction with the three beers.

"Excuse me, Iliana," Stewart said brazenly as he plunked a few pesos on the bar. "Myles here says he started you smoking. Any truth to that?"

Iliana stopped in her tracks, taken aback by the question. She blushed and laughed as she replied, "He's so bad!"

"We know that much," Stewart said. "Is he a liar, too?"

Iliana put her hands on her hips and cocked her head. "The first night he came in here," she said, looking off to the side, "he spent all night buying me drinks and courting me. He was a real gentleman. I must say, I was starting to find him kind of cute. Anyway, at the end of the night, he asked me if I wanted to come up to his room and have a drink. I had had a little too much to drink myself, so I said yes."

"Your first mistake," Stewart interrupted.

"Well," Iliana explained, "he was spending money on me like crazy. When I got up from the table we were sitting at, he told me to grab a pack of cigarettes sitting at the end of the table. I told him I did not smoke. He said after a night with him I would start."

She swept up Myles's ten-pack of Piedmonts from the bar and lit one.

"You sure look like you've started," Sergeant Bates said. "Maybe the colonel was right."

She laughed hoarsely and exhaled smoke through her nostrils as she shook out the match. "A beautiful man started me smoking," she said, pausing for effect. "But I can assure you, he is not in this room."

With that, Iliana turned abruptly and returned to the room behind the bar.

Sergeant Bates broke into a fit of laughter, spraying beer through his nose and mouth, while Stewart just smiled silently in amusement.

"She's always had a flair for the dramatic," Myles said gloomily. "I'll give her that."

* * *

The three eventually retired upstairs for a good night's rest. They would need it for the journey ahead. Henceforth, they would ride behind rebel lines.

Chapter 15

They arose before sunrise the next morning. Myles led them out of town in the predawn stillness, the cool morning air bringing a chill to his bones as he beheld the blood-red sliver of sky being born on the eastern horizon.

He slumped forward on his horse, low enough to feel its warm breath on his face, and shifted his gaze from the sky to the town's center, which, brimming with activity the previous evening, had fallen ghostly quiet. Even the hundreds of jaybirds nestled in the encino trees sat motionless above the small plaza. The platoon of soldiers bivouacking outside the hotel and the refugees in the church courtyard lay sound asleep. Two Federal sentries posted in the corners of the plaza had joined them, no doubt nodding off hours earlier.

The journey north would cover terrain similar to the prior day's ride, taking the Americans deep into the rolling foothills and farmland along the base of the Sierra Madre Mountains. With the town now behind them, Myles, as he had done the previous day, sent Sergeant Bates ahead to scout the route. He watched as the sergeant dutifully rode to the next hilltop the road crossed, carefully picking his way through sleeping refugees and their belongings.

As the morning wore on, the road once again swelled from the southerly exodus and teemed with survivors fleeing the horrors just a few miles north. Lone women and forsaken children with nothing more than the clothes on their backs walked alongside entire families pushing two-wheeled carts piled high with clothes, kitchenware, and everything of value they could carry.

Myles saw no soldiers and few horses. Most of the men interspersed with the other refugees were riding burros.

"One of us should spell Bones so his horse doesn't get tired," Myles said as he and Stewart approached the waiting sergeant at the top of a rise in the road. "We might want to start riding off the road, parallel to this foot traffic, before someone gets a bee in their bonnet and starts begging me for what's left of my money."

Stewart nodded in agreement and rode on up ahead, motioning for Sergeant Bates to join him and Myles. The three rode as far off the road as they could manage.

By early afternoon, they had come upon the village of Montemorelos, which straddled a small river and served as its junction at the base of the mountains. Sergeant Bates, after enjoying a brief respite from his foremost duty, had once again ridden ahead to scout the area, and was waiting under a shade tree on the road that led into the village.

"What'd you find, Bones?" Myles asked, fanning himself with his hat in the midday heat.

"Montemorelos is occupied," the sergeant said. He got off his horse and walked over to the packhorse tied to Stewart's mount to refill his canteen. After guzzling half of it, he removed his tan but dirty cowboy hat and poured the remainder over his head.

"Did you take a look?" Stewart asked.

"No, that's just what I've heard from a few passersby,"

Sergeant Bates said as he remounted. "I decided to wait here for you two."

The three continued on for another quarter mile and dismounted at the base of a hill overlooking the town. The small, rocky hill took little effort to climb, and its top afforded a panoramic view of the village below.

"Looks peaceful from here," Myles said, straining to pick out any movement through his binoculars.

"Siesta," Stewart said. Like Myles and Sergeant Bates, he was lying on his stomach, looking through his binoculars as he talked.

"It doesn't look like anything we should be worried about," Myles said, "but there's no sense in going looking for trouble if we can help it." If Montemorelos were truly occupied, Myles knew, such a revelation would be difficult to divine in the heat of the day, when most towns shut down. "There's a river ford down there somewhere," he said as he lowered his binoculars and reached into his pocket to remove a small rag. He wiped the sheet of sweat from his face and looked up at the scorching sun. "Anyone with any sense is lying under a shade tree right now."

"Somewhere else we can ford the river?" Stewart asked.

"I don't know," Myles replied. "Let me take a look." He pulled a map out of a small bag he had lugged up the hilltop. The map was already folded to expose their current location. "There's a ford about three miles west of here," he said after examining it.

"Why don't we go there?" Stewart asked, still scanning the town with his binoculars.

"We can't do that," Myles answered. "If we have to ride around every town between here and Santiago, it will take us a week to get there." He returned his binoculars to his eyes and peered down at the town. "We're just going to quietly ride around the south side of town until we get to the river, then move up the river until we can cross. Real quietly. Not galloping, but with brevity. Probably get through there without anybody even knowing we're there."

The three hiked back down the hill and remounted. It was only a half-mile ride down the valley to the town, and most of it was well covered. The cropland was fallow, but trees were abundant, and a few small buildings skirting the southern periphery of the town aided their approach.

They reached the river without seeing a soul, and rode slowly along its bank toward the village's center before pausing. The river, though only twenty yards wide and slow-moving, cut through the limestone plane and was abutted on each side by a precipitous rock step.

Myles dropped a small stone into the creek and counted as he watched the pebble plummet to the bed. "Four seconds," he said. "Probably about eight feet deep."

They continued on as slowly and as casually as possible, not wanting to draw attention to themselves. Four colorful adobe buildings fronting the river, each separated by an austere street, sat between them and the village's center. At each building, they made a cautious inspection of the roadway opposite it and crossed.

As they reached the last of the buildings before the village's small center, they paused behind its cover. From there, they spotted the river ford across the plaza ahead, easily identified by a wide, muddy trail leading to the water's edge.

They could hear several loud voices coming from the village's center, and Myles crept his horse to the edge of the building to eavesdrop. Not hearing anything to satisfy him, he leaned forward to take a look.

A few trees obscured his view slightly, but he could see a spacious dirt plaza bordered by three buildings and an old stone church. On the other end of the plaza, he noticed two men in distinctive bright khaki uniforms backed against a wall. With their pants tucked into knee-high leather boots, they were no doubt Federal officers. Three unshaven men in ordinary dress, each equipped with a rifle and two ammo belts crisscrossing his chest, were screaming and gesturing at the Federals. Two of them had leveled their rifles at the officers.

"Get your pistols ready and come on," Myles said quietly to Stewart and Sergeant Bates. Before either man could protest, he proceeded at a slow gallop toward the impromptu firing squad.

"One of them Federals looks like Colonel Sancho," he heard Sergeant Bates call to him softly as the sergeant and Stewart followed him into the courtyard.

Colonel Juarez Sancho was a logistical officer Myles and Sergeant Bates had met on more than one occasion while smuggling out influential citizens. Their interaction had been brief and professional.

At twenty paces short of them, Myles stopped. Stewart and the sergeant paralleled him only a second later.

"Buenas tardes, señor," Myles calmly said to one of the men in ordinary dress.

The man was standing apart from the other two and had his rifle shouldered. All three were young and wore leather sandals, fretted pants, tan shirts, and large white sombreros, their hardened faces sun-parched red.

"Buenas tardes," the man said, and looked up at the three.

"Do you think this is necessary?" Myles asked in Spanish, nodding to the two-man firing squad.

"You better get out of here, *norteamericano*," the man said testily. He was obviously in charge. His two subordinates, one of them in his mid-teens, looked over their shoulders but kept their rifles pointed at the two officers.

"We don't want any trouble," Myles said. "But there's no sense in this. There's been too much killing in this war already." He looked over at the wall where Colonel Sancho and the other Federal officer were awaiting their fate. On the ground beside them were five other corpses. None was wearing a military uniform.

"These two are butchers, not men, and they're about to pay for their crimes," the man said. "You three just move on."

"I'm not trying to get into your business," Myles said, "but we're not going to stand here and let this happen." He was confident that Stewart and Sergeant Bates, flanking him on either side and about a half horse behind, had his back.

"You three can watch or carry on," the man said stubbornly, "but this is not any business of yours."

Myles wouldn't relent. "You can take your rage out somewhere else, but I'll be damned if I'm going to stand by and let it happen while I'm here. Stewart, you and Bones ride over there and get those Federals."

He heard Stewart lightly click his heels against his mount's ribs and start to move in the direction of the two Federal officers.

"Like I said," Myles spoke softly, never breaking eye contact with the man, "we're not looking for any trouble. We'll be out of here in just a minute."

The rebel officer stepped back a few paces in anguish and looked first at the two Federal soldiers standing against the wall and then at Stewart slowly walking his horse toward them. "I don't want to get into a shooting match over this," the man said, his voice rising.

"That would be well advised," Myles calmly replied.

Stewart had always been a much more proficient officer. He was a better marksman, a better navigator, a better soldier when it came to doing things by the book. But Myles never got spooked. He could size up people and situations in the heat of the moment, issuing orders calmly and confidently, his tone of voice reassuring even the most timid subordinate.

"We're not going to let them do this, are we?" asked one of the boys with his rifle raised, panic in his voice.

Before anyone could answer, the young *insurrecto* swung around and pointed his rifle at Sergeant Bates. As he did, he returned the rifle butt to his shoulder and nervously put his finger on the trigger.

His jerky, hesitant movements, whether born of reckless bravado or deadly intent, touched off the lightning response of Stewart's trigger finger. Stewart quickly pulled his pistol and shot the boy in his leg, dropping him to the ground in a writhing heap.

The other man beside him turned and attempted to lift his rifle, but before he could shoulder it, Stewart took aim, delivering a bullet to the man's hip. The young man let go of his rifle and clutched at his hip as he fell to the ground.

Myles leveled the barrel of his Colt .45 even with the eyes of the rebel officer, who was struggling to get his rifle off his shoulder.

The rebel officer froze.

"Drop it and get out of here," Myles said loudly and clearly. He motioned toward the other side of town with his pistol.

The *insurrecto* was standing flat-footed with his rifle above his head.

"I mean it," Myles said. "If you had listened to me in the first place, this wouldn't have been necessary. Now get moving, or I'm going to shoot you—right now!"

The man paused but a second, and then threw his rifle on the ground and took off running across the plaza and out of sight.

The first man Stewart had shot had abandoned his rifle and crawled behind a nearby building. Stewart climbed off his horse, pistol ready, and pursued him until the man had moved to a safe distance. He then rushed to the other rebel soldier, still writhing in the dust from the bullet to his hip.

Myles felt his heart sink. "Did you have to shoot that kid?"

He watched as Stewart, on his knees trying to apply first aid to the young boy, removed the leather ammo bands from the boy's chest and ripped his light cotton shirt off to apply pressure to a three-inch hole in his hip that was gushing blood profusely. The boy was still breathing, but Myles could tell his life was passing quickly. He wanted to express his sorrow and say something to comfort the boy, but he could see it would not be comprehended.

"He's not going to make it," Myles said quietly.

Stewart dropped the blood-covered shirt and gently lifted the boy's head off the ground. He caressed his cheek lightly with the back of his hand and said a quick prayer as he made a cross over the boy's forehead.

The boy, shaking and ghostly white, looked up at Stewart without seeing him. His teeth chattered and then went silent.

Stewart returned the boy's head to the ground and then stood up. "Damn it!" he cursed. He took off his dusty white straw hat and ran his hand through his black hair in despair as he looked down at the boy. "He was about to shoot Bones, but I meant to shoot him in the leg! That damned horse jumped just as I fired! This is getting completely out of hand!"

As he returned his hat in disgust, gunfire from the center of town erupted, and bullets began glancing off the surrounding buildings.

Myles turned to see four men converging on their location from a small store across the *zócalo*. They were about a hundred yards away and firing as they walked. Two of the men brandished rifles, the other two pistols.

"Go get Sancho and the other officer," Myles told Sergeant Bates, "and hurry!" He then reared his mount around and raced behind a building to his rear. "I'll cover you!"

Protected by the building, Myles swiftly dismounted, retrieved his rifle from his saddle, and ran to the edge of the building. From there, he fired three quick rounds in the direction of the men, making sure not to hit any of them. He and his friends had already shot two revolutionary soldiers, killing one. Any more casualties, he knew, would only add to their trouble. His shots managed to send the men scurrying for cover, but did not hinder their firing.

He could see Stewart and Sergeant Bates struggling to hoist Colonel Sancho and the other Federal officer, each with his arms still tied behind his back, over their horses.

"Get a move on!" he hollered from the corner of the building.

"What do you think we're doing?" Stewart grunted as he pushed the colonel onto the back of his horse.

With the Federal officers finally slung over their horses, Stewart and the sergeant raced toward Myles and the protection of the building as bullets whistled over their heads.

As he fired feverishly from the hip into the plaza, Myles was having a difficult time wiping the smirk from his face.

"What's so damned funny?" Stewart asked breathlessly after he and Sergeant Bates had beaten a hasty retreat to the corner of the building.

"This," Myles said, gesturing to the plaza in front of him where the rebels were slowly advancing. "It's kind of stressful being shot at, even if these rebels couldn't hit a barn from the inside."

"Glad you're enjoying yourself," Stewart groused.

"Think about it," Myles said as he raised his rifle to deliver another round of suppressing fire. "Mexicans fighting for anybody are some of the worst shots known to man. No offense, Colonel Sancho." He paused and winked at the colonel, who was still bound and slung over Stewart's horse, staring in disbelief at the gabby American. "Mind you, Mexicans are plenty brave. Their courage even approaches the absurd in some cases. I've seen Mexicans on either side of this war obey almost ludicrous orders, far in excess of what even the most daring American would consider the line of duty. But in the field of marksmanship, they're incompetent."

"What's your plan?" Stewart asked.

"Let me finish," Myles said, feigning indignation. "I have sat in awe watching Mexicans fire their rifles at each other. They rarely aim at their target, and on most occasions never even put the rifle butt to their shoulder. They simply load a round into the chamber, barely lift the firearm above or around whatever they're hiding behind, and fire."

A bullet ricocheted a foot above Myles's head as he reloaded.

"What do you call that?" Stewart asked.

"Luck," Myles said, still smirking. "He was probably aiming at you. I tell you, most Mexicans never even touch a rifle until some officer's kicking their butt into battle." He turned again to the colonel. "We sure as hell saved you a lot of grief, Colonel Sancho. Talk about a gut-wrenching ordeal. You probably would have been on that wall ten minutes before that junior firing squad hit a vital organ."

Sergeant Bates finished cutting the ropes around the wrists of Colonel Sancho and the other officer and tried to rein Myles in. "What you got?"

"I've got them pinned down," Myles said, "but I'm almost out of ammo. Grab your rifle." Myles peeked around the corner to see if there was any truth to his statement.

"How many?" Stewart asked.

"Just those four," Myles said, and fired a few more strafing rounds into the plaza. "But I'm sure if we lounge around here long enough, we'll have the entire rebel army on our hands."

"Why are we waiting?" Stewart asked. "Let's load up and go."

Myles paused to reload and then looked up sheepishly. "The river ford is on the other side of the street."

Stewart threw him an angry look. "What the hell did you come over here for? Now I know why you wouldn't shut up about those damn Mexican sharpshooters. You didn't want to own up to this mess." He fired a shot into the plaza with his gun barrel only inches from Myles's ear.

Myles cringed with such agony Stewart decided to fire a second round.

"If it was such a bad idea," Myles replied with a hand over his ear as he fired two carefully aimed shots at the feet of two of the *insurrectos*, "why in the hell did you follow me over here?"

Two rebel soldiers had gotten more brazen and were exposing themselves in the street. But Myles's latest volley sent them both behind a wall.

"Saddle up and get my horse," Myles said. "I'll keep holding them back."

Sergeant Bates had already untied the two officers and loaded them onto his and Myles's horses, and hearing Myles's order, he walked them to the edge of the building.

"You ready?" he asked, looking down at Myles.

"I'm going to empty my chamber," Myles said, "and we're all going to haul ass across the road and to the other side of the river."

"Sounds pretty chancy," Stewart replied as he climbed on his horse.

"Not really," Myles assured him. "I put the chances at about one in ten that they'll shoot one of these horses. For a skinny gringo like Bones, the chances are almost none. We're somewhere in the middle. Nonetheless, it would probably behoove you to ride as fast as you can. Isn't that right, Colonel Sancho?" He secured the reins to his horse in his left hand and pointed his rifle back around the corner. "You sure that woman is worth all this trouble?"

Stewart nodded.

"You think she's finally going to run off with you after all this inconvenience?" Myles asked, and emptied his chamber. As he did, he motioned for Sergeant Bates to get moving.

Myles squinted into the distance at the long and narrow silhouette of Sergeant Bates, still on horseback. The sergeant had his back to him and was scanning their vanishing dust trail on the horizon for any signs of the rebel soldiers.

They had managed to bolt across the street to the river ford without a scratch, and had ridden hard for several minutes into the hills before pausing under a large scrub oak to catch their collective wind. Myles hadn't heard the rebels fire a shot since they had crossed the river, nor had he heard any horses in pursuit. But he wanted to be sure as he and the others dismounted.

He looked over at Colonel Sancho. "What the hell you want us to do with you now?"

"I don't know," the colonel answered, catching a canteen Stewart had just thrown to him. "I've just been given an extra thirty years. I haven't really decided what I want to do with them yet." He opened the canteen and guzzled the water voraciously.

Stewart shook his head. "Guess this is your lucky day, Colonel Sancho." He turned to the other officer and introduced himself. "Stewart Cook. I assume you already know Myles and the gentleman on the hill up there."

"It is very good to meet you," the lieutenant said in broken English. "I am Lieutenant Pablo Rubio." Lieutenant Rubio, a common mestizo in his late twenties, was tall and thin—and unshaken by his near-undoing.

"I reckon it *is* your lucky day," Myles said disdainfully. "Lucky we didn't find you on the other end of a firing squad; else you might be lying out there sunning in the street right now."

"I always treat my prisoners totally in accordance with

Mexican law," the colonel said in perfect English, and laughed. Thin and in his early forties, Colonel Sancho stood facing Myles, his eyes about even with the American's chest.

"Save that shit for somebody who might believe it," Myles said, "but don't burden me with it. I know better."

As Stewart straightened his saddle, Myles quizzed Colonel Sancho again on his plans. He didn't want any loose ends.

"Maybe we'll try and move south," the colonel said. "Find the army."

"Is there anywhere around here you can get a horse?" Myles asked.

"Allende has not been occupied yet," the colonel answered. "It's about a two-hour ride from here."

"I tell you what," Myles said after taking a sip from his canteen, "we'll take you to Allende, but we have a little job we've got to do. You're going to give us a hand with it, and then you can go south. We've got a couple pairs of extra clothes. You two can change into them. Those bright uniforms you wear can be seen from twenty miles off. But let's get off a piece before you change."

"You asking or telling?" the colonel asked.

"I'd say it's compulsory," Stewart answered for Myles as he remounted. He reached down and offered his hand to the young lieutenant to pull him up behind him.

"You got any money to buy a horse?" Myles asked as he got on his horse.

"No," the colonel replied, "but I'm sure you gringos do. You always seem to have a pocketful of it."

He put his foot in Myles's stirrup and started to climb up behind Myles. Before the colonel could swing his other foot across the horse, Myles took off riding up the hill almost spilling the colonel.

At the top of the hill, Myles stopped to light a cigarette,

still grinning to himself as the colonel finally got situated behind him. "Anybody coming?" he asked the sergeant.

"Doesn't look like it," Sergeant Bates said, still searching their dust trail, now all but gone, for any pursuers. He reached over and grabbed one of Myles's cigarettes and lit it. "Stewart's sharpshooting must have made them think twice."

"Bones, I thought you quit smoking," Stewart said, arriving with Lieutenant Rubio as the sergeant took a long drag off the cigarette.

"He quit all right," Myles said. "Quit buying. Let's get across the next hill and change these Mexicans out of those uniforms before we have a real fight on our hands. This woman-chasing has turned into pure folly. Done shot two *villistas,* harboring two wanted Federals, and we're headed north. We'll be lucky if we're not all out in front of a firing squad before the day's over."

Chapter 16

As Stewart led the group single-file toward the mountains, they entered what was left of an orange grove. He was the first to see the bludgeoned terrain, which opened up a few yards at a time as it rose slowly toward the foothills looming on the horizon.

He had never been a patient man, never one who could sit still in the face of uncertainty. He preferred to act, even if it meant making a mistake. Despite embarking on yet another detour, they were still headed north—and closing the gap on Santiago. But the addition of yet another side trip to their itinerary was almost more than he could bear, and he was surprised by the tension in his own voice.

"Gunpowder," he said between clenched teeth.

The acrid haze hung in drifts in front of him, shrouding the sight of the first body he came upon, a Federal soldier stripped of his boots, rifle, and valuables. The soldier lay contorted in the worn turf, spent ordnance still smoldering in the grass near his blood-soaked, blackened skull.

Stewart looked up at a pair of buzzards circling in the sky, and then turned his gaze to Myles and Colonel Sancho, who were trailing the group at a slow trot through the battlefield.

Myles had plucked a half-ripe orange from a nearby tree and was taking off his gloves so he could peel it.

Stewart did a lazy half turn in his saddle and paused for the others to catch up. "Some of these your men?" he asked Colonel Sancho.

"Yes."

Stewart waited as the colonel eyed a pair of corpses entangled in the grass below.

"About two hours ago," the colonel said, "we were trying to retreat, but they caught us out in the open. My men who survived were taken prisoner. Lieutenant Rubio and I would have been the last ones executed had you three not come along."

Stewart nodded and continued on.

Up ahead, he spied a couple of coyotes, not at all deterred by the sight of men on horseback, feasting on one of the dead soldiers. He methodically pulled out his pistol and fired a few rounds to run them off. He then slowed to look at the fly-covered corpse. He felt little remorse for the dead soldier, only a desire to move on. There was nothing he could do to help the men who had perished on this makeshift battlefield, but he could prevent something similar from happening to Alexia and her family.

"They didn't leave anything for the scavengers, did they?" Sergeant Bates asked.

Stewart didn't answer. "Let's get moving," he said to the group. He spurred his mount and led the way out of the tattered and smoking orange grove.

Two hours later, with Stewart still fixated on finding the shortest route to Santiago, Myles was troubled by a more immediate concern: the rumbling in his belly. After sending Colonel Sancho and Lieutenant Rubio to look for horses, he followed his nose—and the appetizing odor from a grill out front—to Allende's only thoroughfare, which boasted a bakery, a tiny grocery with only a couple of stocked shelves and one refrigerator, and a few open-air stands selling everything from fruits and vegetables to chicken feed.

Nestled in a Sierra Madre pass at three thousand feet and well off the beaten path, Allende was an island unto itself, its 150 residents happily insulated from the war raging in the valley below. The carnage at the orange grove, less than two hours south, was a world away.

Myles stopped alongside the large iron pit in front of the grocery, where two older women, each wearing a casual skirt, a light shirt, and sandals, were tending to an open grill.

As thick white smoke rose from the grill's smokestack, one of the women bent over to inspect the pit from a small door on its side. Her assistant was stoking the fire below with a long wooden stick.

"What you got cooking in there, Señora?" Myles asked in Spanish as he tried to look through the small door. "It sure does smell good."

"Beef brisket," the woman inspecting the grill answered. She closed the small pit door and, using the rag she had just used to protect her hand from the searing iron handle, wiped the perspiration from her weathered face.

"We'll take some," Myles said.

"It won't be ready for about an hour and a half," the woman said, and looked up. She was shielding the sun from her eyes, Myles figured, in an attempt to match his accent with a face.

"We don't have an hour and a half," Stewart said.

Myles turned to see Stewart and the sergeant dismount and head toward the grocery behind the pit.

"I smell baked goods," Stewart said to him, nodding to the tiny bakery next door. "You can load up on flour and sugar."

Sergeant Bates veered right and disappeared inside the

bakery as Stewart entered the grocery, but Myles lingered at the pit.

"May I take a look?" he asked.

The old woman in charge nodded and opened the lid, letting the sumptuous aroma escape.

Myles's mouth watered as he devoured with his eyes the four huge chunks of marinated meat on the grill. He removed his pocketknife and cut a small gash in one of the pieces. To his dismay, he found the brisket still dark red inside.

He sniffed the delicious-looking meat again. "An hour and a half?" he asked in disbelief. "You can't heat this pit up a little more?"

The old woman shook her head.

Myles heard the door to the grocery creak open. "Leave that lady alone and come on," Stewart said.

With the marinating beef still tantalizing his senses, Myles grudgingly turned and followed Stewart to the bakery, where he found the sergeant standing in front of a glass counter housing everything from day-old tortillas and corn bread to freshly made pastries. The sergeant was anxiously looking over an assortment of chocolate, cinnamon, and cream-filled pastries.

"You men look hungry," an elderly woman said in Spanish from behind the counter. "Can I get you anything?" She was short and fat and busily arranging a batch of chocolate-covered pastries under the glass counter.

Myles sniffed at the fried pastries. "Bones, get us a variety, including a couple of those," he said as he pointed to a long, thin pastry filled with chocolate. "I'll go get us something to drink."

After making a quick stop at the grocery, Myles found Stewart waiting for him and Sergeant Bates in a shady spot under a tree, where he was drinking from his canteen. Stewart gazed quietly at the ground as he wiped his mouth with his sleeve, and then nervously looked at his watch.

"What're you so antsy about?" Myles asked as he and the sergeant arrived with a quart of milk in a glass bottle, an assortment of pastries wrapped in wax paper, and five more ten-packs of Piedmonts.

Stewart, in a rare moment of loquacity, strung together more than a handful of words. "We're wasting time. What the hell are we going to do with these Mexicans we've picked up? Seems like unneeded delay and trouble. We've already squandered half a day messing around with 'em."

"They'll come in handy," Myles said, smiling at his friend's relatively prolific outburst. "Don't worry. They know a hell of lot more about what's going on around here than they'll lead you to believe. You worry about this woman, and let me worry about the Mexicans." He finally managed to unwrap the pastries, and joined Stewart in the shade.

Sergeant Bates followed, and Myles caught him eying the mangos Stewart had bought at a fruit stand. "That's all you got to eat?" the sergeant asked.

Stewart didn't answer.

"Sourpuss," Myles whispered to the sergeant, who, to his disappointment, managed to keep a straight face.

With Stewart nervously checking his watch once more, Myles looked down at his own watch and its weathered black-leather band, which looked like it was about to disintegrate. "What I need is a new strap for this watch. I wonder if they've got any watchbands in this town."

"Doubt it," Stewart said gruffly.

"Boss, how many bands is that you've put on that watch?" Sergeant Bates asked. "I know it's got to be at least ten. Why don't you just get you one of those new metal bands?"

"Metal band? That's not very sophisticated. I've got to have a watch that's versatile. I might be tracking a lion by day and attending a royal ball by night. I haven't got time to be packing around a bunch of different watches. Besides, you never know when I might be massaging some princess on the thigh. A metal band might scratch her."

"I thought you were engaged," Stewart said, giving Sergeant Bates a reprehensible look for initiating the conversation.

Myles looked up at his partner and stuffed half of a chocolate-filled pastry into his mouth. As he bit into it, chocolate oozed out of the corner of his mouth, and he could feel it drip southward. "Want one?" he asked, his mouth half full.

"I had my fill of sweets at the carnival," Stewart said as he began slicing one of his mangos. He looked down at the pastries and then back up at Myles. "Disgusting."

"You're as tough as they come," Myles said in mock admiration.

Stewart wolfed down a couple slices of mango and then climbed onto his horse.

"Where you headed?" Myles asked.

"See a man about a horse."

Myles waited until he thought Stewart was out of earshot. "That son of a bitch sure is irritable."

"Seems like for every mile we get closer to Santiago," Sergeant Bates said, "he gets even more worked up."

"Probably just constipated," Myles said as he took up a position of repose under the shade tree.

Stewart found Colonel Sancho and Lieutenant Rubio standing outside a small corral on the other end of town. They were leaning on an old wooden fence, peering over it at two horses. The colonel was so short he could not see over the fence without stepping up on the bottom rail.

Inside the corral, an old man was trying to harness one of the two horses.

"What'd you find?" Stewart asked as he brought his horse to a stop alongside Colonel Sancho at the fence line.

"He has these two here," Colonel Sancho said. He turned around and looked up at Stewart. "He said he would sell."

"How much?"

"I don't know. I haven't asked him yet."

"Vaquero," Stewart hollered across the fence, "how much?"

"Two hundred and fifty pesos each," said the old man, who wore a white sombrero that hid his face from view. He let go of the horse he was trying to harness and walked over to the fence.

Stewart squinted at the withered horses, whose ribs could be seen from the fence and whose stringy manes showed no signs of grooming. "Two hundred and fifty?" he asked incredulously. "Doesn't look like either one has been fed in a week."

"You head off on foot in this heat and you will change your mind in a hurry," the old man replied sternly. He lifted his sombrero, and Stewart caught sight of his steely old gaze.

"If I head off on those two, I'll probably be on foot by the end of the day anyway," Stewart replied, exasperated by all the talking he was having to do. He looked down at Colonel Sancho and spoke in English. "Any more horses around here?"

Stewart waited as the colonel peered at the poor specimens one more time, nearly tripping on the pants Myles had loaned him, the thickly rolled cuffs encumbering his every move. "This is it," he said.

"Got any saddles?" Stewart asked the old man.

"*Sí*"

"Three hundred pesos for both horses, including saddles," Stewart said emphatically. "My final offer."

"Five hundred and you can have them."

Stewart made a counteroffer, but the old man would
not budge.

Stewart agonized over the old man's intransigence for a few
moments, and then reached into his back pocket to retrieve his
wallet. "Extortion," he muttered before turning to the colonel.
"You two better be worth something." He pulled some money
out of his wallet and counted it. As he did, he derided the old
Mexican vaquero as best he could, trotting out a few choice
Spanish expletives. "Get those two horses saddled up," he said
to Colonel Sancho. "I'll be back in a minute."

He handed the money to the colonel and turned to leave.
As he did, he heard the two men laughing.

"That's one angry gringo," he heard Colonel Sancho
saying.

"It's on account of the girl," he heard the lieutenant counter.

Back at the store, Stewart found Myles in a stationary position under the shade tree. Sergeant Bates was beside him,
sharing the pastries. Stewart rode up and stepped his mount
directly over Myles, straddling him broadside.

"You find any horses?" Myles asked without opening his eyes.

"I did."

"Let me guess," Myles said as he opened his eyes and looked
up at Stewart, "there's an old Mexican back there who's going to
spend the rest of the afternoon celebrating because he got some
foolish gringo to pay a fortune for two old scraggly mules."

Stewart shook his head in disgust.

"Don't worry," Myles said. "If we get on down the road a
piece and our Mexican friends disappear, I'll let you hunt
them down personally. Shouldn't be too strenuous with them
on those old mules you just broke the bank for."

Santiago. Ever since Stewart had left the port of Tampico,
entrusting his passage to a waterlogged riverboat and its

pompous but affable sponsor, Santiago had never been far from his lips. Its mere mention was enough to sober even his partner. It had become synonymous with duty, tension—peril. The fate of each man, he knew, had become wrapped up in one eight-letter word that hung over them like an ominous thundercloud.

Five hours after leaving Allende, the group had drawn agonizingly close to their ultimate destination. And the tension had reached a boiling point.

"Hell, we're so close," Stewart said as they paused at a riverbank a few miles from Santiago. "I say we just ride on into town tonight." He dismounted and stormed into the creek in search of a ford.

"No," Myles said earnestly. "We're not going in there tonight. It's too tricky. It's only eight hours till daylight. If she's there now, she'll be there in the morning."

Stewart knew his partner was right, and could only stand stoically at river's edge as Myles hammered the point home.

"I'd like to get as close as we can tonight," Myles said. "But we ain't going to find a river crossing until daylight. We'll just camp on this side of the river and get moving early in the morning." He turned to Sergeant Bates. "Bones, ride back a piece and look for a place to camp. We aren't going to camp on this riverbank. It's too confining. Not many exit options if we need to make a quick departure. Not to mention it's a haven for mosquitoes. Be sure you find a spot with a lot of cover. Colonel Sancho looks like he might not be afraid to snore."

Stewart swallowed the impulse to protest, and followed the men back toward a stand of pines.

Chapter 17

Myles awoke to the sound of Sergeant Bates's voice.

"You ready to get up, Boss?" the sergeant whispered.

Myles didn't move. It had only been a few hours since he had finally fallen asleep. Maybe the sergeant would go away.

"Boss, you ready—"

Myles felt the cool, damp morning air against his skin as he yanked his blanket from his face and stared angrily at the dark outline of the sergeant. "What time is it?" he groused.

"It's about an hour before sunup."

Myles slapped at a mosquito buzzing his ear. "Go get Stewart up and tell him to get everything ready. He's the one that got us into this mess."

He pulled his blanket back over his face and tried to steal a few more seconds of rest.

They had chosen a campsite in a thinly wooded area about a half mile south of the river. The trees had provided posts for the Americans' hammocks and shielded the group from sight. But to Myles's consternation, the local insects had also found the location agreeable.

Myles's blanket, meanwhile, was a foot short. It could cover either his feet or his head, but not both. He had chosen to protect his head, but had still managed to get bitten on the face and neck a couple dozen times during the night.

As his eyes acclimated to the predawn darkness, he lay silently under his blanket and listened to Sergeant Bates roust the group. He scratched his arm and found a checkerboard of swollen mosquito bites. He then reached down and felt his right leg, which might as well have been a relief map. He wondered what his face looked like. He had loaned his mosquito netting to Lieutenant Rubio, assuming that his hammock was more important. But he had traded the ants on the ground for the mosquitoes on the breeze.

Myles finally threw off his blanket and sat up. As he stared at the campsite, he frowned at the layer of dew that had covered all their belongings in a cool, slick film.

He thought about building a fire to ward off the bugs and warm a pot of coffee, but saw that Stewart, who had already helped pack up most of the site, had started a fire of his own and was sitting beside it. Myles stumbled toward the fire and then paused a few feet away to relieve himself.

"Don't you have any social graces?" he heard Stewart mumble from the fire.

"Yeah, but I don't see any use in employing them out here," Myles said after emptying his bladder. He reached for the coffeepot and poured himself a cup of the steaming-hot liquid. He looked down at Stewart, who was staring back up at him. "Well?"

"Well what?" Stewart asked.

"What are we waiting around on?"

Myles's eyes narrowed as he gazed ahead. Located in the fertile Guajuco Valley, where it straddled a river by the same name, Santiago was barely visible in the distance, a few lamps twinkling in the half-light of dawn. Irrigation ditches,

each one home to a row of thick rubber trees and serving
maze of row crops, ran all the way to the town's outskirts an
restricted views along the flat terrain.

"What do you see?" Myles asked Stewart.

His partner had pulled out his binoculars, and was scannin
the town as the group sat on horseback atop an irrigation leve

"Not much," Stewart said as he removed his glasses fro
his eyes. "Not enough light yet."

The deep indigo sky was brightening imperceptibly, an
visibility was improving with every minute that passed.

Myles turned to Colonel Sancho. "What do you know
Colonel?" He lit a cigarette and then handed one to Lieu
tenant Rubio, who had already bummed a pack from him th
day before. "It's a good thing I bought extra cigarettes in Al
lende."

"They had a fight here," Colonel Sancho answered. "Whe
we pulled out of Monterrey, most of the local *hacendados* de
manded we stand here. Not many did, but they coerced
couple hundred. I haven't heard, but I suspect it fell rathe
easily."

"You got any idea where Alexia lives?" Myles asked Stewar
Stewart nodded.

"How well do you know your way around?" Myles asked
inspecting the small town. Their surroundings were startin;
to brighten, and he could make out faint details of the town

"Fine," Stewart said, staring at the town through his binoc
ulars once again.

"How do you accomplish anything in court?" Myles aske
"You can't even connect two words. What's the judge sa
when you rest your case before it's even made?"

"Brevity," Stewart answered, "is the essence of wit."

"Brevity?" Myles repeated. "Cut that in half, and that's you.

"It ain't Paris," Stewart finally said. "Only ten streets in th
whole town." He trained his binoculars on one particular spc

and then continued scanning the rest of the town. "Only a few people up. Best get moving while they're asleep."

"I suppose I agree with you there," Myles said. "We better get moving. Colonel Sancho, you two stay here. We'll be back in a few hours. Don't make me have to come fetch you."

As he looked at Colonel Sancho, Myles put his hand on Lieutenant Rubio's shoulder. The lieutenant, he could tell, had in the last twenty-four hours started to take to him, albeit somewhat reticently. Myles liked to bring young, impressionable men under his spell. The colonel, though, was a different matter. His disposition was tepid, and he was openly uneasy in his current predicament. This, Myles knew, ensured that he would stay put. Heading south alone would not be prudent, and Myles had displayed his man-tracking repertoire to the colonel on several occasions. Any flight was sure to be a short-lived escapade.

But Myles had to be sure. "I mean it," he said, and looked sternly at the colonel, conveying to his captives that he was in no mood to be antagonized.

They bade the colonel good-bye and made their entrance into Santiago, the administrative and social headquarters for the dozen or so haciendas in the surrounding valley, whose farms, settled by the Spanish in the 1650s, constituted some of the first organized agriculture established in Mexico. Presently, the old town was one of the richest in all of Northern Mexico, and served as a perfect paradigm for the war. Its handsome cobblestone streets, lined with huge eighteenth century colonial mansions, amounted to lightning rods in a revolution pitting the interests of the haves against the have-nots.

Myles let Stewart lead, and they cautiously entered the town on one of its cobblestone side streets. Although Stewart had been to Santiago only twice, Myles did not doubt his partner's recollection of the town. There were few places

Stewart had been that he could not recall in great detail. His memory was that sharp.

The town was set in a monolithic grid, from which all signs of civility sprang up abruptly. From the side street, they turned onto a commercial avenue that was bordered by several stores, offices, and the town's only school, all of which had been built in the venerable colonial style. Santiago had not seen any new construction in fifty years.

But the town's gentrified veneer had crumbled into mayhem in the wake of the revolution. This morning the unmistakable signature of the war was evident in abundance: bullet-pocked walls, broken windows, and shattered glass in pieces on the cobblestone streets greeted the Americans. A trail of dead horses, their bloated carcasses swarming with flies, punctuated the deathly quiet streets.

The group paused in front of a hastily built barricade. As Myles slowly surveyed the scene, he instinctively recoiled from the smell, even if there was nowhere to escape the pungent haze—or the buzzing flies massing in the still morning air.

He turned to see Stewart looking away from the carnage as well. Sergeant Bates, for his part, had removed his hat to cover his nose. He dismounted and tore a path through the stone and earth barricade.

After the sergeant cleared the makeshift defenses, they entered the plaza, where they discovered two ghastly corpses lying faceup on the cobblestones. Both men had been shot and stripped naked, and their bodies were pulsating with insects.

Myles cleared his throat softly and spoke, his voice sounding alien to him in the dead calm. "I'd say from the looks of these boys, they've been here at least a day." He turned to Sergeant Bates. "Cover 'em up, and see if you can find somebody around here to bury them."

Myles reached into his saddlebag and pulled out his blanket as he stared at the dead men. He had seen plenty of useless killings in the last three years, but this was the first pure carnage he had witnessed. Things were much worse than he had speculated, he was realizing, and he suddenly felt weighed down by a sense of irrevocable doom. He pessimistically eyed Stewart, who was as silent as ever. How far would his good friend insist on taking this? Would Myles be able to say no to him, if it came to it?

"Where do you think we can find Alexia?" Myles finally asked.

"Over there," Stewart said, pointing ahead. He had an unsettled look on his face, and his voice was raspy. "Where the hell is everybody?"

"Bones," Myles said, "we're going to go back here and see if we can procure some information."

"Sure thing, Boss." Sergeant Bates was busy putting his and Myles's blankets over the two dead men. He was trying to cover the repugnant bodies with the use of only one hand. The other he used to cover his nose.

Myles surveyed the plaza. It was empty, and the looted buildings surrounding it appeared to harbor no one. Two dark plumes of smoke pierced the horizon in the direction Stewart had pointed.

"Let's go find your girl," Myles said as he and Stewart left on horseback for the smoke.

As Stewart led the way along a divided residential boulevard, Myles studied the large juniper trees lining its center and the huge white stone houses on either side. Most of the houses had been plundered or burned. The burnt ones had no roofs, windows, or doorways, and their stone shells were buried in black soot.

Myles stopped at one of the burned-out residences and looked grimly at six dried blood splats spaced a few feet apart and chest high on its front wall. Just then, a pack of wild dogs emerged from the still-smoldering ruins and began to circle the two men on horseback.

"We got company," Myles called ahead to Stewart.

Stewart pulled his pistol from its holster and stopped the growling alpha male in its tracks. The rest of the dogs scattered, yelping as they fled.

Myles pulled even with his partner, who stared back at him blankly, and brought his gloved index finger to his lips. "Shush."

"Right," Stewart said with a wry smile.

A few more blocks down the road, Myles followed Stewart as he turned into a large mansion. Its windows and doors had all been broken, but the house had not been set afire. There were several small residences annexed on the lawn behind it.

"She live in one of them boardinghouses out back?" Myles asked.

Stewart nodded.

Myles dismounted and followed Stewart into one of the small houses. Its door was unlocked, and its interior appeared intact.

"This is her place all right," Myles said as he noted an old black-and-white photo of Stewart on the dresser. "She's got a picture of her Romeo right here."

All was in order: No clothes seemed to be missing, and the bed was made.

Myles, confounded, walked back outside and entered the grandiose house out front. He made a quick check of both floors, but found no clues. As he descended the staircase, he ran into Stewart.

"Well," Myles said, "nobody's here. They've packed up and left. Not many valuables here." He stopped to view an imposing painting of a well-tailored man. "What did you find?"

Stewart shook his head dispiritedly, his face covered in anguish. He dropped his shoulders and led Myles back outside, pausing on the porch to look down the street at the two plumes of smoke.

"There's got to be someone around here," Myles said. "Let's go check out those fires."

As they rode down the street to investigate the two mysterious fires, they discovered that the smoke wasn't coming from buildings, but rather two large piles of debris in the middle of the boulevard. A woman and three young children were picking up litter and rubbish scattered on the streets and burning it.

"Buenos días," Stewart said as he and Myles slowly rode up to the woman. "We're looking for the schoolteacher. Do you know where she is?"

The petite dark-skinned woman gave no reply. She did not even look up, but instead continued to pile debris on the fire.

Stewart got off his horse and asked his question again. His new inquiry elicited no response. He finally grabbed the tiny woman by the shoulders and turned her toward him.

"I am looking for the schoolteacher," Stewart said to her face. "Alexia Garcia. Do you know where she is?"

"I know nothing," the shocked woman said. She did not struggle to free herself.

"She doesn't know anything," Myles said from his horse. "Let's ride back up to the plaza and see what we can find."

Sergeant Bates had located a couple of peasants in the plaza, and was currently employing them to bury the bodies. Stewart and Myles arrived in time to see them dragging the bodies away.

They followed them to a small cemetery on the edge of town where eight fresh graves had already been dug. Sergeant

Bates, who had tied ropes around the bodies to assist in their burial, was supervising the move from horseback.

"Find anything out?" Stewart asked.

"The *insurrectos* took the town two days ago," the sergeant said. "They killed about ten or twelve people. The well-to-do had already fled. They rounded up twenty or thirty people and led them out of town."

"What about the schoolteacher?" Stewart asked.

"What about the schoolteacher?" Sergeant Bates repeated to one of the old men dragging the bodies.

"She was here," the old man said. He stopped tugging on a body and stared up at the sergeant. "Maybe they took her. I don't know."

"Where did they take them?" Stewart interrupted.

The old man shrugged his shoulders.

"They don't know anything," Myles said. "Let's go see if Sancho is privy to any information we're not. Bones, make sure they get started and come on."

"You think that Mexican is still up on that hill?" Stewart asked resignedly.

"I don't know," Myles said as he turned his horse. "Let's go see."

Colonel Sancho had not gone anywhere. He and Lieutenant Rubio rode out to meet them on the town's outskirts, emerging from a small thicket along an irrigation ditch where they had been waiting.

"What did you find?" the colonel asked.

"Nothing," Stewart said curtly.

"Looks like they've taken everybody away somewhere," Myles said. "Do you know where that might be?"

"No," Colonel Sancho said with a sigh, "I don't."

"Where's Villa?" Myles said.

"He has his headquarters set up in the Bishop's Palace in Monterrey," the colonel replied.

"We better go see him," Myles said. "What's the best way to get to Monterrey from here?"

"I would go by the Huasteca Canyon," Colonel Sancho said. "That's the safest route."

"You think that's wise?" Stewart asked.

"Not to worry," Myles said. "I have a good relationship with Villa. The problem is not Villa. It's getting to see him without getting skinned first."

The United States had been passively supporting many of the rebel armies. Myles's direct commander, General Hugh Scott, had been assigned the task of implementing this policy. Myles had at times represented him by proxy. The revolutionary commanders generally respected Myles, primarily because he was the eyes and ears of their most reliable source of supplies, not to mention that he had the credibility of the United States behind him.

Villa was one of the most cordial of the revolutionary commanders toward Myles. He had spent much of the last few years in Juarez, or across the river hiding in El Paso. There, he had often been invited to Fort Bliss, and had become quite enamored with the U.S. Army.

In recent months, reports of his men's excesses had found their way across the border. As a result, General Scott had sent Villa a personal message urging him to curtail the barbarism of his subordinates and warning him of the consequences of harming Mexican Americans. Villa had heeded Scott's admonition.

His men were a different matter. Many were illiterate serfs with little knowledge of the intricacies of diplomacy. They knew only retribution.

Chapter 18

Stewart squeezed the reins and felt his knuckles go white as Myles and Colonel Sancho argued ahead of him on the trail. All evidence thus far suggested that the colonel was a feisty and talkative gentleman, not at all content to let something disagreeable be said without repudiation.

"You Americans are so sanctimonious," said the colonel, who was glaring at Myles. "You think every Mexican you see is decadent. To hear you talk and to read your newspapers, you would think you're all saints. I suspect you're not a whole lot different than we are."

Myles had engaged the colonel in the politics behind the bloody war, priming the Mexican with enough outrageous generalizations to stir up an emotional response. The colonel's willingness to banter, Stewart thought, must be a godsend to Myles on a long ride, but Stewart had run out of patience. Letting the two Federal officers tag along with them was one thing. Listening to Myles prod the unwitting colonel into a tiresome debate was another.

"Enough!" Stewart snapped, his jaw locked. "We got no time for this."

Myles glanced back at Stewart silently and then winked at the colonel, tempting him to continue.

The Americans and their willing captives were slowly wending their way through the Huasteca Canyon, a vast waterless wasteland southwest of Monterrey. Thousands of thorn scrub bushes and yucca, the latter of which spiked the desolate canyon like olive-green bayonets, baked under the suffocating sun. The tangled scrub prevented even a man on horseback from seeing the steep canyon walls, and it made the landscape difficult to traverse. Humans rarely frequented the canyon, which had precious few exit and entry points but plenty of no-man's-land in between. For several hundred years it had served as a forbidding sanctuary for Apaches and bandits on the run.

"Now, Colonel," Myles drawled, "even you have to admit that—"

"Myles," Stewart said, cutting him off again, "don't make me repeat myself. Colonel, he's baiting you."

"Well, he can stir with another topic," the colonel said indignantly, still fuming. "You're the bastards who have raped our country for everything it's worth and left us as nothing but a land full of serfs."

"Colonel Sancho," Myles objected, "you don't have to lecture me or anybody in this party on the principle that a man's actions rarely match his rhetoric. We . . ."

Stewart narrowed his eyes and contorted his face into a menacing scowl. He caught Myles's gaze in time to finally shut him down mid-sentence.

They traveled the rest of the way in silence, with Colonel Sancho, who had recently scouted the canyon, as their guide. After exiting the canyon, they came upon a high plain just south of Monterrey proper. As they rode, Stewart attempted to trace their route using Sergeant Bates's compass and the few identifiable landmarks to plot their course. But the thick brush prevented even this. He finally gave up and reluctantly put his confidence in the colonel.

With ninety thousand residents, Monterrey was the largest city in Northern Mexico. It sat on a flat saddle, the towering peaks of the Sierra Madre Mountains encasing it on three sides. Their apexes were less than twenty miles from the city center, and gave the city a confining feeling. As the group drew closer to Monterrey, Stewart felt the enveloping effect of the ubiquitous mountains grow more intense.

"Where's the nearest bridge, Colonel Sancho?" Stewart asked as they reached the banks of the Rio Santo Catarina.

Most of the year, the river, which bordered the city to its south, could be easily crossed on horseback. But it had swollen to its banks after the spring rains.

The group dismounted to investigate the river and water their horses. It was noon, and the heat had set in on them.

"There is a bridge at the base of the palace," Colonel Sancho said as he filled his canteen. "That should be about a mile east of here."

"Bones, do you have a white shirt in your pack?" Myles asked.

"I think I have an undershirt in there somewhere," Sergeant Bates replied.

"Find a long stick and put it on it," Myles said.

Stewart splashed some cool river water on his face and scowled at Myles.

"Colonel Sancho," Myles said as he grinned at Stewart, "thanks for the debate, even if Stewart was too sullen to let us settle our intellectual differences. And thanks for getting us this far. You and Lieutenant Rubio would be wise to go back to that draw we came into the canyon on and wait there. If we're not back by morning, get the hell out of here. We'll ride down to this bridge. I'm sure we'll run into some of Villa's boys. We'll see if we can get in to see him."

* * *

As the group approached an old wooden bridge at the base of the palace, Stewart spotted four *villistas* patrolling on horseback. He stopped and gestured for Sergeant Bates to come forward with the white shirt he had tied to the end of a stick.

The four *villistas* approached slowly and halted at a distance of twenty yards. By their dress, it was clear they were officers. Each wore the trite white sombrero, but accompanied it with a clean cotton shirt, a neat pair of slacks, and knee-high leather boots. They were well groomed, and instead of crisscrossing ammo belts, they wore conventional waist belts with an accompanying sidearm.

"What do you want, gringo?" one of the men called out bluntly. He stared back at the Americans with a mixture of curiosity and contempt. He looked, Stewart thought, more civil than the common soldier.

Myles spoke casually. "We want to see General Villa."

"What for?" another man in the group asked suspiciously.

"I am a friend of his, and I have some business to conduct with him," Myles answered. "Tell him Colonel Myles Adams, United States Army, would like to see him."

The four men appeared vexed by Myles's response, and began to talk amongst themselves in an indigenous dialect.

"We'll take you up to the top of the hill and send General Villa a message," one of the men finally said in Spanish. He nodded his head to one of his juniors, who rode out to meet Myles.

The man leveled a contemptuous gaze at Myles and jerked Myles's rifle from its holster on his horse.

In response, Myles slowly removed his pistol from its belt and handed it to the man, handle-first. As he did so, he said nothing, but kept eye contact with the man, his stare indicating his disapproval of the look he had received.

After disarming Myles, the man rode over to retrieve

Stewart's and Sergeant Bates's weapons. He started with Stewart, forcefully pushing him aside with his forearm to dislodge his pistol from its belt.

Stewart did not resist, but coolly stared the man down.

After their arms were confiscated, the three were escorted down the river, across the well-guarded bridge, and up a steep hill toward the Bishop's Palace. Two of the *villistas* led, and two followed.

As they approached the palace, Stewart stared up at the large domed limestone structure overlooking the town from its hilltop perch. It had been blessed a hundred years earlier by the city's bishop. During the Mexican-American War, it had at various times served as headquarters and focal point for both armies. Its strategic value lay in its commanding and unblemished view of the city below. After the war, the Mexican Army had not returned it to the Church and, until the Federals' recent expulsion, had garrisoned it with troops.

Fresh bullet holes pockmarked the palace walls, and sandbags filled its windows. All approaches had been worn free of grass, the turf bearing its own battle scars. Surrounded by numerous stone barricades, the palace had so far withstood another war, but its occupants looked impervious to the recent hostilities. A few soldiers could be seen fraternizing outside, and men were entering and exiting the palace beneath its huge stone arches.

The three Americans were taken off their horses outside the palace and put against a wall at gunpoint. One of the men in the group handed Myles a piece of paper and told him to write his name on it. The man then barked a few orders to the men guarding the three before entering the palace.

Stewart slumped down to the ground and leaned against the wall. He tried to free his mind of his worries, but to no avail. Myles finally handed him a canteen, and Stewart took a sip of water.

"Quit worrying so much," Myles said as he reclaimed his canteen. "If she's alive, we'll find her. Hell, I've come this far; I'm not going to desert you now." He paused and looked at Stewart. "If she's dead, there's nothing you can do about it. Get your mind right. We may need you to do something useful before this is over. I don't think I've ever seen you this agitated."

They had been sitting against the wall at gunpoint for about an hour, with Myles ruminating over his good-natured quarrel with Colonel Sancho, when a man exited the palace and approached them.

"General Villa will see you," the man said with a touch of conciliation in his voice. He was not one of the four who had escorted them to the palace. He instructed the two sentries to lower their weapons, and ordered one to retrieve the Americans' horses and weapons. The other he ordered to accompany the three to Villa. "He's at the Hotel Monterrey. Corporal Corral will take you there. The general sends his apologizes for any inconveniences."

The man walked forward and offered a salutation to each of the three. Before he was through, the corporal arrived with the horses and introduced himself in a less agreeable fashion.

From the Bishop's Palace, the center of town was a two-mile ride down a steep decline and then back up a more gradual hill. Myles rode alongside the corporal. Conversation was minimal as the group was swallowed up by the city. They turned onto the elegant Avenida Matamoros, which hosted the city's breweries, butcheries, and glass factories, the basis for much of its wealth. Today, the businesses were idle and showing appreciable damage from the war.

Past the industrial area, they rode by the colossal concrete bullfighting ring and into the city's commercial and banking sector, which had fallen into disarray after being heavily plundered.

The closer the Americans got to the city's center, the closer they came to the epicenter of destruction. Many of the buildings, made of both wood and stone, had been ransacked and burned, leaving just their skeletons in place.

As they wove their way through the rubble, they found the barricaded center of the city largely abandoned, save for the occasional work crews and citizen soldiers. No bodies lay at their feet, but the streets and walls were baptized in dried splatters and pools of blood. The fetid smell of death emanating from the broken buildings and alleys meant that many of the fallen had still to be recovered.

They eventually arrived at the city's Gran Plaza, so named because of its mammoth expanse. At several hundred yards wide and more than a half mile long, it was flanked by Monterrey's most prominent buildings: the Federal Palace, governor's mansion, cathedral, and state bank, all of them grandiose stone buildings displaying the stone columns and marble facades common to viceregal architecture.

Dozens of statues dotted the plaza, which was paved with brown limestone mined from the nearby mountains. It had been patched up since the battle, but bullet holes and missing windows could still be seen in some of the plaza's humbler buildings. Electric streetcars, static monuments to peacetime, sat where they had been when the city had lost power.

The sumptuous Hotel Monterrey sat at the plaza's nucleus in a large colonial building. Parked outside were a number of carriages and a few dozen horses. The corporal leading the three Americans got off his horse and handed its reins to a young man standing outside. He instructed the bellboy to tend to the horses, and strode inside without paying any heed to the three men in his charge.

Myles traded glances with Stewart and Sergeant Bates and then followed. Inside, the vintage hotel's lobby, which was three stories high and easily big enough to house a building, boasted glass chandeliers and mammoth stone columns supporting its fresco-adorned walls.

A man behind a large mahogany desk at the hotel's entrance took notice of the corporal walking briskly by, but after recognizing him he returned to his business. The corporal led the three Americans into a ballroom adjacent to the lobby, where several men were sitting at a large table arguing loudly over some maps.

The room grew quiet as the men looked up at the Americans.

"Colonel Adams," said a man sitting at the end of the table, "it is good to see you."

"How are you, General Villa?" Myles asked in Spanish as he shook the general's hand.

Nothing about the general's appearance suggested his prominence. Dressed in a dirty military jacket without insignia and wearing a black mustache on his sun-seared face, General Villa looked dusty and disheveled as he slouched in his chair in unmilitary fashion. He was a heavyset gentleman, but not fat, and he wore thigh-high chaps, partially unlaced.

As the two greeted each other, the rest of the room watched quietly. Myles broke eye contact for a brief moment to search the table for some recognizable faces. The general's juniors ran the gamut in age and appearance, but all were rough and worn. Myles recognized two or three of the men, and dug deep in his memory to remember their names.

"How is my good friend General Scott?" General Villa asked cheerfully from his chair as he grabbed a beautiful young waitress by the arm and gently patted her derriere.

"He is doing well," Myles said, "as it appears you are."

Several of Villa's men laughed and visibly warmed to the Americans.

"Congratulations on your victory," Myles said. "Let me introduce my friends. You know Sergeant Bates, and this is my friend Stewart Cook. He helped me lick the Spanish over there in the Philippines." Myles had long ago discovered how much General Villa despised Colorados, or Spanish Mexicans, most of whom were fighting on the side of the Federals. He had on more than one occasion entertained the general with personal anecdotes from the Spanish-American War.

"Pleased to meet you," General Villa said as Stewart approached to shake his hand. "What brings you to Monterrey?"

"We're looking for a woman some of your men took from Santiago," Myles said. "She's a schoolteacher."

"Colonel Adams, I don't remember you being the type to journey off after a woman," General Villa said. "Is she yours?"

"She is a friend of Stewart's. We would like to have her and her family released . . . if that is possible. We will ante up for her if need be."

"No, that will not be necessary," the general said. "I will check on her. But no Colorados will be released. Let's hope she is from a well-behaved family."

His men laughed at the remark.

"What is the girl's name?"

"Alexia Garcia," Myles answered.

General Villa gestured for one of his men to write the name down. The general was illiterate, and always had someone with him to read and write his orders.

"If we have her and all is in order, you can pick her up at the theater in the Barrio Antiguo in a few hours."

"Thank you," Myles said. "If I can be of any assistance in the future, let me know. We'll inconvenience you no further."

He turned to leave, but the general stopped him short.

"I hear you shot two of my *insurrectos*," General Villa said loudly.

Villa's men grew quiet.

And Myles felt his stomach leap as he turned around to face the general again. "They threw down on me. I tried to explain to them they were getting in over their heads, but they wouldn't listen. It's not a good idea to rile an Irishman after a hard day's ride."

"My apologies, Colonel," General Villa said.

"You won't have to worry about me in a couple of weeks," Myles said with a chuckle. "I'm going back to Louisiana to be married. It's getting dangerous to be a white man down here."

"Really," General Villa said, his interest piqued. "A Mexican woman?"

Myles nodded.

"This is good. Mexican women make good wives. They are very obedient."

"This one is nothing but a pain in the ass," Myles said, shaking his head.

"You should stick around for a while," General Villa said. "I will show you my headquarters, and we can have a few drinks."

Myles watched as the general looked around the table at his amenable subordinates. An American had called on him, and he had just acceded to his request. He clearly wanted to demonstrate it was by choice, not obligation.

For his part, Myles had no desire to stay any longer than he had to, but he knew that standing the general up in front of his men would be bad precedent.

"I have a few chores that need immediate attention," he said, "but I'm sure Sergeant Bates can handle them. When your meeting is over, I'll be in the lobby. I saw a few señoritas in there that might induce me to compromise my chastity. If I'm not in the lobby when you're finished, I'll be upstairs getting a bath from one of them."

Everyone laughed, and Myles reached up and wiped a finger full of dust from under his eye. He had no appetite or want for carousing, but he knew how to work the general. "Maybe I can survive the rest of the day without another one of your bandits mistaking me for a Colorado."

"Stay away from the redhead," the general warned. "She's feisty."

The Americans left the ballroom without an escort.

"What do you think?" Stewart asked as the three exited the front door of the hotel.

"If she's alive, and he has her, she'll be there," Myles said as he untied his horse. "Villa is as uncouth and barbarous as a wild dog, a mite tempestuous and vindictive, also. But when he makes a deal, he keeps it."

The afternoon sun was at its peak, and the stone-covered plaza amplified the heat.

Myles patted his sweat-laden horse on the neck. "Bones, see if you can find some grain and a shoe man for our horses. They're in dire need."

Stewart was already inspecting one of his horse's hooves.

"I better stick around here and cater to the general a little while," Myles continued. "Stewart, you should probably stay here with me. Bones, meet us at the theater in about two hours. If you can find a few more horses for sale, buy them. We may have a few guests in a couple of hours."

"Let's hope so," Stewart said, and looked out into the plaza. "Somebody could put us up against a wall right now, and nobody in the real world would ever know."

"We're out on limb, no doubt," Myles said. "To tell you the truth, I'm surprised we made it up here as easily as we did. I think we came up in the wake of this recent offensive. I doubt we'll be as lucky on the way home."

He gazed into the crowded plaza and then at several of its occupants, all of whom were staring at the Americans contemptuously. The throng made him feel claustrophobic—and insignificant. He looked around for the abundant and reassuring police he had been accustomed to seeing in the plaza, but found none.

Chapter 19

"You look like you're about to go up in flames," Myles said. "Relax."

Stewart stopped pacing the lobby long enough to glare down at Myles, who was lounging on a cushioned sofa and reading the book he had taken from Stewart's house. He had been reading it on and off for the last few days.

Stewart waited for Myles to begin his reading and then interrupted him. "Like that book?"

"It's not bad . . . though it's hard to read," Myles mumbled without looking up from the book.

"That's because it's written in real English."

"They didn't teach Victorian English at West Point." Myles nodded his head as if he was learned in such matters, and confidently returned his attention to the book.

Stewart continued to study one of the frescoes hanging on the wall.

"This Arabia is a pretty restrictive place," Myles observed. "It wouldn't be conducive to a man with all my talents, but I wouldn't mind being one of these sultans."

"It's fiction, not reality. Some people have trouble differentiating between the two."

"That queen in there sure sounds sexy and cosmopolitan. I bet me and her would hit it off with a bang."

"You're an engaged man. You shouldn't even be thinking about something like that."

"I know. I didn't say I would do anything with her. I just said she seems like the type of woman that would appreciate a man like me. Like you said, it's just fiction."

The two waited in the lobby for another hour until one of General Villa's aides finally came out to confer with them.

"The general sends his apologies," the aide said curtly. "He has urgent business to tend to and will not be available after all."

As the aide turned to leave, Stewart glanced at Myles, who suddenly looked about ten pounds lighter.

"Let's get out of here," Myles drawled, "before he changes his mind."

"Where to?" Stewart asked.

"The theater," Myles answered. "Villa's boys aren't due to drop off your gal for a while longer, but it couldn't hurt to be early."

They took their time walking to the small theater in the Barrio Antiguo, Monterrey's most affluent neighborhood just off the Gran Plaza. As they ambled slowly through the wide boulevards, they took in the rows of now-empty homes, most of which had been defaced and left in disarray.

When they reached the center of the neighborhood, they found the small outdoor theater, a conical-shaped refuge dug into the ground. With its stage backed by towering trees, the empty theater amplified their entry, and the clicks of the Americans' boots reverberated off the limestone steps.

Stewart found a shady spot on the cool floor and sat down with his back against the stage. He looked up as a pair of trogons flew overhead, the birds' metallic chirps tunneling with the breeze through the theater's acoustic confines, and an uneasy feeling washed over him. The gravity of their journey

had finally overtaken him, and it was easier to give in to its
pull than to continue on fighting. He closed his eyes and tried
to think of more obliging times.

As Stewart drifted into unconsciousness, Myles spied the
aristocratic rooflines of several mansions rising beyond the
theater walls and decided to investigate, not bothering to
inform his partner. He walked the vacant quarter a block or
two before entering one of the gutted mansions.

Once inside, he closed the door behind him, and he felt
broken glass from the windows crack and splinter beneath his
boots. Next came a fetid wave of decay that nearly knocked
him off his feet.

"How 'bout that?" he said as he shielded his nose from the
pungent aroma of rotting flesh.

He walked to a window and pulled aside the torn curtains
to open the window and let some fresh air inside. He then
turned and followed the foul odor to the kitchen, where he
found a family of seven riddled with bullets and lying faceup
in a pool of blood. Two of the children were girls outfitted in
humble but fashionable white dresses. Their bodies had
become bloated and were swarming with insects.

Myles lit a cigarette and stared at the family from the doorway. "Noncombatants," he said, shaking his head.

As he viewed the carnage, he thought of the girl they had
failed to find two days prior. What had become of her after
her would-be rescuers moved on without her? Was she dead
somewhere beyond the river her kidnappers had used to cover
their tracks? Would she be left to rot, another anonymous
victim of a war plowing indiscriminately onward?

The cigarette hanging from his lower lip suddenly tasted foul.
He coughed lightly and let it fall from his mouth, snuffing it out

on the tile floor. As he stumbled outside, he reached for his handkerchief and wiped his mouth clean.

He continued on a couple more blocks and then stopped, mystified: Two children were selling ice cream at a makeshift stand on the side of the road, and they beckoned the American forward.

"Would you like to buy some ice cream?" a young girl asked in Spanish.

Myles blinked as he stared at the girl and what looked to be her younger brother, both of whom were sitting behind a table under the shade of a large umbrella. He peered beneath the rectangular table and spied an old washtub with a five-gallon carton of chocolate ice cream inside it resting on a slab of ice.

"Where are your parents?"

"They're working another neighborhood," the boy said. "It's hot out. Don't you want some ice cream?"

"Sure," Myles said. He reached into his pockets and clumsily pulled out a handful of change. "How much?"

"That will do," the boy said.

"I'm sure it will," Myles replied as the boy handed him a scoop of soft but still mostly frozen ice cream in a paper cup with a little wooden spoon. "This has to beat anything I've ever seen." He dealt the boy a severe look. "Do your parents know there's a war on?"

"Of course," the boy said, "but even the revolutionaries like ice cream."

Myles shook his head and laughed. "Leave it to Mexico to find a way to make money off a social revolution."

He said good-bye to the children and found his way back to the theater, where he found Sergeant Bates and Stewart snoring against the stage. He paused at the large stone gate to study the two horses the sergeant had purchased.

"It's a good thing I'm not a group of *pistoleros*," he finally said. "You'd both be dead."

Neither man moved.

"The CO goes off for a brief frolic," Myles groused, "and the whole damn outfit goes to pot."

"If you'd been a *pistolero,*" Stewart said from beneath his hat, "I'd have shot you dead."

"I see you found some horses, Bones," Myles said, squinting in pain after eating his melting ice cream too fast in the hot afternoon sun. "I'm glad somebody in this outfit is doing something. How much did you have to pay for them?"

"Too much," Sergeant Bates replied, and stood up.

"Yeah, this Mexican here is starting to run up a pretty big bill," Myles said, and tossed the empty paper cup on the ground after licking it clean. "If this woman will just run off with him and get him out of my hair once and for all, we'll probably call it even." He wiped his chin with his dirty sleeve and grinned as he looked down at Stewart.

"Where you been?" Stewart asked.

"Just looking around. They worked this place over pretty good. Found a family of seven full of bullet holes. They've been dead a few days. Life is getting cheap around here."

"Haven't seen anybody here," Stewart said, removing his hat and looking at his watch.

"Since you've gotten me up, I think I'll have some lunch," Sergeant Bates said, and retrieved from his pack a sixty-ounce can of pork and beans he had purchased earlier in the day.

The midday heat made cooking the contents redundant. He opened the can and set it on the stage, and his companions grabbed their drinking cups to partake in the feast.

"Damn, those are pretty tasty," Myles said, quickly finishing his cup of beans.

"You know these beans down here will make you impotent," Stewart said.

"Really? Good. Give me another bowl." Myles dipped his cup into the can for another round. "Hell, if I could get impotent, half my problems would be solved. I'd have a bank account full of money and could finally put all my energies into something worthwhile. There ain't no telling what a man like me could accomplish without all these women distracting me."

"These beans really make you impotent?" Sergeant Bates asked. He looked at his half-eaten cup of beans as if he'd suddenly lost his appetite.

Myles smiled. "I wouldn't worry about it too much, Bones. I can't really see where an acute case of impotence is going to affect your social schedule much."

"Speak for yourself," Sergeant Bates replied.

"Someone's coming," Stewart said, getting to his feet.

Before Myles or the sergeant could respond, a group on horseback stormed into the theater. Two men in humble military uniforms were escorting a train of three women whose hands were tied in their laps.

One of the men promptly dismounted, walked back to the other three horses, and grabbed each of the women in succession, pulling them off their horses.

As the last of the three fell to the ground on her bound hands and knees, the man rapidly remounted his horse and aimed his comments at Stewart, who had approached. "They're yours," the man said in Spanish. "I would get them out of here before somebody changes their mind." He turned his mount and, with the aid of his partner, ushered the horses out of the theater.

Myles waved his hand in front of his face to clear the dust kicked up by the horses and gazed down at the three women, each of whom was still bound and struggling to get up. Their long dressers were filthy, and their faces and hands were caked with dirt and oil.

He watched as Stewart rushed to their aid and lifted one of the ladies up by her arm. Dried blood peppered her sleeves and cream-colored face. Her deep ebony eyes stared back at Stewart in disbelief as she struggled to her feet.

Stewart cut her arms loose and took a step back to look at her. "You all right?" he asked as he brushed her long black hair from her face and searched her eyes.

An inch or two taller than most Creole women, but still much shorter than Stewart, she buried her head in his shoulder and said nothing.

Myles looked on approvingly before joining Sergeant Bates and helping the other two ladies to their feet. An older woman and a girl in her early teens, each bore a striking resemblance to Alexia, no doubt her mother and sister.

Sergeant Bates cut their arms free, and Myles dusted their faces and dresses.

"Ladies," Myles said, "I see you've had a rough time of it, but we need to get out of here. Get on these horses, and we'll go somewhere safer."

He stirred the young girl's hair and helped her onto one of the horses Sergeant Bates had purchased.

She could not bring herself to look back up at him. Neither her youthful innocence nor Myles's cordial introduction could ameliorate the shame on her half-hidden face.

Myles stood silent a moment, transfixed by the sheer weight of the women's humiliation, as palpable as the late afternoon heat.

"Alexia," Stewart said, "this is Myles Adams and Sergeant Bill Bates. They've risked their lives to help rescue you."

The women said nothing, perhaps still unable to comprehend what was happening to them.

Stewart turned to Myles and the sergeant. "This is Alexia's sister Alijondra and their mother Señora Garcia."

Myles, hoping to relieve the unbearable tension that had descended on the theater, walked over to size up Alexia. He searched her stoic face in an effort to discern something of her constitution, but found little. He then looked her up and down, openly inspecting her.

"So this is what we fought our way up here for," he finally said, extending his hand. "Your appearance is certainly exemplary, but I'll have to see how your camp-making and babbling skills are before I pass any final judgment on the merits of this journey."

"Thank you for anything you've done," Alexia said barely above a whisper. She extended her hand to Myles and then Sergeant Bates. "Stewart has told me much about you," she said to Myles in perfect, albeit heavily accented, English. "He says you are one ornery and disgruntled soul. I must say that my initial impression does not invalidate this."

"You must have a few endearing qualities for Stewart to come up here and get you," Myles said, warming to his new sparring partner. "But I can see that gratitude is not one of them."

"Knock off the gibberish and load these ladies up before we have to fight the whole rebel army," Stewart said as he led a horse to Alexia.

She backed up and refused.

"Alexia?" Stewart said, mystified.

"It was too kind of you to trouble yourselves with our safety," she said, "but I have no intention of going anywhere. Those bastards still have the rest of my family."

Myles couldn't believe his ears. "Look, woman," he began, "you may have a spell on this half-breed here, but I'm in charge of this outfit." He sized up Stewart's love one more time and then continued, his tone not nearly as harsh as his words. "I didn't fight my way up here to put up with a disrespectful Mexican woman. I've got one of those at home. Now get your ass on that horse, or I'm going to tie you back up and put you on there myself." Myles climbed atop his horse and walked it toward Alexia.

"What are you going to do?" Alexia said, backing up until

she ran out of room against the stage. "Force me to go with you?" She spoke loudly and without grace. Her ragged appearance ran contrary to her outward resolve.

Myles lit a cigarette from atop his horse. "If I have to," he said softly, "I will tie you up. And if you don't lower your voice, I'm going to put a sock in your mouth." He used his horse to gently pin her against the stage, and then reached down to take her arm. "You can make this easy or hard. Either way, you're getting on that horse. I'm a trained killer. I don't think I'll have much trouble subduing an eighty-pound woman." He took her other arm. "What will it be?"

"Alexia," Stewart said, trying not to laugh, "do what he says." She frowned.

"If you've got grievances," Myles said, "we can sort 'em out later—just as soon as we get the hell out of here." Myles smiled wryly as she looked back at Stewart, who was nodding.

"Do what he says, Alexia," Stewart said. "You're safe now."

Chapter 20

A three-quarter moon lit a path through the thorn scrub as they rode at dusk toward the rendezvous point with Colonel Sancho. Myles glanced back at Stewart bringing up the rear, on his horse a single black silhouette against the fading blue horizon, and breathed a sigh of relief. Maybe now, he thought, his partner would finally lighten up on the reins. They still had to make it through rebel territory to get back to Victoria. But they had found the girl, they had cut her loose, and they were homeward bound.

Alijondra, riding just ahead of him, was still catatonic, unable to bring herself to look up from her horse. Like her mother, she spoke little English. And like her mother, her eyes, lost in a frozen sea of pain, told a story of savagery and dehumanization.

Myles turned his gaze from Alijondra to her older sister riding alongside him. "You're lucky to be alive," he said to Alexia.

She shuddered and then spoke, unloosing what her sister could not bear to set free. "They took me four days ago from Santiago. Put me in a prison about twenty miles outside of Monterrey. There were hundreds of us there. I was reunited with my mother and father, my other sister, and one of my brothers. The guards wouldn't tell me what happened to my other two brothers. They told me we were only being held until they could determine our loyalty. They . . . they raped my sister Maria." Her voice cracked, and she paused until she could regain her composure. "They took away many of the men, and we never saw them again."

Sergeant Bates slowed out front, picking a path through the thorn scrub. He was listening to Alexia's tale, Myles knew, but rode on stoically. The lanky sergeant had heard and seen worse.

By midnight, they had found Colonel Sancho and the campsite, the trail to which had been well hidden in the loose sand. The colonel and his lieutenant greeted them quietly and stood by as the three ladies dismounted. Alexia and her sister and mother were asleep on the ground before the horses had been unloaded. Myles watched as Sergeant Bates placed what blankets and jackets they had on the three and left them to rest.

"They sure look like they've had a rough time of it," the sergeant said as he joined the other men.

"Bones," Stewart said, "me and Myles are going to ride up top and refill our water supply. We'll be back shortly."

Myles had already picked out a soft location on the ground, and was removing the saddle from his horse. He looked up to see his partner remounting.

"Tighten that strap back up," Stewart said. "You're not going to bed yet."

"Why don't you go get some water by yourself?" Myles groused, wondering what his partner was really up to. "You ain't done a thing this whole trip but ride my coattails. Unlike you, I didn't get a nap this afternoon in that shady theater."

"Come on," Stewart said, and rode off.

Myles grudgingly rebuckled his garter strap and followed Stewart to the top of the canyon, where he found him sitting casually atop his horse with both legs hanging off one side of his saddle, no doubt to relieve the tension on his groin. He wore a flustered look on his face, as though he was trying to find the grit to say something he knew Myles didn't want to hear.

"Why don't we go bust her family out tomorrow?" he finally said.

"Bust them out?" Myles asked. "I don't recall signing on for any prison busts."

"Bust them out," Stewart repeated, "and get out of here."

"I knew you wanted something. You're not very suave. What do you want us to do? Just ride up there like we're leading a cavalry charge? Shoot up all the bad guys and march off into the bush with the good guys? We do that, there's going to be two hundred Mexicans wanting to come with us and another twenty thousand behind them with horses and guns." Myles trotted his horse past Stewart into the midst of the five-foot-high sage. "I thought we came up here to get some water."

"The creek is to our left," Stewart called out from behind him. "If you didn't have Bones, you'd stay lost. Alexia says there's not but seven or eight guards. You said it yourself: Those Mexicans can't shoot anyway. If it was your family, I would go with you. You know that."

"Yeah, I know that." Myles lit a cigarette and looked off into the brush instead of at Stewart. "You're turning into a real pain in the ass, you know that?"

"Put that out," Stewart said. "The only people out here with cigarettes are Federal officers and rich *hacendados*."

"You're trying to talk me into storming a Mexican prison, and you're worried about somebody seeing my cigarette?" Myles asked. "It didn't take long for her to put a hex on you, did it?"

"So it's on?"

"I don't know. Let me think about it tonight. I'm too tired to think straight right now." Myles sighed and took another drag off his cigarette. "This is serious. We get up there and get in over our heads, we aren't going to do anything but get us all killed."

"Suit yourself. I'm going—with or without you."

Chapter 21

Myles sat up quickly. He stared at the slumbering bodies around him as he vainly tried to shake loose the chilling image of the family of seven gunned down in their kitchen. He closed his eyes and saw faces frozen between terror and nothingness, living souls turned worm fodder.

Slowly, as the campsite came into focus under a dawn-bleached sky, it came to him that he had been reliving the same nightmare for the better part of the night. A chilly, dry breeze from the canyon below brought gooseflesh to his arms, and he reached for the wool sweater he had been using as a blanket. As he did, he remembered the wild gamble Stewart had asked him to take the night before. The thought of charging into harm's way, particularly if it meant advancing civility in the face of repression, always seemed to inspire rapture in Myles's psyche. But he had rarely gone out of his way to implement his convictions. He had stayed alive in dire times by using his head, not his heart.

Such deliberations, he realized, were a waste of energy. But he felt their weight, nonetheless. He was unsure if Stewart would go it alone. He doubted it. But he knew Stewart was often governed by rectitude instead of logic.

Myles shook involuntarily and stood up. His fate would have to wait. For now, somebody needed to build a fire to take some of the chill out of the early morning air. He walked over to rouse Sergeant Bates, who was lying nearby on his back with his coat stretched over his upper body, snoring quietly. Myles smiled down at the man who had been such a loyal friend for so many years, and he wondered how tired the sergeant must be to still be asleep; he was always the first one up. He didn't have the heart to wake him.

Instead, Myles grabbed a few pieces of mesquite wood the sergeant had gathered the night before, and quietly piled the wood up in the middle of the campsite to build a fire. Finally, with the help of some paper from his pack, he got the fire started.

With that accomplished, he retrieved a couple pounds of salted bacon from Sergeant Bates's saddlebag—bought the day before while the sergeant was rounding up the horses—and placed it in an old iron skillet. The simple task of cooking took his mind off the trouble that lay ahead.

As the bacon sizzled in the pan and its pleasant aroma filled the air, Alexia stirred. She quietly came up beside Myles and warmed her hands over the fire.

"Help yourself," Myles said.

"I think I will," Alexia said, and grabbed one of the pieces of bacon. "It has been over a week since I have had any real food. Thank you for what you have done."

"We didn't really have any choice, did we?" Myles dumped the cooked bacon on top of one of his leather saddlebags.

"You're not a bad cook, Colonel," Alexia said as she took another piece. "Maybe you should tend the kitchen and let me run this outfit."

"You and Stewart would make a fine pair," Myles said, and put some more bacon in the skillet. "What with his stubbornness and you being as supple as you are." He chuckled softly and shook his head. "No, it's him you should thank. If it weren't for him, you'd still be in that prison right now."

"You are quite presumptuous," Alexia said, turning away from Myles to gaze at Stewart, who was lying sound asleep on his back.

"Men don't come this far just for the hell of it," Myles offered. "I do believe he is quite fond of you." He looked hard at Alexia. She had been growing on him since their introduction, and he searched for the foundation of her appeal. There was something intriguing and attractive about her. Even putting aside her tattered veneer, he could find no stunning beauty in her appearance, just a reclusive and plain air. But she spoke with abiding passion, locking her eyes on her subject and always pausing before talking to ensure her words were relevant. Her voice radiated something kind and resilient.

"He has never attempted to court me," she said softly.

"He's kind of shy when it comes to things like that."

"Stewart? Shy? Never."

"Sometimes, men who are normally open to women can be shy around a woman they like. Not shy to them, just about their feelings for them. They need and want a push from a strong woman. If I had no concern for his welfare, I would not be telling you about this. You should pursue it. It would make him very happy." Myles stood up. "Stewart tells me he has been trying to get you and your family to come to El Paso for several years now. You should've listened to him. We wouldn't be in this mess right now."

"If everybody who had the means just left when things got bad, what kind of country would we have?"

"I can see you're a contemporary, free-thinking young lady. Few qualities in a woman provide men with more pleasure or torment."

"I am just a poor, insignificant Mexican woman. I do what I can and stand for what I believe, but it is very little. You are a great man. Stewart says you are the greatest leader of men he has ever seen, and despite your front, quite noble. He says it's a God-given gift. We have too few men like you in this country, and the ones we do have are inactive and concerned only with themselves. This is the tragedy of my country. When strong men stand idle, catastrophes happen. I've done all I can; I have no guilty conscience."

"I am just one man," Myles mumbled, and lit a cigarette. "If I try to do too much, I jeopardize what little I can accomplish." He let his voice trail off, and he stood silently, realizing any rebuttal would be inadequate. He then bent over to pick a canteen up off the ground. "Time to wake up your knight in shining armor."

With a skip in his step, he walked over to where Stewart was sleeping, opened the canteen, and carefully dribbled just enough of its contents onto Stewart's face to make him stir. He then tilted the canteen further until Stewart, still asleep, began to shake his head under the steady stream.

Alexia covered her mouth with her hand and giggled quietly.

Myles winked at her, and continued to tip the canteen until Stewart shook his head violently and opened his eyes. Myles was smiling now as he generously emptied the canteen onto his partner's head. Not content to ruin one man's sleep, he playfully kicked Colonel Sancho next to Stewart.

"Let's get up and get moving. You guys can nap all you want when we get back south of the Conchos River."

"Hope you haven't been listening to him all morning," Stewart said to Alexia as he put his boots on. "A good way to debase your soul."

Everyone was up and warming themselves around the campfire. Alexia had taken over the skillet and was cooking a new batch of bacon. Myles and Sergeant Bates were saddling up the horses.

"He looks harmless," Alexia said, smiling for the first time since her liberation as she glanced at Myles. Her pearly white teeth shone brilliantly from her dust-covered face.

Stewart shook his head. He hadn't talked to Myles yet about their conversation from the night before. But he had already made up his mind: He was going to help Alexia break the rest of her family out of jail. The only question remaining was whether or not he would ride alone. He had been trying to gauge Myles's mood since being baptized by his canteen. His partner seemed his usual self: ornery and given to blabbing.

"It's going to be nice to have a woman in camp to talk to," Myles said, still saddling his horse. "I'm always in a chipper mood when I can discuss the artful things in life with someone who can appreciate my physical prowess and worldly wisdom."

Stewart caught Alexia's gaze, but his words were meant for Myles. "Don't encourage him. His idle little mind is the devil's playground. It's always scheming mischief."

"Stewart," Myles said, brushing aside the comment, "if we're going to look for these Mexicans, we'd better get moving."

Stewart felt his heart race. He glanced excitedly at the others around the campfire. Colonel Sancho and Lieutenant Rubio were looking up from their bacon, and everyone had grown silent.

Sergeant Bates let go of the saddle he had been straightening on his horse and turned to Myles. "What Mexicans you talking about, Boss?"

"There's supposed to be a bunch of Mexicans in jail around here somewhere," Myles said casually. "We're going to ride over there this morning and see how much trouble it would be to get them out. I ain't going to make any promises, but we're going to go take a look."

His words earned an appreciative but perplexed stare from

Alexia, who quickly relayed the news in Spanish to her mother and sister.

Myles, clearly relishing the excitement he had caused, spoke authoritatively. "Sergeant Bates, I want you and the lieutenant to stay here and look after these women. Me, Stewart, and Colonel Sancho are going to go scout this prison. Stewart, we'd better bring your *mujer*. She's the only one here who knows where we're going."

"What the hell you need me for?" Colonel Sancho asked around a mouthful of bacon.

"Because I said so, and I'm in charge," Myles said, and tossed the colonel his boots. "It's about time you did something. You haven't done anything the last two days but eat our food and smoke my cigarettes."

"That ain't no bull," Stewart said. He felt a sudden surge in appetite, and reached down to grab another handful of bacon from the skillet. As he stuffed his mouth full, he looked up at Myles, who had already mounted up.

"Damn," Myles said. "These women haven't eaten in a week, and you're going to steal all their bacon."

"They don't have anything else to do all day. They can cook up some more," Stewart said as he threw his saddle on his horse. "I'll be busy babysitting you."

"Sergeant Bates," Myles said, "be ready to move. When we get back, we might be in a hurry. If we decide we're going to give this a shot, it will probably be after dark. Don't waste all your energy sitting around arguing with these women. You can't win."

"Does anything pleasant ever come out of your mouth?" Alexia asked. She had already climbed atop Sergeant Bates's horse. Before Myles could respond, she started riding toward the prison.

Stewart laughed at his partner, who was glaring back at him. "I hope she's a little better behaved at home than she is now," Myles grumbled. "Once we're through here, you should send her over to my place for a couple weeks of training. When you get her back, she'll be much more subservient."

"Why are you stopping?" Myles asked Colonel Sancho, who was riding out front.

"Indians," the colonel said, pointing to tracks in the dusty road.

With Alexia acting as their guide, they had already traveled half the three-hour ride north over turn-rows and pastoral roads.

"Looks like a hunting party," Myles said. "We best be circumspect."

As he spoke, Myles spotted four Huastecan braves on the horizon. The revolutionaries had armed some bands, but this party seemed harmless enough; the four braves were armed only with bows and arrows and were stalking local cattle.

"Let's wait till they're done," Myles said.

"I see more sets of tracks than there are Indians," said Stewart, who was lingering on the side of the road. "And most of these are just about as fresh as the Indians'."

"This road is well traveled," Colonel Sancho offered.

"Maybe," Myles said. "Or maybe we're being shadowed again."

"Jorge?" Stewart asked.

Myles rode over to where Stewart was sitting atop his horse and dismounted. He knelt down and took a long look at the tracks Stewart had spotted. He had seen the same shallow grooves in the horseshoe prints—the distinctive signature of his menace—before.

"Looks like it," he said grimly, and continued to study the tracks. "And he's riding *ahead* of us now. Bastard's persistent;

I'll give him that. Looks like he's riding with eight. He picks up hooligans faster than you can kill them off."

"Who's Jorge?" Alexia asked.

"Nobody," Myles lied with a rare concerned tone. He knew now that Jorge would pursue him until one of them was in the grave. "Just a bothersome gnat that needs a good swatting. He's on our day-old trail to Monterrey, but it won't be long before he doubles back. These tracks look only a few hours old. I should ride ahead and check this out. I know the constable in that little village we passed through last night on the way back. It's right up this trail." Myles nodded up the trail in the direction the tracks were headed.

"You want me to go with you?" Stewart asked.

"No, I'll go alone. I move faster like that, and I won't kick up as big a trail." Myles looked at Alexia and Stewart, then looked down at his watch. "You three find a good place to take cover. I'll be back by noon if I'm coming back."

It had started to sprinkle. Stewart looked up at the sky and grimaced. "We're gonna get wet."

"A good time to travel in hostile territory," Myles surmised.

"Agreed," Stewart said. "We'll move over here and take a breather as soon as these braves are finished."

The raindrops multiplied, quickly turning into a torrential downpour.

Myles took out for the small village—at a trot and in the rain. It took him about twenty minutes to get there. Instead of riding into town, he dismounted and climbed a small hill, where he squatted in some brush to inspect the village, just three wooden buildings, serving a small ferry on a stream.

Through his foggy glasses, Myles could see Jorge and his gang. A few of the men were pacing around the porch of one of the buildings. Myles moved his binoculars to the side of the house. An elderly woman and a young girl were on their knees, at gunpoint. Jorge and another man were chastising them. Myles heard their loud voices, but none of the particulars of the conversation. He steadied his lenses as Jorge violently slapped the older woman. She returned the gesture by spitting in his face.

Myles put down the binoculars. His overwhelming desire to plant Jorge, and what he was seeing, produced an impulse to mount his horse and ride into the village, guns blazing. But he sat on his knees for a few moments, letting his temper settle as the rain trailed off, a rumble of thunder in the distance. As he sized up the situation, he realized there was little he could do. Eight men to one was almost certain to be fatal, and if not, he would reveal to Jorge that he was in the area, thus endangering his entire party.

The realization that he was helpless to do anything but sit and watch Jorge's gang pillage weighed heavily on Myles. He was a soldier, someone accustomed to acting, to making a difference—not hiding and waiting for safety. As he watched, he hoped the bandits would move on. If they started to kill, would he be able to sit and do nothing?

Finally, Jorge's gang mounted up and headed north out of town.

Myles remained on the hill until he saw Jorge and his band disappear a mile out of town. He then rode into the village. The two women were still on their knees, where they had been when the gang departed. Myles got off his horse and walked to the largest of the three buildings, a two-room wooden office. Stepping up onto the porch, he read a sign on the door signifying that this was the constable's office.

He continued inside, where he found a man lying on the floor, a common Mexican in appearance. He was motionless, but breathing roughly. In the half-light of the room, Myles could see his bloody facial wound.

Knowing the wounded always needed water, Myles hurried to the man and knelt beside him. "You all right?" He gave the man a drink from his canteen, then poured some water on his face and swabbed his wounds.

The man groaned while Myles inspected his injuries. He had been hit on the head—twice, probably with a pistol butt.

"You all right, Ramón?"

Ramón shook his head a few times as he regained consciousness. He wiped his face with his hand and looked up at Myles. "Myles Adams, you must be the gringo those bandits were looking for."

"Bad bunch. If I get a chance, I'll get 'em for you."

"Sarina, Sarina," Ramón said nervously, his memory returning. He tried to get up.

"They are fine." Myles put his hand on Ramón's chest and then stood. He extended a hand to Ramón and helped him to his feet. Internally, a huge weight lifted from Myles's soul. No one had been seriously hurt while he was cowering in the bushes on the hill.

Myles led the wobbly-legged Ramón outside to the two women, still on the ground, bawling. He retrieved a small self-contained first-aid kit from his saddlebag and gave it to Ramón.

"It's going to be all right." Myles put his hand under the girl's chin and gently turned her head to him. Her eyes were full of fear. He brushed her hair with his hand. "Hate to leave you like this, my friend, but I've got to get moving."

"Let's get going," Myles called out as Stewart and his group rode out to meet him. "Jorge's about an hour or two in front of us, headed for Monterrey. Probably make it by dark.

Hopefully, he'll wallow in sin there for at least a night—or get shot in a local cantina. But he's looking for us,"

"It was him?" Stewart said, pulling abreast of Myles and continuing to ride.

"Yeah. There's eight of them." Myles shook his hat to remove some rainwater.

The brief deluge turned the silted turn-rows into a quagmire, taxing the horses as they struggled along. Though the rain had stopped, it was replaced by oppressive humidity.

The group finally arrived in sight of a small hacienda around mid-afternoon, and Alexia informed them that the prison was just out of sight. Stewart dismounted first and led his horse and the group into a brushy irrigation ditch beside the turn-row they had been following. The ditch had a couple feet of water in it, but thick rubber trees on its banks gave good cover.

"The camp is about a half kilometer on the other side of those farmhouses," Alexia said quietly.

"Anybody at that farm?" Myles asked from his horse. He had not felt the need to dismount and walk into the rain-soaked shrubs, but instead had ridden into the brush. On horseback, he could still see the four small farmhouses. He studied them with his binoculars.

"Could be," Alexia said. "I don't know."

"What's around this prison camp?" Stewart asked.

"Not much," Alexia said. "It's pretty open for about a half kilometer, but there are plenty of turn-rows around."

"What's the best way to get a good look at this camp?" Myles whispered as he tried to wipe the sweat from his face with his shirt, which was clinging to his arms and back.

He gazed at the surrounding wheat fields, eighty-acre stands that had been planted recently, the spring wheat having grown no more than a couple of feet. The fields were surrounded by thick, brush-covered irrigation ditches.

"Probably around to the left," Alexia finally answered. "Let me show you."

She kicked up a few weeds from the ditch bank, picked up a small stick, and squatted to sketch the prison in the dirt. Myles and Colonel Sancho got off their horses and walked to the edge of the creek to look over her shoulder.

"The prison is here," Alexia said, sketching as she spoke. "The front gate and most of the guards are here—on the side facing those houses you see. Around back are two guard posts, but they are rarely ever occupied. The surrounding ground is just like it is here. There are turn-rows on all sides except the one facing those farmhouses."

Stewart cleared his throat and spoke. "These turn-rows are too low to shield a horse. We should ride back a piece and tie up, then move up where we can have a look."

"Okay," Myles said, "that sounds like a good idea. Stewart, you think your ill-mannered *mujer* can be quiet long enough to come along?" As he often did, Myles finished the sentence louder than he started it, unable to mute his enjoyment and practically bellowing the final words as he reveled in the jab.

"Best I can tell, you make more noise in this outfit than anybody else," quipped Alexia, who looked at Stewart and nearly let out a smile.

Myles pretended to be hurt.

Stewart laughed. "Can't believe I've made it as long as I have with that big mouth beside me."

The four doubled back to a tree line a few hundred yards away and secured their horses to a stand of willows. From there, they entered one of the irrigation ditches leading toward the camp. The ditch held about a foot of muddy water and was buzzing under a cloud of mosquitoes.

As Myles followed Colonel Sancho into the watery ditch, he watched as the colonel inhaled one of the airborne insects and began to choke and spit.

"Don't eat 'em all, Colonel," Myles said. "Leave some for me."

The two men stomped in the mud to ensure the bottom was hard enough to support them; it was. They had almost five feet of cover in the ditch, requiring only a hunch to walk without being seen.

Alexia, still wearing her torn dress and spindly sandals, stumbled as she entered the ditch behind them, making several loud splashes in the process.

Myles turned and glared past her at his partner following her into the ditch.

"Alexia, drag your feet along the bottom when you walk," Stewart said as he slapped at two mosquitoes on his neck. "Don't take your feet out of the water. That way, you won't make so much noise."

Myles continued on ahead another twenty yards before the colonel stopped in front of him.

"They got any snakes around here?" Colonel Sancho asked. He lifted his bandanna over his face, leaving only his eyes exposed to the swarming mosquitoes, and scanned the terrain in front of him, no doubt searching the weed-covered bank for any signs of reptiles. "I would almost rather face a firing squad than a snake. This ditch looks like it might be an appropriate home for a few."

"Yeah, there's all kinds of deadly snakes around here, especially that fer-de-lance," Myles said somberly. "You've got about thirty minutes after he bites you. These ditches are havens for them. They kill a couple dozen of these wheat pickers around here every year."

Myles tried to keep from grinning as the colonel's eyes grew wide. He turned to Stewart to hide his titillation. Even the hundreds of pesky bugs swarming around his face could not squelch the gratification of seeing the colonel sweat.

"Why don't you lead?" Colonel Sancho suggested with anguish in his eyes.

"That's fine with me," Myles said, and walked by the colonel in the narrow ditch. He pulled a rag out of his pocket and wrapped it around his head. "The snake usually bites the second man."

They trudged another five hundred yards down the ditch before they reached the next turn-row, from which they could see the prison.

Myles crawled out of the ditch and up onto its bank. He took up a prone position in the heavy brush and pushed some branches aside to clear his view. Colonel Sancho lay down beside him.

The prison was situated as Alexia had described it, and only a few hundred yards of wheat obstructed their view. Myles pulled out his binoculars for a better look at a large wooden warehouse and two smaller buildings beside it. A simple five-foot barbed-wire fence surrounded the buildings. Three men with rifles could be seen at a gate out front, and four people were cleaning some dishes in the small yard to the left.

"It looks rather benign," Myles said. He lowered the binoculars and began to ponder their options. He turned to Stewart, who had shuffled up the bank behind Alexia and was now lying between her and Colonel Sancho. "I was starting to wonder if you were going to make it, or if I was going to have to send the colonel back to get you. I almost forgot how nimble you are."

"I thought you said your buddy was a soldier," Colonel Sancho said, warming to Myles's banter.

"Well, he was kind of a pseudo-soldier. He used to hang out about five miles behind the fighting. If you needed some artillery support and he and his buddies weren't too busy playing cards or taking a siesta, they might fire a few rounds down-range. They were just as apt to get you as the people they were aiming at."

Myles continued to look through his binoculars. Two of the

guards were sitting on a bench, rifles slung over their shoulders, and one was standing beside them. "Where's everybody at?"

"Everybody is in that big building," Alexia said. "One of the little ones is a kitchen, and the other is where the guards sleep." She pushed aside some brush and pointed.

"Let me see those glasses," Stewart said, reaching over Colonel Sancho and grabbing Myles's binoculars. He trained them on the front gate. "Are those guards regulars?"

"One of them is about forty," Alexia said. "He's fat and lazy. The rest are very young. I would say no older than twenty-three. They talk as if they have been fighting for several years."

"Are there cells in that warehouse?" Stewart asked.

"No," Alexia answered. "About ten rooms, with only small holes in the walls for light and heavy wooden doors, locked. There are probably one or two guards in the hallway serving the rooms. The rest of the guards are in this house up front. There are no more than eight of them, and three are always asleep, except at mealtimes."

"Too far across this field to go during daylight," Stewart grumbled. "Don't care who's guarding the front gate." He paused a moment, and then started talking rapid-fire. "We're going to have to go at night. Late, when they're all asleep, but before the moon goes down. With no more people than we have, I don't see any way around shooting those two guards up front. We'll sneak around the side and shoot them from the rear. The rest of those Mexicans will come pouring out of those building trying to find out what's going on. We'll have them then. Maybe we won't have to shoot them all. It will be imperative to get to that boardinghouse before those guards empty out."

"There is nothing pious about any of these fellows," Alexia assured him. "I don't think you should exert yourself trying to preserve any of them."

"And I wouldn't go formulating any plans just yet," Myles declared. "I ain't even decided whether we're going in yet."

"Maybe we'll get another rain tonight," Stewart said. "That would be perfect." He looked up with interest at the sparse clouds in the sky. The remnants of the earlier storm still hung in the atmosphere, and the clouds were on the move. Stewart pointed his nose to the sky and sniffed a few times.

"Maybe you're right," Myles said. He looked up at the sky and sniffed a few times himself in an animated fashion.

"What are you sniffing for?" Colonel Sancho asked. "You gringos can smell rain?"

"I ain't ever smelled rain before, and I seriously doubt Stewart has, either," Myles said. "But he looked like he knew what he was doing, so I thought I'd give it a try. I've got a reputation to hold up." He lifted his canteen to his mouth.

"I can smell rain," Stewart said.

Myles swallowed some water, then said, "Yeah? Then how come you didn't bother to let us know that big gully-washer was coming?"

"I know how tender you are. If I'd told you, you would've wanted to find some shelter and take a siesta." Steward returned his attention to the prison.

Myles also returned his gaze to the prison. Thus far, he had only agreed to come look at the stockade. Logic was telling him that any raid was a bad idea. But he knew it was too late to turn back. His stomach lurched as an uneasy feeling washed over him.

Chapter 22

"Is this it, Stewart?" Myles asked as they saddled up to return to the jail. "You're not going to wake up in the morning and tell me about some cousin of yours that needs rescuing over in Saltillo, are you?"

Out of sight and away from the mosquitoes, which had left a trail of welts in their wake, they had waited nearby in a stand of trees for the sun to set. Myles, as always, was mining the lighter side of danger.

Stewart just shook his head.

"Alexia," Myles said seriously, "you will stay back a piece, at least until we have the place under control. Then ride up and help us locate your family."

"I can handle myself," Alexia said defiantly.

"I'm sure you can," Myles said with a chuckle.

As they worked their way around to the rear of the prison, hiding amongst the turn-rows, a three-quarter moon once again illuminated their path. They dismounted just beyond view of the prison.

Stewart whispered to Alexia, "Sit tight here until I holler. Then bring the horses up." He brought his index finger to his lips, instructing her not to respond.

Alexia, still on her horse, was ghost white with fear.

"Don't fret so much," Myles whispered to her before friskily pinching her on the thigh. He tied his horse to a tree with a slipknot and handed her the loose rein. "Nobody's going to forsake you."

"I'm not fretting," she said testily.

"It won't be long," Stewart said. Then he and Colonel Sancho disappeared into the darkness.

"Jerk on these," Myles said as he handed the other two sets of reins to Alexia, "and it will free the horses."

He paused as he peered into the darkness. He could hear no voices, only the hum of thousands of popping insects and the deep bellowing of bullfrogs. He casually walked down a turn-row until he found Stewart, who, along with Colonel Sancho, was inspecting the prison.

They could see the small fence encircling the place, and could barely discern the outline of one of its buildings. Two glowing lanterns marked the prison's front gate.

Myles watched as Stewart crawled forward to the fence to get a better look before quickly returning.

"You go right there, Colonel Sancho," Stewart whispered, pointing to the dimly lit building. "If anybody comes out that door, shoot them—unless they're running away. We're going to crawl around to the side and take the guards. Don't shoot until we shoot."

They all checked to make sure their weapons were loaded, and then Stewart instructed Colonel Sancho to move out.

As the colonel struggled to climb the four-foot fence, Myles stifled a laugh. The colonel was only a few inches taller than the fence, and his baggy pants kept snagging on the barbed wire.

Myles followed Stewart to the fence line, and the two lay down on their stomachs. From there, they crawled along the fence's perimeter toward the front gate. The six-inch grass was thick with dew, soaking their clothes. But it provided some cover and muffled their approach.

Fifty paces from the entrance, the gate came into view. They stopped. Two men were sitting on the bench they had observed earlier, casually passing another quiet night at the post.

Myles cupped Stewart's ear with his hand and put his mouth to it as he whispered, "I only see two. How 'bout you?" His heart was beating so wildly it seemed to drown out his words.

"Same," Stewart whispered. "I'll take the one on the left. You take the one on the right. Okay?"

Both men raised their rifles.

"As soon as they fall," Stewart whispered, "we haul ass for that door on the right. On three. You ready?"

"I reckon," Myles said, still wondering how he had agreed to busting out Alexia's family. "This is about the stupidest thing I've done in a while. I know that *mujer* of yours is awful feisty, but you sure she's worth all this?"

"I bet this isn't even the stupidest thing you've done this month," Stewart whispered, and counted down to one.

The two fired simultaneously, but only the guard on the left fell.

Stewart quickly bolted another cartridge into his rifle. "I forgot what it's like to look after you," he said as he pulled the trigger.

The second guard fell to the ground before he knew what hit him.

Myles offered no reply, quickly jumping the fence instead. With Stewart on his heels, he sprinted toward the guards' sleeping quarters. As they approached the small wooden building, they heard a shot from where they had left Colonel Sancho. Simultaneously, three men in their underwear came running out of the sleeping quarters with their pistols at the ready.

"Drop the guns or you're dead!" Stewart hollered in Spanish at the three dark shadows ten paces in front of him.

One man foolishly raised his pistol. Stewart knocked him off his feet with a bullet to the chest and issued the same order to the remaining two: "Drop 'em or you're dead!"

The two men let their pistols fall to the ground and quickly raised their hands.

"I'm going to check the kitchen," Myles said, and took off at a dash for the building next to the house.

He squinted inside and saw that it was empty: an open room with only one large table and no closets.

He immediately returned outside. "Nobody in here."

"There's a dead one out back," Colonel Sancho said after emerging from the prisoners' quarters. "No guards in here." He held up a set of keys in one hand and brandished Myles's spare rifle in the other.

"Go open one of those rooms so we'll have somewhere to put these gentlemen," Stewart said to Colonel Sancho. He waved his pistol to instruct the two men to follow Colonel Sancho, then yelled for Alexia to come forward.

She arrived with the horses at the front gate before he could finish his sentence.

Myles accompanied Colonel Sancho and the two guards into the prisoners' quarters. He followed them down a narrow corridor that had four doors on each side and was illuminated with one lone lantern.

With Colonel Sancho unlocking and opening each door in front of him, Myles stopped at the first one and peered inside. He could barely make out a dozen people huddled together against the back wall.

"We're busting you out," Myles said in Spanish. "You're free."

He delivered the good news to the prisoners in the remaining cells, and then left the two sentries in Colonel Sancho's care.

Outside, he found Alexia sitting horseback at the front door watching the newly freed prisoners exit the building. The former inmates stumbled into the courtyard, disbelieving, unsure of how to react. There were many men amongst them—shadows of their former selves—along with women, children, and the elderly. Unshod and dressed in rags, many looked too weak to embrace their newfound freedom.

Alexia spotted someone in the last group emerging from the building. "Father!" she called to a feeble-looking man in the crowd.

Stiff-jointed and stooped, an old man walked as briskly as he could to her horse. He was followed, as far as Myles could tell, by what had to be his children: Alexia's sister Maria and brother Pablo.

"What's happening?" the old man asked.

Alexia dismounted and embraced her siblings and disoriented father. "We're getting you out of here!" she said. "That's what's happening!"

Myles tried to speed things along. "You got everybody?" he hollered.

Alexia nodded and returned to her horse.

"Then save the reunion for later," Myles said. "Let's vamoose."

"I have to get something first," the old man said, and shuffled toward the prisoners' quarters behind him.

Myles was fervently checking his surroundings for anything amiss. "Whatever it is," he said as he stepped in front of the decrepit figure, "it's not that important. We need to get out of here."

"No!" Julio said, and pushed Myles aside. "I have to get it!"

Myles turned to Alexia. "Get your brother and sister out of here! I'll get him."

He followed the old man to the building and stood at the door, where he watched impatiently as Julio desperately rummaged through personal belongings scattered on the floor.

"What are you looking for?"

"My family jewels," he said. He reached under a cot, but came up empty.

"Maybe we should wait around here until Villa's army shows up," Myles said as he leaned against the door. He folded his arms over his chest. "I'm sure one of his *pistoleros* will know where they are."

"Okay, we can go," the short, gray-haired man said in despair after emptying a laundry bag on the floor and vainly searching its contents. He kicked the pile and walked toward the door.

"You sure you don't want to walk back over and look at your cell again for old times' sake before we go?" Myles asked before leaving.

Myles led Julio back outside, where most of the captives were milling around the prison gate. Stewart was explaining to them that they were free, that they needed to go somewhere. But the prisoners stood silently, staring blankly at the dark figure with an American accent.

"You're free!" Stewart implored the crowd. "You must—"

Several shots rang out as someone opened up on the courtyard. Within seconds, the gunfire managed to do what Stewart's words could not: get the crowd moving. The prisoners started fleeing in every direction.

Myles shoved Julio to the ground and fell beside him. He could see Stewart, who had dropped beside Colonel Sancho, looking around frantically, trying to determine the gunman's location.

"What the hell is going on?" Stewart called across the courtyard to Myles.

Before Myles could answer, a man running between them was cut down by another round.

"He's over here on the fence line!" Myles hollered, pointing in the direction from which the shots had come.

He hugged the dirt as another round careened through the courtyard. He focused his eyes, but could find no one.

Finally, after another volley, he spotted the bright flash from a muzzle. "He's shooting in six-shot intervals! When he pauses, let's get him."

As soon as the gun went silent, Myles leapt to his feet and dashed toward the muzzle blasts. He scurried as close as he dared, Stewart and Colonel Sancho covering his approach with rapid gunfire at the fence line, and then dove to the ground.

Myles desperately searched for the shooter. He was watching for another muzzle blast when Alexia, with her sister clutching her tightly from the back of the saddle, galloped toward the front gate.

"Ah, hell," Myles said.

Another round of gunfire poured forth from the fence line as Alexia and her sister exited the gate, and Maria tumbled from the horse.

Alexia did not slow her horse's stride, but turned in the direction of the gunfire. She closed on a scarcely visible man kneeling on the fence line. He was looking down and feverishly reloading an antique lever-action rifle.

Alexia charged her horse at the man and fired two rounds at him with Stewart's pistol. The man fell to the ground before he could look up.

Myles raced to her sister and knelt over the sixteen-year-old girl on the ground. A bullet had torn through her neck. Blood was pouring from the gaping hole, soaking the neckline of the young girl's dirty blue dress.

He brushed Maria's black hair aside and found her eyes closed. He checked her wrist for a pulse. There was none. Panting in the darkness, he looked up at Alexia, who had just arrived, and shook his head.

"Stewart!" he hollered between breaths. "Get over here!"

Stewart, along with Colonel Sancho and Alexia's family, rushed to Myles's side.

Alexia's father walked feebly to them and collapsed to his knees beside Maria, weeping as he reached down and stroked his daughter's hair. He looked up at Myles, blinded by manic despair.

"I'm sorry," Myles said. He turned to Alexia, whose chest heaved as she tried to catch her breath, tears streaming down her cheeks. "Come," he said as he picked up Maria and lifted the young girl over his shoulder. "Let's go. We'll bury her proper in the morning."

He put his free hand on Julio's shoulder and looked past him at two prisoners lying dead on the ground beneath the ghostly light of the two lanterns hanging from the front gate. He then stared out into the darkness and spoke numbly as he considered the repercussions of their hastily conceived jailbreak.

"There'll be some angry men looking for us in a few hours."

They were anything but home free.

Chapter 23

With the sweat on his forehead glistening in the early morning sunlight, Stewart finished digging the grave and looked up at Sergeant Bates.

"That should do it," the sergeant said. "I'll go wake up the family."

Stewart nodded and plunged the entrenching tool into the sandy earth. As he wiped his brow with his sleeve, he took in the quiet solitude of the surrounding meadow he and the sergeant had scouted minutes earlier.

He had slept lightly all night, certain that a posse or the ever-present Jorge would be bearing down on them at any moment. But the morning had come without further bloodshed. They would pay their respects to Maria and then ride back to Victoria, hopefully still safely ahead of the advancing rebel army.

Myles and Sergeant Bates arrived first, followed by Colonel Sancho and Lieutenant Rubio and then the Garcia family. Alexia's father and brother looked like broken spirits in the morning twilight, their clothes tattered and their bodies bruised. They had surely borne the brunt of their captors' rage.

When everyone had gathered around the grave site, Stewart

crossed himself and then read from an old Bible he lugged with him everywhere he went.

"Yea, though I walk through the valley of the shadow of death, I will fear no evil," he read softly, "for thou art with me."

He finished the psalm and planted a primitive cross he had built from kindling.

Julio lowered his daughter into the shallow grave, covering her face with a blanket. He prayed silently and then, seemingly stifled by grief, stumbled back toward the campsite with his beleaguered family at his side, his son steadying him, and his wife crying quietly alongside.

"Boss," Sergeant Bates said as they watched the family walk away, "it may not look like it now, but you two's excursion last night has done some justice." The sergeant smiled at Myles and patted Stewart on the shoulder.

"We're a long way from being out of this mess," Myles said. "I wouldn't go passing out any accolades yet. I think I'll try and say something of solace to them before we go."

Stewart followed Myles to the rim of the canyon, but he stopped a few paces short of the Garcias and watched with pride as his longtime friend comforted Alexia and her family. Notwithstanding Myles's pretentious nature and occasionally lewd behavior, he was an excellent consoler. His calm and solemn optimism seemed to transcend the darkest hour.

Myles put his arms around Alexia and her brother. "I'm sorry about what happened," he said. "A lot of people have suffered unimaginable horrors in this war, but there is nothing we can do about the past. All we can do is move on and see if we can make a difference in the future. You should mourn, but don't let it prevent us from the task at hand. That is what Maria would want."

After Myles had finished consoling the Garcias, Stewart slowly followed the group back to the campsite, but not before instructing Sergeant Bates to ride north about a mile.

He was still worried a posse might be in pursuit. As he walked, he felt the tension of the last several days slowly lift. The new day and the hope that they would all be safe soon had inflated him with optimism and satisfaction. He arrived at the campsite's edge and lingered there briefly to collect his thoughts.

With Lieutenant Rubio and Colonel Sancho lending a hand, Myles started to redistribute the loads on the horses. The two additions to the party would mandate the abandoning of everything on the packhorse. Even with this, someone would have to ride double. He had gathered all the horses and tied them up to see what would have to be left.

"How many siblings do you have?" the lieutenant asked.

"All I have is a brother," Myles said, "but I'm getting married in a few weeks."

"Your first time?" the lieutenant asked.

"Yes."

"You know anything about marriage?" the lieutenant asked.

"The only thing I know about marriage is that I've broken up a few," Myles said.

The two laughed.

"Can't help yourself," Stewart said as he entered the campsite, "can you?"

"Just over here enlightening these boys on all my matrimonial injustices," Myles said, still unloading the packhorse. He looked up in time to see his partner shoot him a weary glance.

"Everything packed?" Stewart asked.

"Just about," Myles said. "We'll be ready to go in ten minutes."

As he unloaded the packhorse, Myles gazed disappointingly at several of his belongings. The thought of leaving them did not please him. He glanced at Colonel Sancho, who was instructing Lieutenant Rubio to lift a fully packed saddlebag Myles had just finished inventorying. The two made an awkward pair, Myles thought. Lieutenant Rubio was easily a foot taller than his superior, but he moved in step at the colonel's orders.

Myles then eyed his spare rifle, which he had loaned to Colonel Sancho and which was now leaning against a large boulder beside the colonel. He reached over, picked it up, and put it in its holster on his horse.

The colonel looked up at him in dismay. "Why don't you let me keep that, just in case we run into some more trouble? I covered your ass with it last night."

"You shot a fat old man who was probably drunk," Myles replied.

"I shot a competent guard and took that big building all by myself," the colonel said. "I bet you've never done that."

"Colonel, there's nothing I haven't seen or done," Myles said casually, securing his saddle to his horse and carefully looking at a raw spot on his mount's back.

"These boys can finish this up," Stewart interrupted. "Let's go get Bones."

He rolled up his sleeves—something he did even in inclement weather to show off a ten-inch scar on his right forearm, a souvenir from the Spanish-American War—and started to saddle his horse.

Myles knew the maneuver was meant to impress the lieutenant. But Lieutenant Rubio seemed absorbed with his own thoughts.

"You look like you're getting a little restless, Lieutenant," Myles said as he climbed atop his horse. "Come on. If we run into any bandits, I might need a little help. My yes-man here has many times proved inadequate."

The lieutenant quickly saddled up and followed Myles out of camp.

"To be honest, Lieutenant," Myles said, hoping to continue their conversation from earlier, "I'm not sure a worldly man such as myself is cut out for marriage. There used to be this redhead in El Paso. What was her name?"

"Julie," Stewart said as he caught up with the two atop the canyon, where Myles had already stopped and was playing with a small brown lizard he had plucked from the sage.

"Ah, yes, Julie," Myles said. "She was too good-looking. Every time she would rub herself on me, she put me in a trance. Caused me to lose total control of my faculties. I never could think straight when she was around. I didn't really like that too much, so I had to send her on her way."

"Kind of like when somebody sits a big plate of biscuits in front of you," Stewart said.

"Something like that," Myles mumbled, gently placing the lizard back on its perch in the sage before resuming the ride.

As the three rode, they did not attempt to pick up Sergeant Bates's track, but instead carried on a conversation while moving along the canyon rim. After fifteen minutes and no sign of the sergeant, they paused.

"Don't see him," Stewart said. "You reckon he got lost?"

Myles pivoted in his saddle and gazed at the sage-covered open country that unfolded in every direction as far as the eye could see. "Hell," he said, "*we* may be lost." He pulled his pistol from its holster and fired two shots in the air. "There ain't no telling. He'll be along shortly."

"He ain't comin'," Stewart said. He looked over at Myles, who didn't seem to be in any hurry to disagree with him.

"How long has it been since I fired those shots?" Myles asked.

"Fifteen minutes."

"All right," Myles said. "Let's backtrack."

Stewart led Myles and the lieutenant back the way they had come, and it didn't take him long to pick up a track on the rim of the canyon. It led north, and they followed it until it terminated at a dusty single-lane road. The commotion of five men on foot and two motorized vehicles was still evident where the track met the road.

Myles got off his horse and took a long look at the road.

From his horse, Stewart could make out two sets of horse tracks. One dead-ended at the road, and the other led in the direction from which they had come.

"Both sets of these tracks belong to Bones' horse," Myles said as he stood up. "But one set is missing a rider."

"What do you think?" Stewart asked. He waited, still on his horse, as Myles knelt again beside one of the tracks.

Myles grabbed a handful of dry sand and continued to inspect the road. He sighed briefly and shook his head.

Stewart had a queasy feeling in his gut. They had found themselves in a lot of trouble together over the years. But he could count on one hand the number of times Myles had looked this worried. And each time, his partner's apprehension had been justified.

"It looks like somebody got him," Myles finally said. He let the sand sift through his fingers and blow in the breeze.

"Don't see any blood," Stewart said, hoping against hope that Sergeant Bates was unhurt.

He got off his horse and started to examine the two sets of wheel tracks, which continued down the dusty road. All signs indicated everyone present had hitched a ride in the vehicles. "If we follow these tracks, I bet they'll lead us to him."

"Lieutenant," Myles muttered as he looked up the road in the direction the tracks led, "get on back to the camp and tell everybody we'll be along shortly."

"Riding with you two is anything but uneventful," the lieutenant said, turning toward camp. "You sure seem to find plenty of misfortune. This is as bad as riding with the Mexican Army."

"You're right about that," Myles replied. "I can't go anywhere without getting into trouble. If I get out of this fiasco, I'm going to retire from this shit once and for all—lay up around the house and be lazy."

"Doesn't sound like much of a change," Stewart said as the lieutenant rode off. He scowled at the sun, which was already beginning to beat down on them. As he returned his gaze to the horizon, he spotted a plume of smoke to the north. "What's that over there?"

Myles lifted his binoculars to his eyes for a closer peek. "Looks like a Huastecan village. Probably belongs to those young braves we saw yesterday."

"I didn't think there were any of those left."

"There's not many. The Mexicans bred most of them out— that is, the ones that didn't get smallpox or just get shot. They're pretty tame anyway. Probably nobody there but women and children. Most of the men have been requisitioned to the front."

Myles took his glasses off the village, and the two began to ride up the road in pursuit of the car tracks.

As they followed the tracks at a deliberate pace, Myles pulled his maps from his saddlebag to see where the primitive road led. "This is a dead-end road. It forks up into two mountain draws about ten miles ahead."

After a few more minutes of following the tracks in the road, they spotted a black vehicle a half mile ahead. From a distance, it appeared idle and unoccupied; nonetheless, Stewart followed Myles into the sage-covered field beside the road. They approached quickly but cautiously, weapons at the ready.

The car was a Ford wagon, almost as new as the Model-T pickup Antonio Diaz had driven up the mountainside a few days earlier but not nearly as pampered. As it had appeared from a distance, it was unoccupied. Someone had pulled it off the road into waist-high brush, and one of the two sets of tracks they were trailing terminated at its wheelbase.

Stewart dismounted to check the wagon's interior. He found nothing in the cab and sat in the driver's seat, where he found the keys still in the ignition.

"Out of petroleum," he said after trying to start the wagon several times. He looked at the fuel gauge and then searched the cab for any clue about its previous passengers.

"The occupants were either in a big hurry," Myles said from behind the wagon, "or they don't know much about driving."

Stewart stepped out of the driver's seat as Myles opened the aft door of the wagon. "There are two cans of petrol back here."

"Two men got out of this car and into the other one," Stewart said, barely hearing Myles as he stared intently at the tracks. He looked up the road, where the tracks of the other vehicle continued on.

"Let's make up some time," Myles said.

Stewart turned to see Myles remove one of the fuel cans and unscrew the fuel cap on the wagon.

"Go tie the horses up in the bushes."

"Ever driven a car before?" Stewart asked as he grabbed the two horses by the reins.

"Only once. It's not like piloting a cruise liner."

Stewart found a scraggly old tree a few dozen feet off the road and tied off the horses. He returned in time to hear the Ford's starter catch and the engine purr.

As they slowly chugged down the road, Myles handed his map collection to Stewart. "Take these," he said. "You can track our progress."

"Watch the road," Stewart grumbled.

It only took Myles a few minutes to get a handle on the

wagon, after which he steadily increased the speed, slowing down—if only slightly—for potholes.

"Damn!" Stewart said as they bounced over a pothole and he hit his head on the ceiling. "I thought you said you knew how to drive this thing."

"I do," Myles said, turning to give Stewart a devilish grin.

After Myles negotiated the fork in the road without losing sight of the trail, Stewart told him to slow down and pull off. "Road finishes about a half mile ahead," he said, still studying the map. "Just like you said."

"What's next?" Myles asked.

"We'll use this creek," Stewart said, pointing to their location on the map and then to a ridge beside the road. "They can't be too far."

The road sat on the high bank of a small creek and had been gradually gaining elevation for the last few miles, its surface turning from dirt to stone. Rocky hills ran along either side of the small mountain draw containing the creek. The ridgeline above them sat only fifty feet higher than their current location, but it was strewn with boulders.

Myles left afoot, and Stewart chased after him toward the top of the neighboring ridge. As they neared the apex, the climbing became more treacherous. Stewart was soon concentrating only on his next step over the car-sized boulders; a misstep, he knew, could be fatal.

Once atop the ridgeline, they pushed on swiftly without conversation. Tangled sage, abundant on the promontory, concealed their approach. After they reached the edge of a large open field, they stopped and took cover to have a good look.

"Let's move right over there," Myles said, panting heavily as he pointed to a twenty-foot berm about a hundred paces into the opening. "We ought to be able to see something from there."

Stewart nodded his head and continued without comment.

He circled around to a location behind the berm and then led Myles up its rear. Just short of the hill's pinnacle, the two fell to their stomachs and crawled to the top. From the berm, they could view the entire area.

"There," Stewart whispered. He pointed to a Ford wagon, the same model as the one they had requisitioned, about two hundred paces away.

Three men were talking and laughing beside the wagon.

Stewart cupped his right ear, but couldn't make out much. A slight breeze at his back squashed the men's voices, which only cut through while they were laughing or talking loudly.

"I don't see Bones," Myles said as he squinted into his binoculars. "You reckon these three have him?"

"There were five sets of tracks back there," Stewart whispered. "There's two more down there somewhere."

Myles lowered his binoculars long enough to respond. "If it's any consolation, it doesn't look like any of them are armed—at least not with a gun. Wonder where Bones is at."

"Probably in the wagon."

Myles continued to study the men. "Hell, they're just kids, no older than eighteen, tops."

"Those were kids we shot last night," Stewart said. He slowly slid back down the hill until he was completely out of sight. He gazed at the horizon wistfully. The breakneck speed of the last several days had begun to drain him.

"Really," Myles said, still training his binoculars at the clique. "Come look."

"What do they look like?" Stewart asked apathetically as he crawled back up beside Myles.

"They look like some of your Mexican kinsmen." Myles handed the binoculars to Stewart.

"First, I'm not a Mexican. Second, you're a bigot. Every time you see somebody with a different lineage than you, you think they're perpetrating a crime."

Stewart raised the binoculars to his eyes. He zoomed in on a couple of the young men and saw that Myles was right: They were barely in their teens.

Myles removed two canteens and his pistol from his belt. "How can I be a bigot?" he asked. "I let myself be seen in public with you all the time." He pushed a new magazine into his pistol and retrieved a spare from his belt.

Stewart put the binoculars down and glared at Myles. "Haven't we shot enough people for one week?"

"Relax, I ain't going to shoot nobody. I'm going to sneak right there." Myles nodded at a large pit ahead that encompassed almost half the distance between them and the parked wagon they were observing. "When I signal you, fire a few shots in the air. Those youngsters will probably run for cover. When they do, I'll go up there and get Bones. You may have to strafe them a little."

"Sounds kind of shaky," Stewart groused.

"You got any better ideas?" Myles slid a few feet back down the berm. "I'm going to scurry over there. When I'm ready, I'll motion to you."

Before Stewart could protest, Myles hurried back down the berm and into the pit.

"This is going to be a debacle," Stewart muttered to himself as he watched Myles take up a position. "Hope it's not a tragic one."

Chapter 24

With his heart throbbing in his ears, Myles felt cut off. Stewart was crouched on the ledge behind him. The men on the other side of the berm were a vague presence. And everything around him had gone silent—a murky backdrop to his shallow breathing, the sweat in his eyes, the small stone that skidded free beneath his boots.

He turned awkwardly to Stewart and raised his thumb.

Nothing.

He relayed the signal again, impatiently cocking his head and opening his eyes wide. What the hell was he waiting for?

Stewart finally fired three shots in quick succession, cutting loose the anxiety in his partner's gut, but Myles's hastily conceived plan was stillborn. The bandits, instead of running for cover, shouted at one another in confusion before quickly rushing to the wagon.

Myles scrambled to his feet and ran toward the old Ford wagon, pistol at the ready. As the black wagon started to roll down the road, the last of the lads jumping on the rear bumper, Myles yelled at them to stop. He raised his pistol and drew a bead on one of the young men on the back bumper. But he couldn't bring himself to pull the trigger.

"Shit!" he groused, lowering his pistol. He stood in shock as the wagon skidded sideways in the gravel road and then rounded a bend in the road, out of sight and untouchable.

"That didn't work out worth a damn!" Stewart called from the base of the berm.

Myles turned desperately to Stewart, who had made no attempt to join the assault. "Let's get moving!" he shouted. "Maybe we can get back to the car in time to catch them."

Stewart slowly picked up Myles's small pack. "You got any more brilliant plans?"

Myles ran by him without responding and dashed the quarter mile back to the wagon. He arrived out of breath—bent over, hands on his knees, huffing violently as he waited for Stewart.

He finally looked up to see Stewart a few yards away.

"No time to be taking a break," Stewart said breathlessly as he arrived. "Let's get moving."

Myles stood erect, still breathing heavily, and fumbled for the car key. He slowly walked to the wagon as he dug in his front pockets. He stopped and searched his back pockets. "I don't feel a key anywhere."

"Maybe you left it in the ignition," Stewart said, still puffing.

The two were only a few paces apart, and Myles could see that Stewart, like him, was struggling to get the words out— and his wind back. He peered through the wagon's window, but gave no response. He then stared down at the gravel road beneath his feet, and he groaned as he saw tire tracks leading to and from the wagon.

"Looks like they took your key," Stewart said.

"Maybe not," Myles said. He sat down heavily on the front wheel of the old Ford. "They certainly stopped and tried, but maybe there was no key. If it was there, they probably would have taken the car."

"Do you remember if you took the key out or not?"

"I think I did. I must have lost it up on that hill when I was pulling all that junk out of my pockets. Why don't you go back up there and check? I'll see if I can start this thing without a key."

"*Me?* You're the one who lost it."

"That's not a good utilization of resources," Myles said as he opened the small hood of the wagon. "I'm the engineer." He could feel Stewart peering over his shoulder at the maze of parts under the hood.

"I'll be right back," Stewart grumbled and started back up the road.

Myles tried to turn his full attention to the engine compartment, but he had no clue how to start a car without a key. Staring at the engine changed nothing. He kept thinking about the events that had led up to his brilliant plan going south. Where had he put that key? He wiggled the radiator hose and then traced a few wires to the cab.

He finally sat down beside the wagon on the edge of the road and tried to retrace his steps. As he did, he suddenly remembered leaving the key in the ignition. A feeling of powerlessness overtook him, and he leaned back in the grass and closed his eyes, exhausted. What had happened to Sergeant Bates? Was he still alive? The thought of losing his loyal friend, especially on the backside of their adventure, was too much to bear.

He heard Stewart's feet in the gravel as he returned from the berm.

"No key?" Myles asked with his eyes still closed.

"No key," Stewart replied, collapsing out of breath in the grass beside him.

"I kind of figured that. While you were gone, I remembered leaving it in the wagon."

"Thanks for telling me," Stewart huffed.

"I didn't see any harm in you wandering around out there

for a few minutes. There is a chance my memory is corrupt. Besides, it gave me a little peace so I could try and come up with a plan to get us out of this debacle." Unlike Stewart, Myles had caught his breath somewhat and was starting to cool off.

"Any luck?"

"None. I figure we'll lay here for a few more minutes and then take off walking. It's probably a three-hour walk back to the horses."

Myles sat up tiredly and looked over at the small creek, which was nothing more than a dry rock bed, beside the road. It didn't look promising. The temperate morning was every minute turning into a torrid day, with no shade in sight and not an inkling of wind. "Of course, the thought of walking three hours is so loathsome it puts a crimp in my constitution."

Stewart patted with both hands his sweaty shirt, which was clinging to his chest. "We're not going to walk three hours in this heat without water."

"We'll find some water," Myles said, and lay back down in the cool dampness of the long green grass. "I'm going to die one day, but it ain't going to be from thirst."

"Your plan back there sure did go afoul," Stewart said.

Myles did not reply. His eyes were growing heavy as he lay in the cool grass, and he pulled up his white shirt to expose his midsection.

"Don't get too cushy," Stewart said and stood up. "We're about to pull out."

"I'm losing weight, you know that?" Myles said, hoping to prolong his stay in the cool grass by continuing the conversation. He rubbed his stomach with his hands as he stared at it lackadaisically. "There was an old set of scales back at the Bishop's Palace. I weighed myself. I'm only one hundred and ninety pounds."

"You still look like an orange on a toothpick."

Myles sat up and watched as Stewart opened the back door of the wagon and checked the cans to see if any contained water. From where Myles was sitting in the grass, they all looked bone dry.

Stewart then picked up Myles's map pack and put it around his waist.

"Where we going?" Myles groaned.

Stewart looked down the road. "Probably a small creek down here somewhere."

"I don't remember any creeks. That's a long hike in this heat."

Myles slowly got up to follow Stewart, who had already started down the road in the direction the two had come from an hour earlier. He did not attempt to catch Stewart, but trudged behind him at a distance of a hundred paces. As he strolled, he looked up at the sweltering sky and grimaced. Mexican summers were not to be taken lightly. He slowed his pace, eventually shuffling to the shoulder and away from the simmering road, which was threatening to cook the soles of his boots.

They walked for two hours without seeing so much as a lizard before Stewart, just visible ahead on a rise in the road, found a lush, grassy knoll under a large oak tree and sat down to rest. Myles caught up with him and plunked down beside him. He was surprised to see how much the sun had already scorched Stewart, whose face was burnt deep red and whose nose was dripping sweat.

They sat quietly for a few moments trying to escape the debilitating heat before Stewart reached over and grabbed a dirty white towel from around Myles's neck.

"How come you never ask for anything?" Myles said sluggishly, without trying to stop him from taking the towel. "You know it's common courtesy to say 'please' when you want something."

Stewart took the towel and wiped the sweat from his face without replying. He then ran the small towel down his hairy arms, drenching the towel with sweat, and tossed it soaking wet back into Myles's lap.

"What the hell am I supposed to do with that?" Myles asked in a disgruntled voice. "It's no good anymore."

"This is all my fault," Stewart mumbled as he panted in the heat. "Should have known better than to get in that car with you."

Myles found a twig in the grass and tossed it mindlessly into the road. "You know, I'm too smart and handsome for this. Maybe I should have married one of those debutantes up in El Paso. One with a big dowry." He rolled over onto his stomach and propped his chin up on his hands. "Instead of sitting out here sweating like a hog on this lonely road to nowhere, I could be laid up on the beach in Padre spending her daddy's money and letting her rub oil on me."

"Yeah, this is nobody's fault but mine," Stewart continued to himself. "This ranks with your biggest blunders."

Myles noticed something in the distance and debated whether or not he should say something. They were about halfway down the creek draw, and much of the ground below could still be seen. "I don't know if I'm seeing a mirage or not," he said matter-of-factly, "but I think I see a house."

Stewart rolled over beside Myles to take a look. "Where?"

"There," Myles replied, and pointed to a small wooden structure about a half mile distant. "I don't know if it's a house, but it's a building."

"You think anybody's home?"

"I don't know, but I'm sure there's some water somewhere near. Let's go check it out."

The farmhouse, a modest little cottage most likely used only during harvest season, was situated about a half mile off the road. While Stewart peeked inside the front window to make sure it was vacant, Myles wandered around back.

"No one here," he heard Stewart call.

Myles spotted an antique well, its open hole encased in stone. He leaned over the well and squinted into its musty dark depths. Was it dry? He straightened and looked around for a small rock to throw down the well, but found nothing.

Beside the well sat a small, elevated steel tank with a lever pump attached to it and a valve protruding from its side. Myles turned the valve, its rusty threads creaking as it opened, and brown water poured forth. He stuck his hand in the streaming water and watched as it slowly turned clear. He put his lips on the valve, and the cool water rushed into his mouth faster than he could swallow. He drank until his stomach could hold no more and then put his head under the spout, letting the deluge of water rush over his head and face. Gradually, he could feel the temperature change as the last of the cool water at the bottom of the tank began to run out.

"I found the water!" he hollered.

He was soaked head to toe and resting against the well when Stewart rounded the corner.

"Well," Stewart said, sizing him up, "you're good for something."

"I've already drank all the cool water," Myles said, wringing dry his shirt, which had been clinging to his full stomach. "What was left I poured on me."

"Figures," Stewart said before putting his head under the valve. He drank a while and then put his head under the water spout to cool off, although in a more restrained fashion than Myles's full-body shower. "You sure are weak. A couple of hours without water and you're sucking wind."

After cooling off for a few minutes, the two refilled their stomachs and canteens before resuming their march in the midday heat. Instead of taking a direct route back to the road, they chose a path across a sage flat, which would add fifteen minutes to their journey but put them back on the road considerably closer to where they had left their horses.

As they walked, the sage gave way to six- and then ten-feet-high thorn scrub and mesquite, reducing visibility to nothing and slowing their pace down to a crawl. Before long, they were mired in confusion and certain they had lost their way.

"Stop," Myles said to Stewart, who was pushing on blindly through a tangled thicket ahead of him. "Let's try and find our bearings."

"You saying we're lost?"

"Well, we're not on course," Myles said. "I can promise you that." Myles squinted up at the sun, which had reached its apex, and shook his head. "Hell, we can't even use the sun to point us in the right direction."

"Get on my shoulders," Stewart said.

"What?"

"Get on my shoulders. Maybe you can see over these god-forsaken weeds."

"You sure you can hold me?" Myles asked. "I swallowed half the water in that tank back there."

Stewart knelt down and signaled for Myles to climb atop his shoulders. "Get on."

"Okay," Myles said, and gingerly sat atop Stewart's shoulders. "But don't go complaining later that your back's all outta whack. I gave you fair warning."

As soon as Myles was aboard, he heard Stewart exhale loudly beneath him, and then, as he felt Stewart jerk him skyward in one violent motion, the ground dropped several feet.

"What do you see?" Stewart groaned.

"Well," Myles said, pausing long enough to notice Stewart start to struggle beneath him, "I don't see much. Maybe you could turn some."

"Which way?"

"Hmm," Myles said in a stilted voice. "Let me think about that." His view atop Stewart's shoulders wasn't any different than the one on the ground: All he saw was brush.

"Don't think long," Stewart huffed.

"How 'bout left?"

Stewart turned left about ninety degrees.

"No, not your left," Myles said, "*my* left."

He could feel Stewart start to turn and then pause. "Wait a second. We're both facing the same way. You can't see anything up there, can you?"

"Actually, I—"

Before Myles could answer, he felt Stewart jerk forward, and he closed his eyes as the ground came up to meet him.

"I was wondering how long it would take you to figure that out," Myles said, looking up at his partner and chuckling.

Stewart found a stout stick on the ground and stuck it in the dirt. He studied the shadow briefly and then pointed behind him. "That's north."

"Well," Myles said, "I reckon that helps a little."

The two trudged through the brush for another ten minutes before finally stumbling upon a tiny hill protruding slightly above the brush.

Myles stopped at the base, exhausted and out of breath. He sat down in the suffocating heat and struggled for air amidst the dry, dusty sage. His arms and face were covered with small cuts inflicted by the thorn scrub. And he was beginning to think that Sergeant Bates wasn't the only one who needed saving.

"I can see the farmhouse we just watered at and the road we're trying to reach," Stewart said from atop the little hill, "but I'll be damned if can find something to shepherd us through this tall sage."

Myles looked up the hill to see Stewart studying a map. He waited a moment and then asked, "You got it figured out?"

"Nope."

Myles lit a cigarette and leaned back to rest his head on the hillside. He stared blankly at his cigarette lighter and flicked it on and off repeatedly. "I think the fundamental problem with our navigation is that I turned the map reading over to you."

Myles spent a few more minutes playing with his cigarette lighter and examining the flint.

Stewart walked back down the hill and looked at Myles and the cigarette lighter. "That little feeble cranium of yours is easily confounded, isn't it?" He walked over beside Myles and stood directly over him.

"I'm not heading back out in that brush until I have a look from that hill myself." Myles discarded his cigarette and stood up. He turned and looked at Stewart, who had taken a seat on the small hill and was brushing some dust off his arms and face.

The fresh red patch on Stewart's face and the exhausted look in his eyes disconcerted Myles. There were few specimens more equipped for hardship than Stewart, and the sight of him near his limit reminded Myles of their desperate dilemma.

Myles looked up at the sultry sky and started up the hill. "I'm the navigator here. That's my job—to get the inept through uncharted country like this."

"If that was your job, you would've been fired a long time ago." Stewart slowly followed Myles back up the small hill. "You got the talking part down pat. I'll give you that."

Atop the small hill, Myles stared at the impasse below. The dense and tangled mass of thorny bushes was disheartening, so he unfolded a map, hoping it might yield a clue.

"Hell," he said as Stewart joined him atop the hill, "we could walk for an hour and end up more lost than we are now."

"Could end up right back here," Stewart groused. "We—" His voice trailed off as he caught sight of something in the distance.

"What?" Myles asked.

"What's that?" Stewart said, pointing into the scrub.

"I don't see anything," Myles said.

"There's a line there," Stewart said, "where the vegetation's greener. Leads straight to the road."

"Could be an old ditch," Myles ventured.

"I'm going to scurry down there and see," Stewart said. "If I get disoriented, I'll holler, and you can guide me back."

"That's fine," Myles replied in a fatigued tone. "I'll find a comfortable place to collapse."

Before Myles could fall asleep, Stewart returned, out of breath but excited. "Not going to believe this," he said as he gulped for air.

"You find the ditch?" Myles asked from beneath his hat.

"That and our misfits. They're headed back this way."

"No shit."

"Take a look."

Myles hustled to his feet and looked out over the thick brush toward a rapidly moving dust trail on the road. "You reckon it's those same banditos?"

"We're in the middle of nowhere," Steward said. "There ain't no more cars out here."

"They sure are some dumb asses. Where do they think we went?" Myles stared at the dust trail. It had passed them and appeared to be turning in the direction of the farmhouse they had recently left. "How in the hell are the Federals losing a war to these guys?"

"Training from Americans like you. Let's head back to that farmhouse. We can backtrack there."

"Just hold on," Myles said. "Let's make sure they stop there for a while before we head back off into those thorns. It'll only take a few minutes."

Chapter 25

Myles raced after Stewart, his partner's back disappearing and reappearing in front of him as they zigzagged through the maze of thorn scrub and sage. They followed their tracks back toward the house, hastily taking cover in a cornfield as soon as the farmhouse came into view.

The cornfield, several hundred acres in size, encompassed the one-room farmhouse on three sides. After snaking through its outer edge as far as they dared, they stopped and hunched over in the corn rows, stealing a glimpse of the Ford wagon they had been chasing all morning. Hands on knees, Myles squatted next to Stewart, and both men gasped for air as they sized up the situation.

"Peons must be inside," Stewart said between breaths.

As Stewart spoke, Myles removed his pistol from its holster and made sure a round was in the chamber. "Let's crawl the rest of the way and then bust in the house."

Myles glared at the house over Stewart's shoulder. "If they spot us before we get there, we just go in firing. We tried to let those little bastards off the hook."

"I don't think any of them is armed," Stewart whispered.

"Don't go shooting them if you don't have to. But if you do, try aiming before you shoot. It helps."

"You sure are talkative these days," Myles grumbled. "I liked you better when you were sullen and taciturn."

"I should have brought Alexia instead of you," Stewart fired back. "She's a better shot—and doesn't complain as much as you do."

"I tell you what," Myles said with a grin, "she sure didn't take any crap from that *pistolero* last night, did she?"

"No, she didn't," Stewart replied before getting down on all fours and moving toward the farmhouse. He turned to Myles and opened his eyes wide for emphasis. "I'm gonna move fast. Keep up."

Myles followed him silently through the corn rows, stopping beside him when they had reached the field's edge, which fell only a few feet short of the farmhouse. The front door was on the side of the house opposite them and out of view.

Stewart nodded and then dashed for the front of the house. Reaching it, he hunched down and looked back at Myles, still squatting in the corn, to see if he had been seen.

Myles gave him a nod of approval and then raced to his side. He held still a moment, trying to hear the voices inside above his own panting.

"I'm going to look in this window," Stewart whispered. "Sit tight."

Myles watched as Stewart slowly stood up to sneak a peek through one of the house's two windows. He glanced inside for a split second before returning to his knees beside Myles.

"There's two sitting at a table eating bananas," he whispered excitedly. "Bones is against the back wall. Shouldn't be a problem. Let's go."

They quietly crawled past the window and then stood up on either side of the door, which was closed but had been kicked in.

Opening it would take one good push, Myles figured. Before he could do the honors, Stewart moved in front of the door and kicked it with all his might. It swung open violently, and Myles rushed in after Stewart, pistol at the ready.

"Put your hands over your heads!" Stewart hollered in Spanish as he pointed his pistol at one of the two young men.

Myles drew a bead on the other one as the two lads jumped from their seats behind a small wooden table in the middle of the house's only room. Each was holding a banana, instead of a gun. The only thing loaded was their mouths.

Sergeant Bates sat on the floor leaning against the wall to their right. His feet and hands were tied, and a piece of cloth was wrapped around his mouth.

"I'm itching to pull this trigger," Stewart continued in Spanish as he approached the young men.

He carefully removed a pistol from the holster of one of the young men. The other was unarmed. After tossing the pistol out the open door, he instructed the young men to sit down.

"How you doing, Bones?" Myles asked. Still keeping his pistol trained on the upstarts, he leaned over to Sergeant Bates and lowered the taut rag from his mouth.

"I was starting to wonder when you were going to get here," Sergeant Bates said, taking a deep breath.

"We got a little sidetracked," Myles said as he tried to retrieve his knife with his free hand while keeping his pistol leveled at one of the young men.

He could see Stewart masking a smirk as he struggled to grab hold of his knife. Finally, his partner pulled his knife from his pocket and handed it to him.

Myles cut the sergeant's hands loose and handed him the knife to finish up. He returned his eyes to the two young men.

"This has been one disaster after another," he said, making sure to speak in Spanish. "Let's get out of here before any more of these little misfits show up." He shoved his pistol into the chest of the young man in front of him. "I ought to shoot your worthless little ass, but I'm not going to."

The man stared coolly back at Myles.

"They thought I was a Creole," the sergeant said as he finished cutting the last rope and stood up. "They were going to turn me in for ten pesos, or shoot me. They were waiting on the boss to show back up. The other three took off with six or seven more looking for the gringos that made the prison bust last night. There's a big reward on their heads. From listening to them, they're just scavenging the country."

"They all this young?" Stewart asked.

"No, these are the pups. I'd say the rest of the crew are in their mid-twenties."

"I'd have given ten pesos for you," Myles said. "But I'm not going to ask how you let them apprehend you. I'm afraid I'd fire you if you told me."

Myles paused and looked at the two again. "You two *niños* don't look too repentant. I'm hoping it's the circumstances and not your character. You two should be in school learning how to read, or chasing a young señorita, not out here getting in all this mess. That's a good way to get shot, especially if you mess with me."

Sergeant Bates stepped outside to retrieve his pistol, the one Stewart had thrown out the front door, and then reappeared in the doorway. He stopped in front of one of the bandits.

"What you want to do with them, Boss?" he asked Myles as he reclaimed his pistol belt from the man's waist.

"I'd like to let them go," Myles said, still staring at the two men, "but I'm afraid they've pestered me too much already. Find something to tie them up with."

Myles finally looked away from the two and frowned. Their adolescent faces, still smooth and whiskerless, and their slender waists and arms belied their aspirations. They were, in fact, aspiring killers. He could see it in their eyes, which like those of a predator locked on its prey, stared back at him with simple, uncomprehending, amoral lust.

"If I ever come across you two again," Myles said gravely, "make no mistake: I will shoot you dead."

Sergeant Bates found a piece of rope outside and tied the two boys' hands together as Stewart held them at gunpoint. On Stewart's instructions, the sergeant tied the knots so they could be worked loose, but only after some effort.

While they finished up, Myles walked out back and sat on the well's stone ledge. He watered and doused himself and then sat silently in the baking sun.

"Let's get out of here, Boss," Sergeant Bates said as he and Stewart approached the well. "I've put in a month's worth of labor for my wages this week."

Myles did not respond. He took a drag from his cigarette, slowly exhaling the light gray smoke from his nostrils, and gazed at the cornfields.

"Get out of the way and let me have some of that water," Stewart said, pushing Myles aside and turning the valve of the water tank, which was just above Myles's head.

The splashing water finally startled Myles from his thoughts. He slowly slid over a couple of feet to escape the streaming water.

"Something the matter with you?" Stewart asked.

"Yeah," Myles said. "Those two little villains in there. I've seen some bad stuff since I've been down here, but they take the cake. They would have shot Bones over ten pesos. I'm trying to decide if I'm going to go back in there and shoot them. I know that doesn't sound like the Christian thing to do, but if I don't do it, there's no telling what kind of wicked deeds they'll end up perpetrating."

Stewart removed his mouth from the water tap and took a long look at Myles. "You're serious, aren't you?"

"Yeah, I'm serious, but I ain't going to do it. I could never live with myself if I did. But I can assure you in a day or two there will be some helpless little girl or abandoned old man who will wish I had." Myles paused a second, stood up, and started walking toward the cornfield beside the house. "I guess this is no business of ours anymore."

Stewart called to him from the well. "Where are you going? We're going to take the car back to the horses."

Myles was walking aimlessly through the corn rows. "I dropped my pack over here somewhere."

"If it was a bucket of my mother's biscuits," Stewart hollered, "you wouldn't have any problem finding it."

"Hell, no, I could smell them." Myles had located his pack. "But I sure could use some biscuits. Can Alexia cook?"

"You don't think I would consent to a week on the trail with you for a woman who couldn't cook, do you?"

"I don't know. You've been known to let morality cloud your judgment from time to time."

Myles put the pack over his shoulder and waded through the cornfield toward the car, where Stewart and Sergeant Bates had spread a map over the hood. But as he emerged from the corn rows, Myles noticed a dust trail hurtling up the road toward them. He stopped in the middle of the grass, out in the open and easily visible to the ten men on horseback racing their way. His eyes narrowed as he recognized the man out front.

He was no boy. Shimmering jewelry, brilliant red bandanna, six-inch goatee—Jorge Trevino, like recurrent cancer, had returned for one final go-round.

"Take cover and get ready!" Myles yelled as Jorge and his thugs reached for their pistols.

He raced behind the wagon and was quickly joined by Stewart and the sergeant, bullets ricocheting off the Ford's spindly frame as the Americans ducked for cover.

"Something you forgot to mention about these boys and their boss, Bones?" Myles said as he glared at the sergeant.

He stood up to get a better look at their attackers, and rested his pistol on the roof of the wagon.

Stewart and Sergeant Bates jumped to their feet beside Myles, and all three returned fire on Jorge and his posse, now within a hundred yards, dropping four of them from their horses.

Jorge and the other five paused but a second before veering off the road and separating into the corn rows on either side. As they disappeared on foot, a deadly hush descended on the farmyard.

Myles stood nervously behind the old Ford, his ears ringing and his heart pounding.

"I heard 'em say the name Jorge a few times," Sergeant Bates whispered. "But I didn't put two and two together."

Myles shook his head. "I'm getting too old for this, Bones."

He looked at Stewart, who was coolly searching the corn rows for Jorge and his men, and then back at Sergeant Bates, who still had a sheepish look on his face.

"Why don't we make a run for it in the wagon?" the sergeant suggested.

Before he could finish his sentence, a bullet cut through the front tire, which began hissing.

"I reckon that answers your question," Myles said. "This thing's starting to look like a pincushion. Let's take cover inside."

Myles took off running for the house, and as Stewart and Sergeant Bates followed him toward the open door, a lone shot whistled over their heads. Inside, they paused in front of the two boys, who were still tied up and sitting against the wall.

"The stove!" Myles yelled, quickly grabbing one end of a large cast-iron stove against the back wall.

With Sergeant Bates taking the other end, they pushed it below one of the windows, and the three knelt behind it.

"I don't like this," Stewart said as they reloaded their

weapons behind the stove. "They know where we are, and this stove only shields us from one direction."

Stewart peeked out the window. He raised his pistol and fired a random shot into the cornfield outside.

His action drew a volley in response that sent the three Americans to the floor belly-first, a mass of wood splinters raining down on them as the gunfire reached a deafening crescendo.

"What the hell did you do that for?" Myles asked as the shooting spree subsided.

"I was trying to locate their position."

"It looks like Jorge and his boys have dispersed pretty good," Myles said, gazing at the bullet holes in all four walls.

Myles looked over at the two boys against the wall, who were feverishly struggling to get prone on the floor. He crawled over to them and jerked each by the leg, tumbling them to the floor in succession.

"Jorge may be nasty, but he sure ain't smart. Those jack-asses are shooting at chest level," Stewart said as he tussled his jet-black hair, now a brownish gray, and released a cloud of dust. "I reckon they're too stupid to realize we're on the floor."

He tried to sneak another peek out the window, but he drew more gunfire, and the sergeant grunted in pain behind Myles.

Myles rose to one knee beside Stewart and returned fire into the cornfield. "You hit, Bones?"

"Yeah," Sergeant Bated mumbled in pain.

"Go check on Bones," Myles said. "I'll keep them at bay." He had located the general vicinity some of the shots were coming from and was searching for movement.

He finally spotted a figure and shot at it. "I got one!"

He turned excitedly to Stewart, but could see he was busy.

"Where you hit?" Stewart asked Sergeant Bates, grabbing him by his pistol belt and pulling him behind the oven.

"The leg."

Stewart found an inch-wide hole in the sergeant's pants just below the knee, and ripped the blood-stained fabric open to inspect the wound. "Hell, Bones, you're barely hit. It just got an inch of meat. You'll be fine."

"He all right?" Myles asked. His deadly shot had brought the firing to an end, and Myles was looking into the field again for anything else to shoot at.

"He's all right. Just a little flesh wound."

"Myles," the sergeant said.

"Yeah?" Myles turned to look at Sergeant Bates.

"Let's take care of Jorge once and for all."

"Here, Bones," Myles said, ignoring the comment and tossing the sergeant a small bottle of iodine from his pack. "Put some iodine on the wound and make a tourniquet to put some pressure on it."

Stewart was cutting up part of Sergeant Bates's pant leg to make a pressure bandage. "Wash it out good first," he said without looking up.

Myles grabbed his canteen, took a large gulp, and poured the remnants over the wound. He then inspected Stewart's work. As he did, all three flinched from two rounds zinging through the window.

"We're going to have to go get them," Myles said. "That's our only chance. Pretty soon, they're going to figure out this house doesn't stop bullets, or they're going to hit us, even if by accident." Panting heavily, he wiped the sweat from his eyes with his shirtsleeve. He then looked at his ammo belt. "We've only got about forty rounds left. How many of them are there?"

"I counted ten, and we've already downed five," Stewart said. He finished applying the bandage and took a drink from his canteen.

"I think there's two over here," Myles said. "I'm going to

sneak around behind them—get in that little ditch we crossed. If you keep their attention, I should be able to get a shot at them."

Myles looked at Stewart for approval. He removed the magazine from his pistol and reloaded it. Stewart and Sergeant Bates were doing the same.

Stewart looked up from reloading and caught Myles's gaze. "You want me to go instead?"

Myles pondered the question a moment as the two studied each other's dust-covered faces. For the first time in his life, he was facing what felt like an almost hopeless situation, and he felt a rare sense of panic. He paused to take account of the unusual sensation before quickly regaining his composure. "No, I'll get 'em. Don't worry."

"Why worry?" Stewart said as Myles crawled to the door. "I'm just sitting in a building that's getting filled with bullets."

Myles laughed.

"Do some of that soldiering stuff you're always bragging about," Stewart said.

Myles removed the spare magazine from his belt, secured it in his left hand, and signaled to Stewart he was ready.

Stewart replied with a nod, and he and Sergeant Bates fired a few rounds through the two windows. As they did, Myles ran for the cornfield. He reached it unscathed as a flurry of bullets rattled the house.

Myles scrambled through the corn rows to a small irrigation ditch. There, he fell to his stomach and, able to see twenty or thirty yards ahead, crawled through the corn until he came upon two men on their knees with their backs to him. Stewart and Sergeant Bates were keeping them preoccupied by firing into the cornfield every ten or fifteen seconds.

After waiting to be sure he was alone and undetected, Myles drew aim and put a round in the back of each man. Both fell, and Myles ran forward to make sure they were dead, quickly putting an extra bullet in each man's skull. He then gathered up their weapons and ammo.

"I got these two!" he called to Stewart and Sergeant Bates. "I'm coming back in. Cover me!"

As his partners covered his retreat, Myles rushed back to the house. He dove inside, dropped the extra weapons, and slid up beside the two boys on the floor. A shot from the recent barrage had hit one of them in the stomach and splattered blood all over his comrade, who was frantically struggling to free himself.

Myles looked at the wounded boy, still breathing. "What happened to him?"

"Just unlucky," Sergeant Bates said from behind the stove. He and Stewart had pulled it away from the wall and were now hunkered behind the opposite side.

"I think the other three are all grouped up on the other side of the house," Stewart said as he and Sergeant Bates fired a few rounds through the window.

The return fire sent Myles scrambling for cover. "I'm back inside now," he said testily. "You two cut that shit out."

As he spoke, a shot whizzed through the siding and ricocheted off the stove, its jolt sending the three Americans closer to the floor.

"You got any idea where they're at?"

"Not really," Stewart said. "Been too busy covering your ass."

"I think they're somewhere out there by that road leading in here," Sergeant Bates said.

Stewart looked at Myles. "Jorge?"

"Still on the loose," Myles said. "But I've got a plan to flush him out."

"Not another plan," Stewart said. He was wedged between Myles and the sergeant, with all three resting their backs against the stove.

Myles cupped his mouth and hollered out the broken window in Spanish, "You worthless little wetbacks, come out and fight like men."

His words were answered with bullets.

"What are you doing?" Stewart asked. "You don't think they're mad enough already?"

"Zealous little bunch, aren't they?" Myles said. "I'm trying to stir them up. Get them to come out into the open or charge us. Jorge has never been one to be cool on his feet." Myles shouted outside again. "You punks, come on. You scared?"

"Pipe down," Stewart said, wiping his eyes in the smoky room. He peeked over the stove to take a look.

"My remarks do any good?"

"Doesn't look like it."

"Well, I'm not going to wait around here to get shot. We're going to go get them. Here's what we're going to do." Myles began drawing an imaginary sketch on the back of the stove. "Stewart, you go hide behind the car. Me and Bones are going to head out into this field over here and either kill 'em or flush 'em out in the road. When we do, shoot them. Any questions?"

Myles looked up at his companions. Each had a somber look on his face, and, like him, was covered in dust, sweat, and splinters.

"What about these two?" Stewart asked.

"Shoot the wounded one," Myles said. "We'll be doing him a favor. Just leave the other one. Come on."

The three glanced around the stove, and Stewart drew his pistol on the wounded man, silently staring at him for a few seconds without pulling the trigger.

Myles finally raised his pistol and shot the boy in the head. He then led the two out of the house and into the adjacent cornfield. Their exodus drew no gunfire, and they dove to their stomachs to take inventory.

"What you think?" Sergeant Bates whispered as Myles

lifted his head and searched the corn rows frantically. "Did ol' Jorge haul ass?"

"I don't know," Myles said, "maybe." He fired three quick rounds in the direction he thought most of the gunfire had come from.

He looked and listened again. But nothing came.

"Maybe we ought to just make a run for it," Stewart said.

"Okay, let's head back through this cornfield across the road and get out of here," Myles said. "There's six horses out there somewhere."

Stewart took off across the road toward the cornfield, and Myles and Sergeant Bates started to follow. But before they could reach the road, three horsemen rose from the corn rows like ghosts in the bewitching afternoon sunlight, their shooting arms extended, each hand gripping a pistol, fingers on triggers, the sun at their backs, Jorge in the middle. All three men jerked back on their reins, bringing their mounts to sudden stops.

Myles and Sergeant Bates quickly drew a bead, but both aimed at the same man, cutting Jorge down before he could fire a single shot. He fell from his horse, his brilliant red bandanna slipping over his eyes as he tumbled lifelessly to the ground, and the two men beside him unloosed a salvo at Myles and the sergeant.

Chapter 26

Ears ringing. Cottonmouth. Stewart stared at his still-smoking gun as he let it slowly slip from his grip and fall to the ground. He had overrun Jorge and the other two, and when he had heard their horses snort as they thundered to a stop behind him, he had reeled and dropped Jorge's men without wasting another round, his deadly aim toppling both men from their saddles before they could reload.

He looked up from his gun at Sergeant Bates, who was still standing in the haze of burnt gunpowder, his bone-skinny frame suddenly looking stout without Myles beside it.

Everything had turned golden in the late afternoon sun, the corn stalks rustling quietly in the warm breeze. Stewart could feel the blue sky closing in on him, squeezing his lungs, and he stumbled toward Myles, who was sitting in the bottom of the ditch with his back resting against its bank, his arms away from his body, extended exactly as they had been the moment he had crumpled in the dust.

Stewart hesitated as he noticed the blood-black rosette spreading from a single hole in Myles's saturated shirt above his belt. "How bad you hit?" he rasped.

"I'm busted up pretty bad," Myles replied quietly, looking down at his stomach.

"Let me take a look." Stewart hurried to his partner's side after shaking off the disorienting fog that was threatening to freeze him in his tracks.

Sergeant Bates was still standing in the center of the road, mouth open, knees buckled.

"Bones," Stewart called out, his voice catching in his throat, "go fetch up some horses! Hurry!"

He knelt down beside Myles, untucked his shirt, and lifted it above the two-inch entry wound. He looked away briefly at the sight of the blood generously pulsing from the wound, and then hurriedly removed his shirt, which he proceeded to tie into a ball and place on the wound to stop the hemorrhaging. His hands shook as he removed his belt and put it around Myles's midsection to secure the rough bandage.

Myles was losing too much blood to last more than a half hour. Moving him would only hasten his death.

"I don't think you're going to make it," Stewart said, choking out the words.

"I already knew that," Myles calmly replied as he caught Stewart's gaze.

Stewart nervously pulled his canteen from his belt. "Here," he said, his hands shaking as he lifted the canteen to Myles's mouth. "Drink some water."

Myles made little effort to drink, and the water spilled onto his chin. Stewart gently whisked the excess water onto Myles's face to cool him.

"That's enough," Myles said, turning his head away from the canteen. "Fetch me my cigarettes, if you don't mind."

"Where they at?" Stewart asked hurriedly.

"In my right pocket."

Stewart gingerly stuck his hand into Myles's pocket, trying not to disturb him as he did.

"*My* right, not yours, jackass," Myles mumbled, and shifted to his left. "Get the lighter while you're there."

Stewart removed the Piedmonts and lighter from Myles's pocket.

"Ouch," Myles complained gruffly.

Stewart put a cigarette in Myles's mouth and lit it. He then leaned back against the other side of the ditch as Myles took a few drags.

Myles lifted his hand slowly to remove the cigarette from his mouth, holding it a few inches from his lips a moment before returning it to his mouth.

"You need a hand with that?"

"Nah," Myles huffed.

Stewart sat quietly and watched as Myles's eyes turned glassy. "You feel dizzy?"

"Not really, just a little light-headed. My mind is as clear and alert as ever." He looked up at Stewart. "You're not going to get teary eyed and all gushy on me, are you?"

"I don't think so," Stewart said quietly.

Myles squinted up at the deep-blue sky. "Good. That's not how I want to spend my final moments in this world." He dropped his eyes from the heavens and gave Stewart a small grin.

"What're you thinking about? You want some more water?" Stewart scooted over beside Myles. A benevolent and humble feeling engulfed him, and he wanted to do something for Myles. He brushed some dirt particles out of Myles's hair and straightened his collar.

"Nothing in particular. Thousands of things are just rushing by. It's quite pleasurable, actually. I feel really alive. All my senses are exaggerated." Myles paused. "You know, of all the things we do in this world, our entire lives are bigger than any of them. But this life's the one thing that's guaranteed to end in tragedy. Don't really make a lot of sense, does it?"

"No, it don't," Stewart muttered. "It doesn't make any

sense at all." He could not take his eyes off Myles. "What do you want me to tell Carmen?"

"Concoct some good heroic tale for her. Something I would come up with. To tell you the truth, my only ill thought right now is how crushing this news will be to her. I can see the permanent agony on her face right now, and that thought hurts me more than my predicament. You need to help her out. Make sure she gets back to Texas and doesn't spend the rest of her life grieving over me. You know how I bring the emotion out in women. I reckon I was just blessed." Myles finally looked at Stewart and gestured for another cigarette. "If I'm getting too sentimental for you, I'm sorry. Dying brings out the honesty in me."

Stewart lit another cigarette and handed it to Myles. "Sorry about getting you into this mess."

"I came by my own accord. There's seven people waiting for us right now that would be dead if we hadn't come up here. Besides, it was an enjoyable way to spend my last few days." Myles leaned his head forward to take the cigarette.

"You," Stewart began as he fumbled for the words. "I'll always . . . Even with all the complaining . . . It was good riding with you again."

He removed his shirt from Myles's wound and saw that the gushing blood had slowed; he knew Myles's blood pressure was almost at the minimum to support life.

"You were an eccentric," he said, finally finding the words, "no doubt."

"I already know how much you admire me, but it still means a lot to hear you say it. My sentiments to you are similar." Myles paused and looked at Stewart. "You should marry Alexia. She's a fine woman. I know you like her a lot. You should have already told her that. Quit being so rigid."

Myles looked down at his chest as Stewart felt for his heartbeat.

"Do me a favor. I figure I've only got about ten minutes. Go catch up with Bones and get out of here before some more of Jorge's little devils show up. Get that chain out of my pocket and make sure Felipe's mother gets it, will you?"

Stewart complied, and then removed his hand from Myles's chest. "I'll stay."

"No, go. I want to pass this world thinking about all the good things that my life has been about, and you're distracting me. Times like catching fireflies with my brother when I was a kid, or you getting me thrown out of the officers club in the Philippines. Boy, those were good times." He chuckled and coughed a shallow cough, blood trickling from his mouth. "Don't worry, you'll be here in many of my thoughts. Tell Sergeant Bates thanks for everything." He reached up and put his hand on Stewart's shoulder. "What happens at the end of that book I've been reading?"

Stewart stood and sidestepped to move his shadow over on Myles, the dark man-shaped silhouette falling on his body. "That sexy queen you were so high on saves herself." He looked down at Myles's eyes, which were fixed skyward. "So long, my fine friend. It has been a pleasure. You should have no regrets. You did it your way and honorably."

Chapter 27

Stewart stumbled through the corn rows until he reached the road. His mind was racing, but everything around him seemed to be moving in slow motion. He stopped at the road's edge, turning to take one last look at the farmhouse, which gleamed rust red with the afternoon sun behind it.

He knew he should go, but something—perhaps the hunch he would never return to this, his birth country—held him where he stood. Until now, he had never noticed the desolate beauty of this rugged landscape that was, whether he liked it or not, in his blood. It was haunting country forever tied to his soul. He closed his eyes and saw the ghosted image of the farmhouse. Savage and unyielding, the Mexican sun would own a part of him until he died.

As he opened his eyes, he noticed something moving by the farmhouse. He squinted until the shadowy figures of an Indian woman and her two children came into focus. The old lady was dancing between the corn rows, chanting a prayer as she tidied the fallen men.

Sergeant Bates, ever faithful, came galloping up the small rise with two horses in tow.

"No need to hurry," Stewart mumbled while still staring at th Indian woman dancing in the corn rows. "The colonel's dead."

He dug into his pocket for a cigarette. As he put one to hi mouth, he noticed a speck of blood on it, and he wiped it o his bare chest.

"You sure?"

"Yeah," Stewart said and lit the cigarette. "How's your leg?

"Hurts like hell, but I'll make it."

"I hope so. We're going to have to ride all night to get bacl behind Federal lines."

"What's going on down there?" Sergeant Bates asked, mo tioning to the ritual unfolding at the farmhouse.

"Old Indian woman sprucing up the dead." Stewart took long drag off the cigarette. "You know, this was probably pretty peaceful place before the white man showed up."

"You don't think these sons of bitches were killing eacl other down here for a couple thousand years before we cam along?" Sergeant Bates handed the reins of one of the horse to Stewart.

"Yeah," Stewart said, still staring at the woman, "but tha was different. It was for things they believed in, not greed an materialism."

"I know you don't really believe that horseshit."

"I don't know what I believe anymore." Stewart discarde his cigarette.

"Let's go get him," said Sergeant Bates. "We'll bury hir up there where we buried that girl."

"No, we're going to bury him right here," Stewart said, f nally turning around and looking at Sergeant Bates. "I thin he enjoyed his short stay here." He grabbed the reins of th horse. "We'll leave the rest of those bastards to the buzzards.

* * *

"Let's get moving," Stewart said as he dismounted at the campsite.

Alexia rushed up to him. "Where's Colonel Adams?"

He pulled a fresh shirt from his pack and buttoned it over his bloody chest. Part of him was still in the corn rows, watching his friend die.

"He's dead," he finally said.

He turned and walked to the edge of the campsite, which sat atop the canyon, and gazed silently out at the setting sun. He could hear Alexia's footsteps behind him, and then felt her hand on his shoulder.

"What happened?"

"It doesn't matter," he said, still staring at the sun, deep orange and hanging just above the rolling hills receding on the horizon.

"You want me to leave you alone?" Alexia asked softly as she rubbed his back.

"No, we'd better get going. We made it. That's all that matters now. We need to make sure some good comes out of all of this." Stewart paused momentarily. "Maybe in the end, some good will come out of this wretched war."

He turned around to face Alexia and her family, Sergeant Bates, Colonel Sancho, and Lieutenant Rubio, all of whom he could see were searching his eyes, waiting for him to somehow set things right. He could feel the burden of their hopes, something he realized Myles had selflessly carried with him to his death.

"Everything's going to be all right," he said, his voice sounding alien to his ears. "We'll be safe tomorrow."

Epilogue

I hesitated to ask the question as we sat in her dimly lit living room, two souls connected by one fateful adventure in the remote backcountry of Mexico.

"Do you feel like it was somehow your fault?" I finally got up the courage to ask the recently widowed Mrs. Cook.

Alexia stared back at me and smiled the sort of smile that looks like it should have been a frown. "There's not a day that doesn't go by," she said softly, "that I don't. He died because of me."

I shuddered as she spoke, instinctively knowing her answer ahead of time. "I have only one goal in coming here," I said.

"What's that?"

"To relieve you of any guilt."

She smiled again, the corners of her mouth pointing southward as she tried to bury the wellspring of anguish that had tormented her since the revolution.

"It's not just Colonel Adams," she whispered.

"What, then?"

"My sister, too. Perhaps, had we not tried to break my family out of jail, she would have—"

"Been killed in captivity?"

"If I had only listened to Stewart before the rebels reached Santiago. He was right about everything."

"But you said it yourself: What sort of country would Mexico have become if everyone had left when things got hard?"

"But I *did* leave," she said. "We ended up leaving anyway." Her eyes welled with tears, and she blotted them with a tissue. "It was all for nothing."

"All for nothing? Stewart put his life on the line—and Myles lost his—for *everything*. Everything that matters, anyway. Stewart risked everything for the woman he loved. And Myles—he died for his best friend." I could see my glasses fogging up and clumsily removed them. "Look," I said, "I can guarantee you my grandmother never blamed you. She would have wanted Myles and Stewart to do the same for her. For love."

Alexia straightened herself in her chair. "It was good of you to come. I appreciate the kind words."

"You really are stubborn, aren't you?" I said with a smile.

"I will never forget your grandfather," she said.

"Neither will I."

Alexia Cook died two years after her husband, the last living link to those bloody, heady days. Whether or not she found peace, I doubt my visit, now more than two decades past, played much of a part. But at least I did what I could.

The Mexican Revolution raged on for three more agonizing years after Myles met his fate, a bit player on that stage, incidental to the thousands who died acting out the end of their own separate tragedies. One out of every eight Mexican citizens, in fact, perished in the war, which, although it continued to flare up for years, finally yielded a new constitution to the Mexican people in 1917. From it, a new and modern Mexico emerged from all the suffering.

The U.S. never intervened, at least not overtly, drawn instead into the war in Europe. While the war to end all wars stole the world's attention, Mexico smoldered in obscurity, each man and woman dying under the same clear blue sky to which Myles said good-bye in his final hazy moments.

In the wake of the revolution, thousands of Americans and other foreign nationals living in Mexico were stripped of their property and forcibly deported, including Stewart's father, who had stayed on to look after the ranch in Victoria. And Pancho Villa, for his part, eventually turned his wrath on America, forcing the U.S. Calvary to cross the border in pursuit of him for eleven months. Villa was assassinated by a Mexican national nine years later. I wonder if he saw the same sun as he drew his last breath.

More Western Adventures
From Karl Lassiter

First Cherokee Rifles

        0-7860-1008-8   **$5.99**US/**$7.99**CAN

The Battle of Lost River

        0-7860-1191-2   **$5.99**US/**$7.99**CAN

White River Massacre

        0-7860-1436-9   **$5.99**US/**$7.99**CAN

Warriors of the Plains

        0-7860-1437-7   **$5.99**US/**$7.99**CAN

Sword and Drum

        0-7860-1572-1   **$5.99**US/**$7.99**CAN

Available Wherever Books Are Sold!

Visit our website at **www.kensingtonbooks.com**.

THE MOUNTAIN MAN SERIES BY
WILLIAM W. JOHNSTONE

__The Last Mountain Man	0-8217-6856-5	$5.99US/$7.99CAN
__Return of the Mountain Man	0-7860-1296-X	$5.99US/$7.99CAN
__Trail of the Mountain Man	0-7860-1297-8	$5.99US/$7.99CAN
__Revenge of the Mountain Man	0-7860-1133-1	$5.99US/$7.99CAN
__Law of the Mountain Man	0-7860-1301-X	$5.99US/$7.99CAN
__Journey of the Mountain Man	0-7860-1302-8	$5.99US/$7.99CAN
__War of the Mountain Man	0-7860-1303-6	$5.99US/$7.99CAN
__Code of the Mountain Man	0-7860-1304-4	$5.99US/$7.99CAN
__Pursuit of the Mountain Man	0-7860-1305-2	$5.99US/$7.99CAN
__Courage of the Mountain Man	0-7860-1306-0	$5.99US/$7.99CAN
__Blood of the Mountain Man	0-7860-1307-9	$5.99US/$7.99CAN
__Fury of the Mountain Man	0-7860-1308-7	$5.99US/$7.99CAN
__Rage of the Mountain Man	0-7860-1555-1	$5.99US/$7.99CAN
__Cunning of the Mountain Man	0-7860-1512-8	$5.99US/$7.99CAN
__Power of the Mountain Man	0-7860-1530-6	$5.99US/$7.99CAN
__Spirit of the Mountain Man	0-7860-1450-4	$5.99US/$7.99CAN
__Ordeal of the Mountain Man	0-7860-1533-0	$5.99US/$7.99CAN
__Triumph of the Mountain Man	0-7860-1532-2	$5.99US/$7.99CAN
__Vengeance of the Mountain Man	0-7860-1529-2	$5.99US/$7.99CAN
__Honor of the Mountain Man	0-8217-5820-9	$5.99US/$7.99CAN
__Battle of the Mountain Man	0-8217-5925-6	$5.99US/$7.99CAN
__Pride of the Mountain Man	0-8217-6057-2	$4.99US/$6.50CAN
__Creed of the Mountain Man	0-7860-1531-4	$5.99US/$7.99CAN
__Guns of the Mountain Man	0-8217-6407-1	$5.99US/$7.99CAN
__Heart of the Mountain Man	0-8217-6618-X	$5.99US/$7.99CAN
__Justice of the Mountain Man	0-7860-1298-6	$5.99US/$7.99CAN
__Valor of the Mountain Man	0-7860-1299-4	$5.99US/$7.99CAN
__Warpath of the Mountain Man	0-7860-1330-3	$5.99US/$7.99CAN
__Trek of the Mountain Man	0-7860-1331-1	$5.99US/$7.99CAN

Available Wherever Books Are Sold!

Visit our website at **www.kensingtonbooks.com**